A Tangle of
SPELLS

Also by Michelle Harrison

A Pinch of Magic
A Sprinkle of Sorcery
Thirteen Treasures
Thirteen Curses
Thirteen Secrets
One Wish
The Other Alice

A Tangle of
SPELLS

BY MICHELLE HARRISON

CLARION BOOKS

An Imprint of HarperCollins*Publishers*

Clarion Books is an imprint of HarperCollins Publishers.

A Tangle of Spells
Copyright © 2022 by Michelle Harrison
All rights reserved. Printed in the United States of America. No part of this
book may be used or reproduced in any manner whatsoever without written
permission except in the case of brief quotations embodied in critical articles
and reviews. For information address HarperCollins Children's Books, a
division of HarperCollins Publishers, 195 Broadway, New York, NY 10007.
www.harpercollinschildrens.com

ISBN 978-0-35-868233-2

The text was set in Berling LT Std.
Cover design by David Hastings
Typography by David Hastings
22 23 24 25 26 PC/LSCC 1 2 3 4 5 6 7 8 9 10

First U.S. Edition, 2022
Originally published in the U.K. by Simon & Schuster in 2021.

For Lucy Rogers, my sister in editing,
and for sisters everywhere

Prologue

Hocus pocus, hubble bubble,
Magic always leads to trouble.
Three brave sisters, one fresh start,
How long till it falls apart?

From Crowstone's damp and swirling fogs
To hidden rooms and hopping frogs.
A pretty village, so serene,
But something lurks beneath, unseen.

Shuffle-shuffle. *What's that sound?*
It's in the air and all around.
A pinch of magic—use it quick!
There's danger here in Pendlewick . . .

Chapter One

Blackbird Cottage

THE WIDDERSHINSES LEFT CROWSTONE just
after breakfast.

Granny had popped her head in to wake the girls
at sunrise, but Betty Widdershins was already up. All
night she had been too excited to sleep, twisting in her
sheets and staring at the cracked ceiling. The old building creaked around her, drafts whistling and pipes groaning as they always did. But on this, her last night in the
Poacher's Pocket inn, the familiar sounds felt different.
Like a goodbye.

Betty had dressed quickly, then stuffed her nightclothes into the bulging trunk at the foot of the bed she
shared with Charlie. Her younger sister slept on, snoring

softly. Betty glanced around, expecting a wave of sadness that never came. This had been her room her whole life, all thirteen and a half years of it. But it didn't feel as if it belonged to her and her two sisters anymore. Not with all their things stowed in the trunk. The closet and drawers were empty, picture hooks were bare, and so were the surfaces normally covered in clutter. There were none of Betty's maps or Charlie's toys or Fliss's doodled poems and rosewater scent.

Fliss stirred in the smaller bed on the other side of the room, then sat up suddenly. Her short hair stuck out in dark, glossy tufts around her pretty, oval face.

Betty grinned at her older sister. "Today's the day, Fliss," she whispered. "We're leaving. We're really, *really* leaving!"

"I know," Fliss whispered back, trying to smile but sharing little of Betty's excitement. Instead, her large brown eyes filled with tears.

There were more tears later from Charlie. She had spent the morning chasing a scruffy black cat around the pub, pleading with it to no avail.

"Come *on*, Oi," she coaxed, as the cat leaped on to a barstool. Charlie bravely tried to pick him up, her small hands almost vanishing into the matted fur. Oi hissed and sank his claws deeper into the stool. "You'll get left behind!"

"Yes, with a bit of luck," Granny muttered. "I've been trying to get rid of that mangy cat for years."

"Granny!" Fliss said reproachfully. She was arranging a handful of flowers in a beer glass filled with water on the bar, ready for when the new owners arrived later that day.

Granny waved Fliss away. "Those boxes need loading onto the wagon. And check my lucky horseshoe's been packed. Mustn't leave that behind."

"It *is* packed, Granny," said Betty, giving the counter a last wipe down. "Checked it myself."

A golden-haired boy, only a year or so older than her, appeared, dragging the heavy trunk from upstairs.

"She did, Bunny," the boy put in. "Twice." He grinned at Betty as she helped heave the trunk outside. It was now that Betty felt the first pangs of sorrow. The boy, an orphan known as Spit, had lived and worked with the Widdershinses at the Poacher's Pocket for the past few weeks. During that short time, the girls had grown to care for him very much. Betty was going to miss him dreadfully.

"It's not too late to change your mind, you know," she said. "Come with us, like we planned."

Spit's grin faded. "Can't. Not yet, anyway. Not . . . now."

Betty nodded. She understood Spit's reasons for staying and knew he was torn. Especially when she saw him gazing at Fliss, even though he pretended not to whenever she caught him.

"Leave it there," said a deep voice. Betty squinted up through the early-morning sunshine at her father's unshaven face. Barney Widdershins beamed back at her, sweat already beading his forehead as he loaded boxes onto a wagon they'd borrowed from a neighbor. "Is that the last of it?"

"Yes." Betty stared at the stacked boxes. It was a surprise to see how little the family owned, even though they'd started packing everything up weeks ago. Most of the furniture and fixtures had to stay in the pub. Some of their belongings had already been shipped to their new home. The rest were so shabby that they probably wouldn't survive the journey. The Widdershinses had never had much money—well, not until recently when a small windfall had unexpectedly come their way. It was this that had finally given them a much-needed change in luck and a chance to move away from the unappealing prison island of Crowstone.

Betty had longed to leave the place all her life, but now that it was happening, she couldn't quite believe it. Finally, she was going to get the opportunity to see somewhere new, somewhere different.

"We'll buy new things," Granny had announced grandly. "Lovely new things for a lovely new start!"

One by one, they clambered onto the wagon and Granny handed the keys to Spit. It had been agreed that he would stay on at the Poacher's Pocket, which was a comfort. Betty stared back at the ramshackle pub. She couldn't help feeling fond of the old building, with its flaking shutters and a slightly drunken lean to the left. It may have seen better days, but it was all Betty and her sisters had ever known. It was home.

"It really does look worn-out, doesn't it?" said Betty, turning to her sister.

"Poor old thing," Fliss murmured, dabbing at another tear. "I wonder if it'll miss us?"

Betty snorted. "Don't be silly. It's a building. They don't have feelings."

"Maybe not feelings," Fliss said, "but they have a *feel* to them."

"Wonder what feel the new place will have?" said Betty, eager to distract Fliss from her gloom. Granny had been annoyingly tight-lipped about the new house and wouldn't tell them a thing about it. She insisted she wanted it to be a surprise.

A small crowd of people had gathered in front of the Poacher's Pocket, despite it not being open yet—and despite having been at the inn the night before. Among them were several lovestruck boys who had come for a last glimpse of Fliss before waving her off.

An older man with a leathery face and grizzled hair only had eyes for Granny, however. He blinked forlornly at her through the gray morning light.

"Seamus Fingerty," Granny sighed. "We said our good-byes last night. You should have stayed in bed—look at the state of you!"

"Had to see yer off proper, Bunny," Fingerty grunted, used to Granny's insults by now. He gave her a loyal wink. "Best landlady this place ever saw!"

"Oh, stop," said Granny, looking secretly pleased.

Charlie was howling now, her cheeks red and blotchy. She didn't even quiet when the sweetshop owners, Henny and Buster Hubbard, handed her an enormous paper bag stuffed with candy.

"There, there, Charlie," said Henny, patting her hand. "This is the start of a new adventure!"

"We don't need any more of *those*, thank you," Fliss muttered under her breath, but everyone except Betty was too busy fussing over Charlie to catch it.

"It's n-not that," Charlie said. "Oi won't come! What if he doesn't like the new owners?"

"He never liked *us*," Betty pointed out.

"But what if they don't feed him?" Charlie's eyes were as round as buttons. To someone as fond of food as she was, the thought of hunger was simply unbearable.

"I'll feed him," said Spit. He winked at Charlie. "Pirate's honor."

Charlie leaned over the side of the wagon and flung her arms around Spit's neck. Then, before they knew it, the wagon was rumbling away in a cloud of dust. The girls and Granny waved frantically as Nestynook Green and the Poacher's Pocket slowly grew smaller in the distance. Fliss was sniffling now, too, and even Granny's eyes were suspiciously damp as she rubbed them and griped about dust. Betty didn't cry, but there was a hard lump in her throat at the sight of Spit and everyone else they were leaving behind.

"Goodbye!" they called. "We'll miss you!"

"Jumping jackdaws," Fliss said, startled out of her tears. She pointed. "Is that what I think it is?"

A black blur was racing after them through the dust

cloud. Before Betty could blink, it launched itself at the wagon in a scrabble of claws and clambered in.

"Oh *no*," Granny said in horror.

"Oi!" Charlie cried, laughing through her tears. "I knew you'd listen!"

Granny glared at the cat. "Chose not to starve, more like."

Oi stalked toward Charlie and sniffed at her interestedly before settling down on her lap with one yellow eye firmly on her pocket.

"Is there food in there?" Granny asked.

"No," said Charlie. "Only Hoppit."

Betty nudged her hard in the ribs, sharing an exasperated glance with Fliss, but they needn't have worried. Granny merely rolled her eyes.

"Still got the imaginary rat, then?"

"Yep." Charlie grinned, revealing a large gap where her front teeth had fallen out. She stared at Oi, overjoyed. "He's never sat on my lap before."

"And probably never will again," said Betty. "Don't even think about stroking him—he's just waiting to ding you."

"Don't care," Charlie breathed, too thrilled and terrified to move.

Betty stared back along the road until finally they

rounded a corner, and the Poacher's Pocket was lost from sight.

"He'll be all right," Fliss said softly. "Spit, I mean. Maybe Fingerty really *can* help him."

Betty nodded. "Fingerty does know a lot of people — and places. If anyone can trace whether Spit has any remaining family, it's him." Her voice caught on the word 'family.' For a while, she had thought that *they* would be Spit's family.

It was a typically drizzly day. Even though it was late June, the girls were used to dampness and marsh mist all year round in Crowstone, and it rarely felt properly warm with coastal winds whipping up all the time. There were still traces of morning mist lurking about, which was bad news for Betty's wild hair. Already she could feel it frizzling on her forehead, but she was determined nothing was going to spoil her hopeful mood. The future lay ahead, and it seemed every bit as sunny as Betty felt.

Granny shuddered as they approached the crossroads.

"Hurry up, Barney," she moaned, linking her thumbs and fanning her fingers like birds' wings over her heart to make the sign of the crow. "We shouldn't have come this way! It's asking for trouble."

Father said nothing but shook his head with a bemused expression. Granny always made a fuss about avoiding the crossroads. It was here, she said, that gallows once stood that were used to carry out the island's hangings and where people suspected of witchcraft were buried. Thankfully, those sorts of punishments took place inside the prison walls now.

Soon they reached the harbor where their own little boat was moored. It was a pretty sea-green color, with its name painted in white letters on the side: *The Traveling Bag*. Betty felt a bubbling thrill at the sight of it. This was it! A journey that would change everything!

"All aboard," said Father with a grin. He began loading the boxes and trunks onto the boat as the girls and Granny clambered onto the swaying vessel. Oi skulked inside the wheelhouse, tucking himself under a bench, but not before exchanging hisses with Bandit, the harbor cat, perched on top of a neighboring boat's cabin.

"Ooh," said Fliss, clutching her tummy as she stepped aboard.

"You can't be seasick already," Charlie snickered. "We haven't even moved!"

"Want to bet?" Fliss said unhappily, her rosy cheeks losing color by the minute.

"Here," said Charlie, offering her the bag of sweets. Her own cheeks bulged with candies rattling against her teeth. "Have a marsh-melt."

Fliss shook her head tightly. "Maybe later."

Betty helped herself to a jumping jackdaw. The delicious sweetness spread over her tongue before the popping candy fizzed in her mouth. She sighed happily as Father unwound the mooring rope and steered the little boat out of the harbor. She joined him at the wheel, dodging a swipe from Oi, and peered at the map her father had spread out in front of him. As she studied it, the fizzing sensation spread to her tummy. Maps were to Betty what sweets were to Charlie. All those places just waiting to be explored! She and her sisters had hardly traveled outside Crowstone until now, which hadn't much bothered Fliss —but seeing the world was the thing Betty craved above all else.

"Where are we going?" she asked slyly, hoping to catch Father off guard now that he was concentrating on steering the boat. It was the same question she'd asked many times since the pub had been sold, but both he and Granny had remained infuriatingly silent. Even now, Father refused to tell her, his only response a cheeky wink. Betty gave up and went outside, too restless to stay in one place. There was a light breeze now that they were moving. She gazed into the distance at the gray, marshy water.

Even if the sun had been shining, nothing could make the prison appear cheerful. It was a huge, squat building that dominated Repent—the closest neighboring island to Crowstone. Hundreds of dangerous prisoners were shut inside, just a ferry ride away. Behind it, just visible through low-hanging cloud, was the island of Lament, where Crowstone's dead were buried. The final island was Torment, a place the Widdershins sisters had never been to. Banished folk lived there, and it was forbidden for anyone to visit—or leave. Together, Crowstone and its three neighbors were called "the Sorrow Isles." Betty wasn't at all sorry to be leaving them behind and heading for the mainland.

As they passed the prison, the boat fell into shadow. Under her thick woolen shawl, goose bumps broke out over Betty's skin as the temperature plunged. There was one part of the jail that didn't fit with the rest—a high tower that loomed above. This was the oldest part of the prison, partly built with ancient cairns gathered from the graves on Lament. It was here that anyone guilty of witchcraft or sorcery was imprisoned, for magic could not be performed inside its walls.

"Crowstone Tower," Charlie murmured beside her,

slipping a sticky hand into Betty's. "I won't miss it. Will you?"

"No way." Betty stared up at the darkened windows. She had been inside the tower with her sisters only once, but she'd remember it forever. It was a long way up . . . and an even longer way down. She gave Charlie's hand a small, secretive squeeze. "I hope we never see it again."

By the time they reached dry land, warm sunshine had broken through the clouds and Fliss had been sick three times. They climbed off the boat in a bustling harbor, where their pale skin and heavy traveling cloaks looked out of place next to the tanned, lightly dressed fishermen. Betty gazed around, thrilled with the newness of it all, and then Father revealed a rather lovely surprise. He beckoned them over to where a fellow stood by a pony and cart. Father shook his hand and then the other man left.

"Where's the driver going?" Fliss asked.

"He's not the driver," Father explained, gesturing to the pony cart. "I am. This is ours."

"A pony?" Charlie squeaked, looking like all her birthdays had arrived at once. She pulled up a handful of grass and fed it to the animal, as fearless as ever.

"A *working* pony," Granny put in. "Not a pet. Now that we're on the mainland, we need a way to get around.

There's more land to cover here, even though Pendlewick is only slightly larger than Crowstone—" She stopped, clapping a hand over her mouth, but it was too late.

"Pendlewick?" the girls shrieked in excitement. "Is *that* where we're going?"

Granny smiled, and Father roared with laughter. "Secret's out now," he said, locking the trunks and boxes in the wheelhouse of the boat. "I'll come back for those— they won't fit in the cart with us."

Indeed, it was a squeeze, but none of the girls minded.

"We're still a good hour away from the new house," said Granny, passing around jam sandwiches that were both squashed and delicious. Afterward, they shared the last of the sweets, and even Fliss was in a cheerful mood.

"I wonder what our new home is like?" she said, sucking happily on a marsh-melt. "I'm on tenterhooks!"

"What's that mean?" Charlie asked.

"It means when you're in suspense about something," Betty explained.

"Oh, yes." Charlie agreed. "I'm on tentacles, too!"

For once, Betty didn't correct her. She was too busy thinking about where they were going and imagining what they'd find there. "Pendlewick," she whispered, liking the taste of it. It made her think of fairy tales, of ticking clocks and flickering candles. It sounded familiar, as if she'd seen it on one of her many maps as a dot or a scribbled word. Never a place she would have thought she'd visit, let alone live.

"Pendlewick, Pendlewick," Charlie sang. *"Take us there and make it quick!"* She winced as the cart went over a bump and Oi, who was on her lap, yowled and sank his claws into her arms.

"The beast!" Betty exclaimed, seeing rows of red pinpricks on Charlie's skin. "Look what he's done to you."

"I don't mind," Charlie said bravely, but her eyes watered every time they hit a pothole.

Betty leaned over the side of the cart, eager to see as much as possible. The pony's hooves clip-clopped ever closer to their new home, taking them over tiny stone bridges and past farms and fields and towns and villages. Even the air was different here: heavy and sweet with summer and hope. Fliss seemed enchanted by it all, exclaiming at the variety of wildflowers and birds nesting in the hedgerows.

"Whoa," said Father to the pony, slowing the cart as they began to go down a steep hill. "Slow there . . . no, *slow*. Not stop!"

But the pony *had* stopped and was refusing to budge.

Granny woke from a long doze and sat up. "Oh, we're here."

"Are we?" asked Fliss doubtfully, looking around. The only thing visible among the hedgerows and fields was a church spire in the distance. "Where's the house?"

"You go ahead and take the girls," said Father to Granny. "I'll follow when I can get this stubborn creature to move."

"This way," said Granny, joints clicking as she set off down the lane. "First place on the right—"

But the girls had already raced past her, laughing and elbowing, each wanting to be the first to see their new home. The gate came almost without warning, tucked in a leafy nook set back from the road. Betty stopped dead and stared as Charlie and Fliss almost skidded into her. Their giggling was cut off abruptly.

"*This* can't be it," said Fliss, her lip curling in disgust. She tugged Betty's arm. "It must be farther on."

"No, that's right," called Granny, puffing along to catch them up. "This is it."

The girls stared past the rickety gate. **BLACKBIRD COTTAGE** said the weathered sign on the house. A house absolutely *nothing* like what Betty and her sisters had been expecting.

Chapter Two

The Crooked House

"IT'S *CROOKED!*" FLISS BURST OUT. "It looks like it's about to fall down!"

"Well . . . the Poacher's Pocket was crooked, too," Granny objected, but Betty thought she detected a hint of worry.

"No, the Poacher's Pocket had a bit of a lean," Fliss argued. "This is wonky!"

Charlie wrinkled her nose. "*Really* wonky."

"I think that's the least of our problems," Betty said, gazing at the cottage in dismay. True, it might have been pretty years ago, but now the whitewashed walls were filthy and gray. The garden was choked with weeds, and a thicket of dying roses and brambles hung in a curtain over a peeling, black door. The thatched roof sagged, and the windows were caked with dirt. Some of them were broken.

"It looks like a witch lived in there," said Fliss.

"It looks like a witch *died* in there," said Betty.

"And after we were on tentacles to see it, too," Charlie added, releasing a struggling Oi from her arms. He vanished into the wild greenery.

"Oh, for crow's sake." Granny glowered. "Can't you at least *pretend* to like it?"

"Crows," Fliss repeated faintly, pointing to the roof.

There, next to the chimney, was an old iron weathervane shaped like two black birds. As soon as she saw it, an old crow superstition Granny was fond of repeating popped into Betty's head.

One for marsh mist, two for sorrow . . .

"Not crows," Granny said impatiently, tapping the wooden sign. "Blackbirds."

"Blackbirds," Fliss whispered. *"Black birds . . .* don't you think that's strange, Betty? It's almost as though the crows from Crowstone have followed us here."

Betty did find it a little odd, but she wasn't about to say so. She prided herself on being the sensible member of the family, not one to dwell on superstitious nonsense like Granny and Fliss. She was determined that the sight of the crumbling cottage wouldn't ruin her excitement, though she had to admit bad luck had a way of following them.

Granny stooped and took a key from under a cracked flowerpot.

"Who left that there?" Charlie demanded.

"One of the neighbors." Granny shoved the brambles aside to unlock the door. "Farther down at Rose Cottage. Or was it Lark Cottage? A key was left with them so our things could be taken inside."

"Why couldn't this one have been called Rose Cottage?" Fliss said unhappily. "Or Lark Cottage, or . . ."

The door creaked open and a musty odor wafted out. Charlie took a wistful sniff.

"Smells like the creepy cupboard back home."

"*This* is home now," said Granny, barging into the darkened cottage. Fliss and Charlie followed, but Betty held back, pausing to take in the sights and smells of their new home. How unfamiliar it all was, just begging to be explored!

She went in, feeling a peculiar swaying sensation as she moved. Granny was throwing back makeshift curtains and opening windows, letting light and air inside.

"Don't just stand there," she snapped at Fliss. "Help!"

"It'd be easier if the house wasn't making me seasick," Fliss grumbled, motioning to the sloping floors.

Betty had to agree. Once, a traveling fair had visited Crowstone and one of the attractions had been a Crooked House. The strange, unbalanced feeling she had now was exactly how she'd felt then.

"Seasick!" said Granny. "Don't give me that piffle." But again Betty thought she detected a note of doubt in her grandmother's voice.

"It really *is* wonky, Granny," she said.

"I have to say, I don't remember noticing that when I viewed the cottage before," Granny admitted, looking uncomfortable.

"How can you not have noticed?" Fliss asked.

"Perhaps we'll get used to it," said Charlie, brightening as she wandered into the kitchen. "Look at the size of the larder. It's enormous! And *oh*—" Her foot scuffed something on the floor, sending it rolling across the tiles. She pounced on it gleefully and held up a silver coin. "Look! Money!"

Betty turned around slowly. Now that the open windows and fresh air had chased away the shadows and mustiness, she was getting a proper look at the cottage. It was full of cobwebs and dust. But it wasn't as unpleasant as she'd first thought, and it was far roomier than she'd expected. The kitchen had plenty of space and a wide window that looked out onto an overgrown garden. There was a large fireplace with bread ovens on either side, and another smaller fireplace in a living-room area where several boxes and some of their furniture sat waiting for them. At the back of the kitchen was a sturdy wooden door that presumably led to the garden.

"Maybe it's not . . . *that* bad," Betty said.

"Not *that* bad?"

Her father ducked in through the front door, thumping a hand against the wall approvingly.

"Good solid house, this is. Built two hundred years ago."

"Bit of a mess, though, ain't it?" said Charlie, blowing at a thick cobweb.

"Mess we can deal with," said Father. "A good clean and a few licks of paint and this place will feel like new, trust me. All it needs is some love, and we've got plenty of that." He scooped Charlie into his arms, tickling her mercilessly. "And you haven't even seen the best part yet."

"What's the best part?" the girls asked together.

Father put Charlie down. "This way."

They followed him back in the direction of the front

door, discovering a narrow staircase set in an alcove. The cottage had been so dark when they entered that they had missed it completely. Father took the lead, having to stoop under the low ceiling, and the girls went after him.

"Stop it," Fliss scolded, as Charlie scrabbled to get to the front. "Don't you know it's bad luck to cross paths on a staircase?"

"Not if we're going the same way," Charlie said, pushing past her.

At the top of the stairs they found a galleried landing with a cupboard, and doors to three bedrooms. Each one was as crooked as the next. They were also full of cobwebs, but not quite as gloomy as the downstairs had been, for the windows were bare and warm sunlight streamed in. The air was fresher up here, too, wafting in through some of the broken windowpanes and bringing the scent of summer.

"Dibs on this one!" Charlie yelled, racing from room to room. "No . . . *this* one!"

Father led them into a room on the right, which looked out over the back of the house. It was bare, except for a built-in closet and its own little fireplace.

"There," he said, pointing to the window. "See that?"

The girls gazed out through the buttery-yellow light.

Betty felt her breath catch. Beyond the window was the small walled garden she had seen from the kitchen. Overgrown, but now she could make out vague rows and sections, and a few broken canes sticking out of the dirt. A cottage garden. Past that, through a leafy archway, there was a path leading to a large area of grass and wildflowers and trees and even a small pond. It stretched back, a thick hedge separating it from a vast expanse of cornfields and meadows. Betty could see the heat from them shimmering on the horizon. One or two buildings were dotted in the distance.

"It's ours," Father said. "All this land—ours, right up to the hedge. Know what that means?"

"Chickens?" Charlie said hopefully. She pointed at a rotting mass of wood that might have been an old coop. Oi was prowling around it, sniffing.

Father laughed, ruffling her messy hair. "It means we can grow things."

"Flowers," said Fliss dreamily.

"Food," said Father. "But yes, flowers, too." He put his arm around Fliss's shoulders and squeezed. "I know how much you like them, so that little patch there in the sun is just for you to fill with roses and lavender." He winked at Charlie. "And we'll see about getting some chickens. Imagine that—fresh eggs every day."

"Yes!" Charlie whooped and began a ridiculous dance, flapping her arms like wings. "Buck-buck-*buck-erp!*"

From the corner of the room, Father picked up a long, thin tube and handed it to Betty.

"Here," he said. "I got this for you weeks ago. I've been saving it for today."

Betty took the tube with a familiar rush of excitement. She could already guess what this was—one of her favorite things in the world. From inside it, she withdrew a thick, crisp roll of creamy paper and held her breath as she unfurled it.

"A map," she whispered. "My very own map of Pendlewick." Fliss and Charlie peered over her shoulder as she greedily scanned the inked surface. A twisting stream, a church, a village green . . . and, beyond that, a vast expanse of thick woodland. "Tick Tock Forest," she murmured, once again thinking of fairy tales and magic. "What a lovely name."

"What do *I* get?" Charlie complained, pouting jealously. "Betty got a map, and Fliss got a rose garden. And don't say chickens, 'cause there ain't any yet!"

Father chuckled. "Well, you see that big tree?" He pointed through the window to the land beyond the cottage garden. "Looks like it could do with a swing to me."

"A SWING?" Charlie looked as though she might

sprout feathers herself at this point. "Let's make it now! Can we, *please?*" She grabbed Father's hand and pulled him from the room, leaving Betty and Fliss alone.

Betty tore her gaze from the map and placed it carefully back into the tube. Her eyes roamed over the golden land beyond the window. A garden! A proper garden—something they'd never had before. Back at the Poacher's Pocket there had only been a scrappy yard full of crates and beer barrels, and a couple of patchy flower beds that never bloomed. But *this* . . . For the first time since they'd entered Blackbird Cottage, she began to believe that Granny had chosen well.

"Oh," said Fliss. "Look at the windowsill—there's something on it. It looks like chalk dust." She shuddered. "I really hope this place doesn't have an ant problem."

Betty frowned, pressing a finger into the white substance. There was a line of it running all along the ledge. She rubbed her fingertips together. "It's grainy."

"Sugar?" suggested Fliss.

"I think it's . . . *salt*," said Betty, half remembering something Granny had once said. "That's odd." She stepped back from the window, and as she did, she saw a flash of silver on the floor, an object caught in a beam of sunlight. She moved closer to investigate. "Another coin, like the one Charlie found downstairs."

"Whoever left this place was careless with their money, then," said Fliss. She went to pick it up.

"Leave it," said Betty. She felt a flicker of something, though she didn't quite know what. Not worry exactly, but *something.* "Look," she said, "over there." She crossed the room, the crooked floor making her stomach lurch. There were a few dry leaves in the corner that she swept aside with her foot. "Another coin."

"And a fourth," Fliss finished, pointing. "How peculiar!"

Betty went into the next room. "More in here. And salt on the windowsill again." She ran into the third bedroom with Fliss on her heels. "And the same in here. A silver coin in every corner of every room."

"It *has* to be something to do with ants." Fliss gazed out of the window, her eyes full of summer and longing.

"Chestnuts keep spiders away, don't they?" Betty said, suddenly recalling this from a particularly spidery autumn a few years back. "It must be something like that. Come on, let's go outside!"

When they got downstairs, Betty saw another line of salt by the door, which they'd disturbed as they'd entered the cottage. They found Granny standing by the kitchen window, staring at another white, powdery trail and muttering to herself. She'd unpacked the kettle, but it dangled half-forgotten in her hand. She looked up as Betty and Fliss approached.

"Salt," she said, her voice hoarse. "On all the window-sills down here and by the doors. And silver coins in every corner."

"It's the same upstairs," said Betty. "In the bedrooms."

"I don't like it," Granny muttered, shaking her head. "I don't like it at all."

"Granny, whatever is the matter?" Fliss asked, reaching out to touch their grandmother's arm. "You look worried."

"I *am* worried." Granny banged the kettle down on the table and started rummaging through one of the boxes. "Where's my lucky horseshoe? Who packed it? I want it out, now."

"It's among the things we brought with us this morning," said Fliss gently. "On the boat. Father has to go back for it, remember? You wanted it with us on our journey."

"What's wrong, Granny?" Betty asked. She had only seen their grandmother anxious like this a handful of times, and it was no less unsettling now. Like everyone else, Betty was used to seeing Bunny Widdershins as the fearsome landlady who could keep even the most unruly locals in check. *What was it Granny had said about salt?*

"It's to keep bad things out," Granny said, almost as

28

though she'd heard Betty's thoughts. "People used salt for protection. Harmful things can't cross it."

Betty nodded, remembering now. When the girls were little, both Granny and Father had told them plenty of stories. Father's were mostly of smugglers and adventure, but Granny's had always been spookier. Tales of wicked witches, vengeful ghosts, and mischievous fairies. One night Betty had been thrilled by the story of a hobgoblin who was trying to get into a house but was prevented by a line of salt in the doorway.

"Surely that's not what's bothering you, Granny?" she asked. "How is it any different from you hanging up hagstones and horseshoes? It's just superstition, isn't it?"

"There's a difference between a few lucky charms in the windows and sealing up every entrance like this," said Granny. "And then there are those coins . . ."

"What do *they* mean?" asked Fliss, looking a bit nervous now.

Granny hesitated. "I'm not sure exactly. But I think I remember hearing something once about silver coins and . . . and selling souls to the Devil." She whispered the last word and made the sign of the crow, then pulled out her pipe and began stuffing it with tobacco.

A horrid little prickle shot up Betty's back. The flicker she'd felt earlier returned as she recalled what Fliss had

29

said about places having a feel to them. Right now, Black-bird Cottage definitely had a feel, and it wasn't good.

"Who lived here before?" she asked, half fearing what she might hear.

"They never said," Granny replied, shrugging help-lessly. "The place had been empty for months. I'll tell you one thing, though. Whoever it was must have been scared. *Really* scared. Someone only goes to all that trouble"—she gestured to the windows—"when they're afraid of what might get in."

Betty felt herself tense at Granny's words and, before she could help it, an even darker thought popped into her head.

Or afraid of what might be let out.

Chapter Three

Magic

*M*EDDLING MAGPIES, BETTY WIDDERSHINS! Betty scolded herself and pushed the thought away—along with the feeling of dread. She'd always refused to get swept up in Granny's superstitions, but it was something that rubbed off no matter what, and she was annoyed with herself for letting it. This was their new start and she wasn't about to let it be ruined by silly, old folk tales.

"Listen, we're all tired and we've had a long journey," she said. "We're bound to feel a bit strange in a new place, but it's like Father said. Once it's cleaned up and painted, it'll feel like new. Like *ours*."

"Betty's right," said Fliss, patting Granny's hand. "I'll put the kettle on, and we'll have a nice cup of tea. And then I'll sweep up all that salt and start on the cobwebs."

Granny patted down her pockets for her matches. "Just the salt," she said. "And the tea. The rest can wait. I'm sure you girls want to go out and explore."

"Can we?" Betty asked hopefully.

"Just for an hour or two," said Granny. "There's a farm your father's hoping to find work at, so it wouldn't hurt to go over and introduce yourselves."

"I'll go and call Charlie," said Fliss, heading to the sturdy wooden door at the back of the cottage.

Betty was about to follow her, but Granny placed a wrinkled hand on her arm and lowered her voice.

"Betty? Get rid of all those silver coins. But *don't* spend them."

"Don't spend them?" Betty repeated.

"Give them to charity," Granny said. "Chuck them down a wishing well—I don't care. I want them out of this house." She stuck her pipe in her mouth, signaling an end to the matter and went to the door Fliss had vanished through. When she unlatched it, Betty was surprised to see that it didn't lead outside as she'd thought it would. Instead, it opened into another room.

"Oh," said Betty, peering in. "I thought this led to the garden."

"It probably did once," said Granny. "This is a newer part that's been added on, most likely for storage." She removed the pipe from her mouth and pointed with it to the back of the new room. "That's the outside door there."

Fliss appeared in the doorway, eyes shining. There was a tiny flower in her hair that looked like a fairy crown. "I like it in here. It's so bright! And the floor isn't crooked. Can this be my room?"

"I don't see why not," said Granny.

Fliss did a twirl in the middle of the room, then went to the largest window. It looked out onto a small paddock and a stable at the side of the house, where Father had left the pony.

"That's ours, too?" Betty asked in amazement. She was starting to see why Granny had been so taken with the place.

"I love it," said Fliss happily. "Right next to the garden. I'm going to call it 'the Snug.' Actually, no. 'The Nest.'"

"It's right next to the kitchen, too," said Betty. "Handy for brushing up on your cooking."

"Hey!" Fliss objected.

"Wait, does that mean Charlie and I are sharing

again?" Betty asked, trying to keep the disappointment out of her voice. "There are only three rooms upstairs." It wasn't that she minded sharing with Charlie, but she had so hoped for her own bedroom.

"No," said Granny. "You and Charlie will have a room each, and your father, of course. I'll sleep down here on a fold-out bed in the sitting room. My knees and stairs don't get along nowadays." She gave Fliss a shrewd look. "Besides, someone needs to keep an eye on you when it comes to garden doors and boyfriends, young lady."

"I don't have a boyfriend," Fliss muttered, going red.

"Yet," said Betty. "Just think—a whole village of boys you haven't kissed."

"Oh, shush," said Fliss, scuttling off to the kitchen to fill the kettle.

Betty grinned to herself as Granny went outside and lit her pipe, wandering through the garden to find Charlie and Father with a cloud of gray smoke trailing behind her. The smile faded when she went back to the kitchen and found her sister sweeping the salt from the windowsills.

"Will you collect all those coins?" Fliss asked. "I don't want to touch them."

"You're as bad as Granny," Betty retorted, though privately she didn't want to touch them, either. She took a dusty glass jar that had been left in the kitchen and began popping the coins into it. They were little slivers of cold against her warm fingers. She wondered how long they had lain there undisturbed. And, more importantly, *why*.

"Do you think it's true, what Granny said about them?" Fliss asked in a low voice. "That they have something to do with selling souls?"

Betty shrugged. "Granny's the expert on superstitions. What we need to remember is that just because whoever lived here believed it, doesn't mean it's real. We can't let ourselves be scared by what someone else thought."

"But, Betty," Fliss said, her voice quieter still, "we know that . . . that certain things *are* real, don't we? When just a year ago, we didn't. We know *magic* is real—"

"Yep."

The voice came from the door that led to Fliss's room and startled them so much that Fliss yelped and Betty almost dropped the jar of coins.

"Charlie!" Betty exclaimed. "Why are you creeping up on us like that?"

"Practice," said Charlie, looking mightily pleased with herself. She strolled into the kitchen importantly. "You know, for when you're talking about 'big sister' stuff. And for when we're playing hide-and-sneak."

"Hide-and-*seek*!" Betty and Fliss chorused.

"Same thing," Charlie said impatiently. Her green

eyes sparkled with mischief. "This place has so many good hidey-holes!" She paused. "Why were you talking about magic?"

"Er . . ." Fliss shared an awkward glance with Betty. There wasn't much that scared Charlie, but they both knew that talk of selling souls wasn't for the ears of a seven-year-old.

"Fliss was wondering where I'd packed the dolls," Betty said, thinking quickly.

"Where *did* you pack them?" Charlie asked.

"I didn't." Betty reached into her pocket and removed a set of wooden nesting dolls, the kind that hid away inside one another, each a little smaller than the last. They were smooth and beautifully painted, with auburn hair and freckles. "I kept them with me the whole time."

"Let me have them," Charlie begged. "Just for a minute."

"Charlie," Betty said in a warning tone. "Granny could come back."

"She won't," Charlie said. "She's too busy nagging Father to go and fetch her horseshoe off the boat. *Please*, Betty!"

"All right." Betty handed her the dolls. "But be quick."

Charlie took them eagerly.

Betty had received the dolls from Granny on her thirteenth birthday. Ordinarily, a gift like this would have been better suited to Fliss, who liked pretty things, or Charlie, who loved toys but had very few. But these were not toys, and they were certainly not ordinary. For, by placing a small item such as a hair or a tooth inside the dolls and lining up the halves perfectly, the person to whom the object belonged would vanish. They were the sisters' most valuable possession; their magical power, a secret from everyone. *Their pinch of magic.*

And as Charlie had discovered, the dolls could make other things vanish, too. She twisted the outer doll so the two parts were no longer aligned, then passed them back to Betty. With gentle hands, she removed from her own pocket a three-legged brown rat, who yawned and stretched. Charlie tickled his ears and placed him in the collar of her dress, giggling as he scampered across her shoulders.

"I've missed you, Hoppit," she said.

"Missed him?" Betty rolled her eyes. "He's been in your pocket the whole time! Even if you can't see him, you can still *feel* him."

"It's not the same," Charlie insisted. "I miss seeing his little whiskers and his little nose, and . . ."

"His wormy tail," Fliss finished with a shudder. "You know, one day Granny's going to find out that your 'imaginary' rat is real. It's only going to take one mistake with those dolls and she'll see him. That's if Oi doesn't get to him first."

"Poor Oi," said Charlie. "He can smell a rat, but he can't figure it out at all."

"Lucky for you," said Betty. "And Hoppit. Now we need to hide him again before Granny comes back."

"All right," said Charlie, pouting a little.

Betty twisted the dolls back into place. Instantly, Hoppit, whose pink nose had been whiffling through a curtain of Charlie's unkempt hair, disappeared. Betty felt a familiar buzz of excitement to see the magic work. Even though the sisters had used the enchanted nesting dolls countless times, she always remained in awe of their power.

"Don't sulk," said Betty. "We're going out to explore Pendlewick in a minute. Perhaps there might be a tea-room where we can buy a late lunch."

"Ooh," said Charlie, her pout vanishing as swiftly as Hoppit. "Lunch!"

Chapter Four

The Hungry Tree

BETTY GOT RID OF THE SILVER COINS by poking them into a crack in the church wall. She figured that this was the best place for them, if there was any truth in Granny's suspicions. She hadn't realized how heavily they'd been weighing on her mind until she prodded the last coin out of sight and then stuffed some moss in after to seal the gap. *There.* She instantly felt lighter. No one would find them anytime soon, if ever. And yet . . .

Perhaps it would be sensible to make a note of where she'd put them, just in case. It was a bit like how Fliss described feeling when she saw a spider scuttle out of

sight—that it somehow felt worse not knowing exactly where it was. Betty stood up, memorizing a small, round window of stained glass in the church and, in the graveyard on the other side of the wall, a headstone upon which there was an angel with a broken wing.

"Come *on*, Betty," Charlie called. "What are you doing?"

"Just . . . tying my bootlace," Betty called back, brushing dirt off her knees. "Anyway, you're the one who stopped to stroke that cat!"

"Tell you what," Fliss said, as Betty joined her sisters, "I'm not looking forward to getting back up that hill."

"Hmm." Betty eyed the tree-lined lane that led to Blackbird Cottage. The slope had seemed gentle enough on the way down, but it was rather a long way to the house. Despite changing into lighter summer clothes, she was already sweating, unused to the sweltering heat. "*Bread and Cheese Hill,*" she read from a wooden sign pointing back up the lane. "I like that name."

"I'd like it more if I wasn't starving," Charlie huffed, impatient now that the cat she had stopped to pet had abandoned her.

The church had been the first thing they'd encountered at the bottom of the hill. So far, they hadn't seen a single person. Now they crossed a small bridge that took them over a merrily bubbling stream. While Fliss and Charlie exclaimed with delight at the crystal-clear water, Betty stopped to examine her map. There was nothing more exciting than seeing landmarks inked on paper springing up around her. On the other side of the stream, in a narrow, cobbled street, there were the first signs of life. Well . . . sort of.

"Oh!" said Fliss in horror as a bell jangled on a door nearby. Betty looked up at the shiny, black shop sign. In gleaming gold letters, it read: DIGGINS & SON, UNDERTAKERS. In the window, a spray of white flowers lay on a coffin, which had various wooden finishes nailed to its side and a selection of casket handles.

"Yuck," said Charlie, wrinkling her nose.

"That can't be a good sign," Fliss muttered, tugging Betty and Charlie past the black door. "The first place we encounter—an undertaker's!"

"It wasn't the first place," Betty said, determined to look on the bright side. "The church was."

Fliss ignored her and made the sign of the crow for protection.

"People don't do that here," Betty hissed, batting her sister's hands down. "Stop it! We're being stared at."

She jerked her chin crossly to a group of boys who were standing by a smithy a little way along from the funeral parlor. They had stopped their chatter to gawp. Strangers, especially pretty ones, drew attention. As the girls approached, two of the lads, both younger than Betty, smirked and placed their hands over their chests to flutter their fingers in an imitation of Fliss.

Charlie stuck out her tongue at once.

"You stop it as well, Charlie Widdershins!" Betty scolded. "We can do without making enemies the moment we arrive."

Charlie glowered, all the tetchier for being hungry. "They started it."

The eldest boy—a young man, in fact—was tall and strapping. He set down the crate of horseshoes in his arms and wiped his forehead with a dirty hand, leaving a black streak across his skin. He looked about eighteen and had thick, black hair down to his shoulders and the twinkliest blue eyes Betty had ever seen. Unsurprisingly, they were fixed on Fliss, and his chest puffed out a little at the sight of her. Despite this, he had such an open and friendly face that Betty couldn't help liking the look of him. He grinned at them good-naturedly, lightly cuffing the lad nearest to him on the head.

"Pack it in, the pair of you. That's no way to treat visitors."

"We ain't visitors," said Charlie. "We live here."

"That right?" The boy shielded his eyes from the sun, then offered a grubby hand to them before thinking better of it and giving a little wave instead. "I'm Todd Berry, and these are my cousins." He scratched his neck. "No point in telling you their real names 'cause everyone calls them Scally and Wags." Todd nodded to the taller of the two boys. "That there's Scally—he's the one you need to watch out for. And this is Wags. He's the eldest, not that you'd think it."

"I'm Betty Widdershins," said Betty. "And these are my sisters, Felicity and Charlotte, but everyone calls them Fliss and Charlie."

Todd nodded at them.

"I'm seven," Charlie announced, evidently sizing up Todd's cousins as possible playmates. "How old are you?"

"Seven and a half," said Scally, not to be outdone. "Wags is eight, nearly nine."

Charlie gave Wags a quizzical glance. He was staring back at them with a rather glazed look on his face but said nothing.

"He don't talk none," said Scally, the boy whom Todd

had cuffed. He had the same dark looks as his cousin, but his black hair was untidy and his eyes were not warm like Todd's. He chewed a blade of grass, eyeing them slyly. "Not since the accident."

"Oh," said Fliss, her brown eyes curious, though she was too polite to ask for details. Betty shot a warning glance at Charlie, who was also curious and not at all polite.

"He's not said a word for two years now," Todd added. His blue eyes suddenly seemed a shade darker, fading with his smile. "Copies everything Scally does."

"Everything," Scally repeated proudly. "Never used to, but now *I'm* the one in charge. And the biggest."

Betty watched him chewing up the grass and spitting it out. She didn't like what she'd just heard or how casually Scally had said it. As if Wags's bad luck had somehow been a stroke of good fortune to him.

"Well," she said, "nice to meet you all. No doubt we'll bump into you again sometime."

"We were just looking for somewhere nice to eat," said Fliss, tilting her head to one side as she addressed Todd. "Is there anywhere you'd recommend?"

Inwardly, Betty groaned. She knew that look. Sure enough, Fliss seemed to be blinking twice as much as usual, her dark lashes fluttering against her cheeks. In return, Todd had puffed out his chest even further. Betty felt a flicker of annoyance. Why, the two of them had only just met and they were practically strutting around each other like a couple of peacocks!

"I can do better than that," said Todd with a charming grin. "I'm finished here for the day, so I'll show you." He took a rag from a nearby hook and wiped his face and hands, then motioned for them to follow him past the blacksmith's gates and along the cobbled road.

"Scally, Wags, go on with you," he said, flapping them away. "Scoot away home now. You know your ma expects you straight back after school."

Scally made one last mocking hand flutter at Fliss before taking off, with Wags lumbering after him, wearing the same dazed expression. They headed down the twisting street and vanished around a corner.

Todd led the way, with Fliss falling easily into step beside him. Betty and Charlie followed, rolling their eyes as Fliss giggled and played with her hair.

"For crow's sake," Betty muttered, feeling suddenly deflated. Here they were, free to explore an exciting, new place, and some of the mystery and fun was being taken away by being shown around. She knew she was being silly, and that Todd was only being kind, but Betty couldn't help wishing that she and her sisters had been left to discover everything for themselves. It was like being on a treasure hunt and finding that someone else had found all the clues first. New places didn't stay new for long, not when you lived there.

"Where did you say you were from?" asked Todd.

"We didn't," Betty said shortly.

Fliss looked back at her and frowned. "Crowstone. It's a little island on the marshes. Well . . . there are four islands, actually, but I doubt you'll have heard of them."

"Can't say I have," Todd answered, shaking his head. "Oh, wait. Isn't there a prison there?"

"You *have* heard of it!" Fliss exclaimed.

"I remember a story about a woman leaping from a tower." Todd lowered his voice. "A sorceress, they said. Only she never hit the ground. She escaped, somehow, by conjuring imps from the marshes. Something like that anyway." He shrugged. "Every place has its stories, I guess. My aunt used to tell me that one."

Charlie took Betty's hand and gave it a squeeze. Betty squeezed back. They knew this story better than anyone. It was part of the history of Crowstone—and of them. Betty was surprised, and rather thrilled, that the tale was known this far afield, although she wondered why Todd had lowered his voice at the mention of witches. Perhaps he felt foolish talking about them.

"There's not much here in the way of shops," he went on as the street opened out. "But most of them are here, around the village green."

A triangular area of lush grass stretched away from them. It reminded Betty a little of Nestynook Green back in Crowstone. Like Nestynook, there was a large tree at the center, but this tree was far wider. It had an ancient, knobbly trunk and stood at the edge of a murky, green pond with a thick root twisting down into the water. Curiously, there was not a single leaf or blossom on its branches; it was completely bare. There were several tall stones surrounding the tree in a circle, as though they were protecting it. Or perhaps . . . imprisoning it.

Betty shook the thought away and scanned the rest of the green. Unlike Nestynook Green, which was boggy and damp, the grass here was springy and fresh and alive with bees buzzing around little pink clovers.

"The Splintered Broomstick over there is the only inn for miles," Todd went on, pointing to a little pub on the corner. It had neatly whitewashed walls and blue paintwork. Pretty yellow flowers tumbled out of window boxes. There was bunting strung up outside and a banner that read *Celebrating 100 years—join us for a party on June 21st.*

"Ooh, a party," said Charlie. "When's that?"

"End of next week," said Betty, thinking of the Poacher's Pocket, which was well over a hundred years old. She wondered whether the previous Widdershinses had thrown a party for that. There had never been much to celebrate in Crowstone.

"It seems nice," said Fliss brightly. "And look! They sell home-cooked meals."

Betty glanced at the pub sign. It showed a small crowd of people gathered around a broomstick that had snapped in two. Beneath was a chalkboard with a list of food on offer, but before she could even finish reading the first line, Todd shook his head vigorously.

"The food's lousy," he said. "Whatever you do, don't eat there."

"Why's it so bad?" Betty asked, feeling hot little pinpricks of embarrassment as she recalled that the Poacher's Pocket hadn't exactly been well-known for good food, either. She suddenly imagined similar whispered conversations about their meals—however hard Fliss and Granny had tried.

"They can't keep the staff," said Todd. "Brutus Crabbe is bad-tempered—that's the landlord, by the way. Best place to eat around here is the Sugar Loaf, next door but one to the Splintered Broomstick. It's a tea shop and ice-cream parlor—but it's getting late now. You might just make the last of the lunch trade before the food's sold out if you're lucky." He glanced at his watch, eyes widening. "Got to dash, late for work! Oh—and the village shop's that way. It's got everything."

"Work?" Fliss repeated, confused. "I thought you'd finished?"

"At the blacksmith's," said Todd, already several steps away from them. "But I've got another job over at Peck-ahen Farm." He gave another one of his charming grins. "This was the quick tour, but I could show you the rest tomorrow? It's my day off."

"Oh, yes," twittered Fliss, flicking her hair as though it were down to her waist instead of merely skimming the tips of her ears. "I mean, I *think* I could. I might be busy . . . cleaning the new house."

Todd didn't seem put off. "Where *is* the new house?"

"Blackbird Cottage," Fliss replied. "Up Bread and Cheese Hill."

Todd stared back at them, the grin freezing on his lips.

"Do you know it?" Fliss asked. "I mean, it looks a little ramshackle now, but once we get to work on it—"

"I . . ." Todd's voice faltered, and he simply nodded.

"I'm late," he mumbled, then took off without another word.

"Well, that was strange," said Fliss, frowning as Todd vanished around the corner.

Betty had to agree. The look on Todd's face had been troubling. It was the same kind of look he'd worn earlier, when Scally had been speaking about Wags's accident. Like he was remembering something unpleasant. "What do you think—?"

"*Excuse* me," Charlie interrupted. "Someone is HUNGRY!"

"Poor Hoppit," Betty joked. "Charlie really should feed you more."

"I'm talking about *me*." Charlie shot her a mutinous look.

Fliss stared after Todd. "I wonder why he took off like that?"

"Perhaps he thought you were going to kiss him to death," Betty teased.

"Oh, be quiet," said Fliss, her cheeks coloring.

The Sugar Loaf was a dear little place that was much larger than it appeared from outside. The girls stepped into the shady tearoom, glad to be out of the afternoon sun. They made their way through a rabbit warren of rooms and found a table in a cool, shaded courtyard in the back. There they ordered a jug of iced raspberry lemonade and sandwiches so enormous that even Charlie couldn't manage to eat all of hers. Afterward, they took their time choosing ice cream from dozens of flavors, each sounding as irresistible as the next.

"It's the best ice cream I've ever tasted," Charlie sighed happily after scrounging several samples. "All of them."

Betty had to agree. She felt pleasantly full as she watched the smiling staff bustling from table to table. Everyone was so friendly and chatty in a way people had never been in Crowstone. It was hard to believe they weren't simply on vacation, but now lived in this pretty, perfect village.

When Fliss paid with some money Granny had given her, the rosy-cheeked lady at the counter tweaked Charlie's nose before giving them their change. The three of them pored over the unfamiliar coins.

"No more crows and ravens or rooks and feathers," Betty murmured, picking up a silver coin with a beautiful etching of a fox. "This is our currency now."

And it was: golden stags, silver vixens, and bronze hares. Betty's eyes lingered on one of the vixens, and she thought about those other silver coins they'd found in the cottage. They were so old and dirty, she couldn't remember whether they'd been engraved or not. Had they been vixens, too? Just as beautiful as this once? She thought of them now, stuffed in the crevice of the church wall. She didn't suppose they would ever know.

They strolled through the cobbled streets, licking their melting ice creams.

"We should head back," said Fliss, popping the last of her cone into her mouth and crunching contentedly. There was a tiny blob of pale-pink rose ice cream on the tip of her nose, and she smelled so flowery that it was a wonder there wasn't a swarm of bees buzzing around her.

"Already?" said Betty, disappointed. "We've hardly been anywhere."

"All right. Well, you and Charlie stay out for a bit longer, then," said Fliss. "But Granny and Father haven't eaten, so I'll pick up a few supplies to take back before the shops close for the afternoon."

They made it to the village shop just in time. **PIL-LIWINKS AND LIGHTWING** read the sign above the door, followed by **PENDLEWICK STORES & POST OFFICE**. Outside, an old, long-haired woman was preparing to wheel a cart of wilting plants inside.

"Oh, are we too late?" said Fliss. "Are you closing?"

The woman squinted at Fliss through thick spectacles that were so smeary it was a wonder she could see at all.

Behind the glass, her watery, gray eyes were enormous and very blinky, like she had dust in them. The glasses were perched on a thin nose that curved hawkishly, and Betty found herself imagining that, when she removed them, there'd be a permanent dent where they'd rested.

"No, dearie." She had a quiet, scratchy voice like a creaking door. "Five minutes yet. You take your time."

She watched them go in, looking them up and down approvingly. It was cooler inside, with a light breeze that Betty supposed must be coming from an open door at the back, although she couldn't see one. There was a rhythmic tapping noise coming from somewhere, too. She wondered what it was. Fliss took a basket and began browsing the shelves, picking up bread, eggs, and flour and putting back the cakes and cookies that Charlie had sneaked in.

Betty picked up a jar of jam. *Pilliwinks' Finest Berries and Cream Preserve*, the label said.

"Homemade, that is."

"Oh!" Betty started, almost dropping the jar. She managed to save it just in time and turned around to see the blinky woman staring at her. "I didn't hear you come in."

The woman smiled at her, not answering. Betty felt awkward. The old lady probably wanted to close the shop and get home and the girls were holding her up. "It . . .

er, looks very nice," she mumbled, glancing down at the label on the jam jar. Then she frowned. "Berries and . . . *cream?*"

"Not real cream," said the woman. She was still watching Betty so intently with her huge eyes that Betty was starting to feel like a mouse being watched by an owl. "But you'd never believe it. It's my secret ingredient."

"You're Pilliwinks?" Betty asked. "I-I mean Mrs. Pilliwinks?"

"Miss," said the woman. She grinned, revealing teeth that looked like a wobbly picket fence. "You take that home, dearie. Housewarming gift. You're the Widdershins girls, I assume?"

"Yes, we are," said Betty, puzzled. "But how did you know?"

"Three girls new to the village? It had to be." Miss Pilliwinks gave a little hoot of laughter, and Betty realized that she didn't look as old as Betty had first thought. "Your grandmother popped in here when she came to view the cottage. And funnily enough, we're neighbors. My sister and I live in the cottage next door but one."

Betty smiled politely, still aware of the tapping noise coming from somewhere. She had thought it was from the back of the shop, but now she wasn't so sure. The noise had sped up, and she wanted to know what it was. Still clutching the jam, she edged around Miss Pilliwinks.

Like the tearoom, the village shop was surprisingly large inside, with smaller rooms tucked away seemingly everywhere. A little, Betty thought, like a set of nesting dolls opening up to reveal another and another. Todd had certainly been right when he said the shop had everything. As well as fresh fruit and vegetables, baked goods and sweets, there were many household items: from tea towels and kettles to broomsticks and gardening tools. There was even a section of yarns and threads, once again bearing the same label as the jams. Only this time the name on it was Lightwing instead of Pilliwinks.

It was here that Betty found the source of the mysterious tapping. A miniature spinning wheel sat on the topmost shelf. It was so small that Betty thought at first that it must be a child's toy, but then a tiny spindle flashed silver, as sharp as a thorn. The tapping came from the little wooden pedal going up and down, up and down, as though an invisible foot were working it, making the wheel spin around. It must be caught in the cool breeze that was drifting through the shop. As Betty watched, the pedal stopped abruptly and the wheel slowed, then stopped. Perhaps it was the memory of the fairy tales

Granny used to tell them or the way the tiny spinning wheel had seemed to be moving of its own accord, but Betty felt there was something rather magical about it.

She moved to the door to wait for Fliss, who had finally allowed a pestering Charlie to add a bag of cinder toffee to the brimming basket. Outside, the hot, heavy air shimmered with heat. Betty gazed across the green. Not far from the shop, there was a set of wooden stocks, the kind used in olden times to throw rotten fruit at wrongdoers. Far beyond that was the strange, old tree by the pond. A sign was nailed to it, but it was too far away to read.

"Why are there two bells?" Charlie asked, pointing up at the door curiously.

Miss Pilliwinks smiled. "What a funny thing to notice! Well, the little silver one is very old. It's been here since the shop opened and we didn't like to get rid of it. We get quite attached to old things—silly, I know." She gave a tinkling laugh. "And the larger one made of brass is newer. That's the one that works.

"Of course, you must come for supper one evening," Miss Pilliwinks went on as Fliss paid for the goods. "Mrs. Lightwing, my sister, makes it her business to personally welcome everyone to Pendlewick."

"How kind," said Fliss politely, no doubt knowing as

well as Betty did that Granny detested invitations from strangers. Thanking Miss Pilliwinks, Fliss and Charlie approached the door, but before they could leave, the shopkeeper called out to them.

"Just a moment, dears." She hurried over and pushed a jar into Betty's hand. "You forgot your jam."

"Oh," said Betty, her fingers closing around the warm glass in surprise. She didn't even remember putting it down. "Thank you."

"Keep away," said Miss Pilliwinks, her owl-like eyes unblinking for once.

"I-I'm sorry?" Betty stuttered.

"The sign on the tree over there," Miss Pilliwinks replied. "You were looking at it earlier, dearie. That's what it says: *Keep away.* None of the locals go near the Hungry Tree."

"The *Hungry* Tree?" Charlie repeated, staring out the window in fascination. "What does it eat?"

"Anything in its path," said Miss Pilliwinks. "Look a bit closer and you'll see things half-swallowed by its bark. A statue. A bench. A shoe." She paused, briskly rearranging the jams on the shelves. "It's one of Pendlewick's little . . . oddities. A bit like Tick Tock Forest."

"Oh, yes," said Charlie. "We saw that on Betty's map. That's a funny name."

"Yes, dearie, it is. And you'd do well to stay out of there." Miss Pilliwinks lowered her voice secretively. "People have been known to get lost in that forest. You lose all track of time in there. Some even say it's"—she hesitated—"*enchanted.*"

Charlie's eyes widened at this, and Betty felt a tingle of excitement. Pendlewick was turning out to be even more intriguing than she could have hoped for.

"But . . . *how* can a tree be hungry?" Betty asked. "Trees don't eat."

"Everything eats." Miss Pilliwinks smiled, showing her crooked teeth again. "Or feeds, at least. There's a story behind it, of course."

Betty could tell Miss Pilliwinks was itching to tell it, too.

"It's said that many years ago, a witch with a wooden leg was buried on that spot," said Miss Pilliwinks. "She was a bad sort when she was alive, and that didn't stop even after she died. The Hungry Tree grew from her wooden leg, and to this day, it's slowly devouring the rest of Pendlewick, so they say."

"How peculiar," said Fliss, looking bemused. "It seems as though there are stories of witches everywhere."

"Quite." Miss Pilliwinks's voice suddenly became hushed. "Even now, it's believed there'll always be

witches in Pendlewick, but folk here don't talk about it."
She smiled brightly, looking directly at Betty in a way
that made her feel rather fidgety.

"Everyone knows magic and trouble go hand in hand
—and we don't want any trouble here, do we?"

Chapter Five

The Ghost

"THEY'RE WEIRD," SAID BETTY the next morning. "*Really* weird."

"Shh!" Fliss scolded, frowning down the ladder at her sister. "Someone might hear."

Betty gave a defiant shrug and blew a frizzle of hair off her sweaty face. It wasn't yet midday, but already the heat was sweltering. She'd always dreamed of living somewhere warmer than Crowstone, where the damp mist played havoc with her frizz-prone hair, but as it turned out, Betty's hair did not like the blazing heat of Pendlewick, either. Not one little bit. It was making her bad-tempered, especially when she could be dipping her toes in the cool stream that cut through the village. Instead, she was around the side of Blackbird Cottage, standing at the bottom of a ladder and holding it steady while Fliss hacked at the ivy growing up the walls of the cottage.

"Who cares if they're weird?" said Charlie, who was wandering through the garden, barefoot and sticky-fingered. She had a slice of bread and jam in her hand and was humming as she ate it. "Miss Tiddlywinks makes *really* good jam."

"*Pilliwinks*," said Fliss. "And yes, we noticed. You've scoffed half the jar."

Betty glanced at the pink stain around her little sister's mouth. "And you seem to be wearing the other half."

"It really does taste like raspberries and cream, though," said Charlie, producing a sticky spoon and scraping a morsel of jam off the bread. "Want some?"

"I tried some already," said Betty. "I still think it tastes like merrypennies, not raspberries."

"No, it's bumbleberries," Fliss argued. "How could it be anything else?"

"Maybe it's all of them," said Charlie between sucks of the spoon. "The jar only says 'berries,' after all."

"I suppose it is a little strange how none of us can agree on the flavor," Fliss pondered.

"Exactly," said Betty.

They all agreed, however, that Miss Pilliwinks's jam

tasted of cream, which had even bamboozled Granny. Betty thought this was odd, too. In fact, she'd found Miss Pilliwinks quite odd altogether.

"I'm telling you, it's almost like she *knew*," Betty said, lowering her voice. "When she started talking about magic leading to trouble, it's as though she sensed there was something different about me—about *us*. The dolls were right there, in my pocket."

"Piffle," said Fliss, sounding remarkably like Granny. "How could she have known? *Really*, Betty. You're always telling me off for being superstitious and now you're the one talking about people sensing things and jam that changes flavors!" She lifted the shears and snipped again, showering Betty with ivy leaves. "She was just being kind."

Betty spat out a leaf indignantly. "I suppose." But the thought niggled at her. If people *did* find out about the magical dolls, it could spoil things for them before they'd even had a chance to settle in. And she wanted the chance to be part of Pendlewick. To *fit in*.

"Anyway," said Fliss, "we haven't even met her sister yet. Mrs. Lightwing might be perfectly ordinary."

Betty frowned. "I wasn't talking about her sister."

"You were," said Charlie helpfully. "You said, 'They're weird.'"

"Well, they must be, mustn't they?" said Betty. Why

had she said "they"? She hadn't even been thinking about Miss Pilliwinks's sister. "Whoever heard of sisters living together like that?"

"We do," said Charlie, offended.

"That's different. We live with Granny," said Betty. "Miss Pilliwinks, well, she's . . . *old*."

"I'd want to live with you and Fliss when *I* grow up," said Charlie, wiggling her grubby toes in the grass. "I wouldn't even mind having the smallest bedroom."

Fliss lowered her shears. "Oh, Charlie. You are sweet. But wouldn't you like to have a home of your own, without us bossing you around?" She gazed down the lane into the hazy distance, a faraway look in her eyes. "A home with your own family and children?"

"Nope," said Charlie at once. Her green eyes widened as she considered something. "Then again, if I had my own house, I could fill it with pets. And eat as much jam as I liked. *Ooh* . . ."

Betty waited expectantly as Fliss started snipping again. "Aren't you going to ask *me*?"

Fliss snorted. "No need. You wouldn't even have a house. You'd live on one of those boats, so you could go wherever you wanted with those itchy feet of yours."

"Too right." Betty grinned, her mood lifting at the idea of sailing from place to place. She was rudely interrupted from her thoughts as another shower of ivy leaves and twigs rained down on her from above.

"Meddling magpies, Fliss!" she began, brushing greenery from her hair. "Can't you at least *try* to aim it—"

"*Aaaaaaaaaargh!*" Fliss shrieked suddenly. "Spider!"

The ladder jerked and Betty stopped flapping at her hair and grabbed it, afraid her sister would topple off.

"Yuck, yuck, *yuck*!" Fliss exclaimed, shaking her hands. "This ivy is full of them. Spiders and slugs and beetles!"

"I don't know why you insisted on being the one to go up the ladder if you're going to keep screeching every time something wriggles," Betty said crossly. "I told you I'm happy to do that while you stand at the bottom."

"It's fine," said Fliss, gritting her teeth determinedly. "I'm *fine*."

"No, come on," said Betty. "Let's swap. I'm bored down here, anyway. And you're hogging all the breeze up there. This garden's a bleedin' sun trap."

"I said I can manage." Fliss snapped the shears violently with a quick glance down the lane.

Betty narrowed her eyes, watching her sister. Fliss's short, dark hair was ruffling in the light wind. She had tied a red ribbon into it to sweep her bangs away from her pretty, oval face. Her skin was flushed and rosy next to the white cotton sundress she wore. Betty glanced down at herself—grimy, clammy, and frizzy-haired. A sudden realization hit her.

"You're looking pretty today, Fliss," said Betty pointedly.

"Am I?"

"You know you are. And don't think I haven't guessed why."

"I can't imagine what you mean." Fliss concentrated on a knot of ivy, working the shears into the greenery.

"There's only one reason you'd volunteer to go up a ladder, Felicity Widdershins," said Betty. "Or anywhere near spiders. You're looking out for Todd Berry—hah!"

"Am not," said Fliss with another telltale glance down the lane.

Betty and Charlie looked at each other and said, "Fliss kiss," in unison, earning a tut from their big sister.

"I bet he doesn't even turn up," Fliss muttered, not bothering to deny it any longer.

"He said he would," Betty replied, but she knew what Fliss was getting at before her sister even spoke again.

"That was before he took off like his boots were on fire."

"He was probably late for his other job," said Betty, but she'd also thought it was strange how Todd's face seemed to change at the mention of Blackbird Cottage. She was wondering if she could have been mistaken.

Fliss made a huffy sound. Then, as though making a point, she came down the ladder and moved it farther along, toward the back of the house, before clambering up and attacking the ivy once more.

Despite their first impressions, the place was already looking much better. Granny and Father had unpacked most of the boxes by the time the girls had arrived back the day before, and they'd made a start on giving everything a good clean inside. While Betty had swept out dust and cobwebs and aired the rooms, Charlie had shirked off, claiming to be looking for Oi, insisting he was lost when he was, in fact, snoozing in a patch of long grass. Later, Betty had found her sharing an apple with the pony and making her a flower garland, which the pony ate, too. Fliss had also made flimsy excuses to be outside and water the drooping flowers, which Betty had been rather cross about at the time. However, the watering had done the plants good and perked them all up. Even though it was still wild, it was exciting to see that a beautiful garden was starting to emerge.

Their first night in the cottage had felt strange. Father had not yet assembled the beds, so they'd slept on their mattresses on the floor. Betty had lain awake for hours, staring at the moon through the uncurtained window. How odd it was to be in a room of her own for the first time and to listen to the creaks and groans of an unfamiliar building like it was speaking a language she did not yet understand.

The room she had chosen (after Charlie had claimed the largest) was the one on the right of the house, through which they'd first looked out on the back garden. Unlike the other bedrooms, there was only one window, and the built-in closet was surprisingly poky, but Betty didn't mind. It was bright, with a sweet little fireplace and plenty of space for her treasured maps.

She had been staring at the moon for perhaps an hour when Charlie crept into her room and cuddled up to her under the blankets.

"What's the matter?" Betty asked. "Bad dream?"

"Can't sleep," Charlie had mumbled. "Feels strange not sharing a room with you and Fliss. Can I sleep in here, just for tonight?"

"Course you can," said Betty, smiling in the darkness and secretly happy to have her little sister snuggling up to her, something familiar among the newness of everything in Pendlewick. "Just for tonight." But Charlie was already snoring in her ear.

"Why do we even need to cut all this ivy back?" Charlie asked now. "It looks nice growing up the cottage." She climbed onto the fence bordering the paddock and clicked to the pony, who ignored her and lazily continued to munch on a patch of dandelions.

"It might look nice, but Father thinks it's not good for the brickwork," said Betty. "Especially when a house is this old."

"Where are Father and Granny, anyway?" Charlie asked.

"Asking around for work," said Fliss. "Father's gone over to that farm they mentioned, and Granny said she was going to ask in the shops."

"They said they'd be back in time for lunch," Betty replied. "So they must be due soon. Any sign of them, Fliss?"

Fliss turned and shielded her eyes as she scanned the lane like a pirate from a crow's-nest. "Nope." She hacked at another tangle of ivy.

"Speaking of lunch," Betty remarked, "will you be able to fit anything else in, Charlie? Seeing as you're stuffing your face instead of sweeping up these cuttings like you're supposed to."

"I've finished now," said Charlie. She tossed a remaining crust to a nearby robin and picked up a broom, straddling it like a witch. "Say, d'you think that story about the Hungry Tree was real? You know, the witch with the wooden leg?"

Betty shrugged. "Hard to say. Those sorts of stories —old legends and folk tales—they normally began with *something* real. Even if the truth gets twisted along the way—"

She was cut off as Fliss gave an ear-piercing scream, the kind that sliced right through any thought of spiders and told Betty that something was seriously wrong.

"What the—?" she began, but the ladder wobbled dangerously. She looked up in alarm to see a flash of light, and Fliss rearing back from the ivy. A long strand of it was wrapped around her hand and her face was a mask of fear.

"There's some—" Fliss cried out, breaking off as the ladder fell away from the wall.

"Fliss!" Betty yelled, wrestling with the ladder. But her sister was too heavy, and the ladder was moving too fast for Betty to control. She barely had time to yank Charlie out of harm's way before the ladder fell one way and Fliss the other, plummeting down toward the fierce hedges surrounding the cottage. The shears, which she had thrown up in shock, sailed through the air and followed Fliss's path, blades glinting silver.

"No!" Betty cried, as Fliss fell into the tangled greenery with a sickening crack and vanished. The shears somersaulted and pierced the hedge . . . right where Fliss had entered the bushes.

"FLISS!" Charlie shrieked, her hands flying up to her mouth.

"Fliss, no!" Betty gasped, clattering over the fallen ladder. *Not my sister. Not Fliss* . . . Her legs felt like someone else's, every movement no longer her own as she scrambled over to the still and horribly silent hedge. "Please, Fliss! *Please* be all right!"

Betty shoved the greenery aside, terrified of what she was about to find—and of what Charlie might see.

Fliss lay on her side in a heap of branches, eyes closed and lips slightly parted in a little O of surprise. For a moment, Betty couldn't breathe. A sickly red stain was smeared across the middle of Fliss's crisp white dress. Then Betty spotted a patch of squashed red berries, juices leaking where Fliss had flattened them. Next to her, the shears had pierced deep into the soil. They'd missed Fliss by a whisker.

"Fliss!" Betty took her sister's hand gently, afraid to make any sudden moves. How badly was she injured? She'd fallen such a long way.

"*Oh,*" Fliss moaned. Her dark eyes flickered open groggily. "*Oh . . . ouch!*"

"Careful," Betty urged. "Don't move too fast—you might have broken something."

Fliss rolled over, wincing.

"You landed in a patch of berries," Betty said. "And lucky you did—the bush broke your fall."

"Looks like your fall broke the bush, too," said Charlie, pointing to a snapped branch.

"Jumping jackdaws, Fliss!" Betty exclaimed, her heart racing. "You scared me half to death!"

A disturbing look crossed Fliss's face as her dazed eyes cleared. For a moment, she hardly looked like Fliss at all. She was disheveled and ashen faced, the mess of berry juice on her dress making her face seem even paler.

"What is it?" Betty asked, alarmed. "Fliss, what's wrong? You look like you've seen a ghost."

"I . . . I think I *did,*" Fliss whispered. She stared up with haunted eyes, and Betty followed her gaze, suddenly remembering her sister's broken cry as she'd fallen.

There's some—

"I saw a girl," Fliss finished shakily. "In your room, Betty. I saw her through the window. That's why I fell."

An icy fear stole over Betty's skin, turning her sweat cold.

As far as they all knew, there was no one in the house.

Chapter Six

The Secret Room

"BUT . . . BUT THAT DOESN'T MAKE any sense," Betty said at last, confused. "You couldn't have seen anyone in my room, Fliss. My window looks out over the back garden."

"There *is* a window," Fliss insisted, her voice rising. "And your room is on this side of the house. I know what I saw! She was there—a girl. She was looking straight at me." She shuddered violently.

Betty glanced up, remembering the flash of light she'd seen just as Fliss had toppled backward. Was Fliss right? Had the flash been sunlight reflecting off glass? At once, her mind settled upon a practical conclusion: Fliss could well have uncovered an old window and simply seen her own reflection. Already Betty felt calmer.

"I ain't scared of ghosts," said Charlie, rolling up her sleeves. "I'll go up the ladder."

"You won't," said Betty at once. Carefully, she took Fliss's elbow and helped her out of the hedge. She was covered in scratches and clearly shaken but seemed otherwise unharmed. "Come inside and sit down. I'll make you a nice cup of tea."

"No," Fliss said quickly, alarmed. "I'm never setting foot in that house again and neither are you."

"It might not have been a *dangerous* ghost," Charlie put in. "Most ghosts just want help, don't they?" She stood back, shielding her eyes from the sun, and peered up into the ivy. Betty got the distinct feeling that now the shock of Fliss's fall was wearing off, Charlie was secretly excited about the prospect of the cottage having its own ghost.

"For crow's sake," Betty muttered under her breath. There was only one way to put to rest this talk of ghosts, and she knew it was down to her. She collected the ladder from where it had fallen and heaved it up against the cottage wall.

"Betty, no," Fliss began. "Don't go up there. Wait till Father's back home."

But curiosity had taken hold of Betty, and she wanted to know for herself what it was that Fliss had seen.

"I'll be fine," she said. "In five minutes, we'll all be laughing about this, you'll see."

Fliss stared back at her, unsmiling. There was a streak of dirt on her nose and a leaf in her hair, and the mess of red berries on her tummy looked very nasty indeed.

"Well, maybe not the falling-off part," Betty mumbled, hurriedly climbing up the rungs. "Just hold on to the ladder."

"Like you did?" Fliss said scathingly.

Betty didn't reply. She was halfway up now and not feeling quite as brave as she had a minute ago. For one thing, she wasn't sure how sturdy the ladder was, especially now. Father had found it abandoned in the garden and, though it seemed solid, it was also old, with one or two rungs missing. For another, Fliss's fall had set her nerves on edge, and she realized too late that she probably should have waited until they'd stopped jangling before doing something as silly as climbing a ladder.

It was, at least, nice and breezy. For the first time that day, a light wind lifted Betty's thick ponytail and whispered through the ivy, making a *shush-shushing* sound. The green leaves were several layers thick, reaching right up to the thatched roof. She could now see thinner areas and gaps where Fliss had chopped it back, and a darker space behind a swaying curtain of vines. Betty reached out and lifted it with one arm, holding tightly to the ladder with the other.

There, hidden behind the leaves, was indeed a small, dark, and dirty window. Betty stared through the glass, holding her breath.

A face stared back at her, one that was not her own. The face of a girl, just as Fliss had described, perfectly still and gazing directly at her through the gloom. Betty's breath came out in a shocked *whoosh*. She let go of the ivy and gripped the ladder tight with both hands.

"Jumping jackdaws!" she whispered. *Who was she?*

"What?" Fliss called, her voice croaking. "Did you see her, too?"

"Y-yes," Betty answered, frozen on the ladder. She couldn't seem to catch her breath. "I saw her!"

For a moment, she didn't trust herself to move, even though she badly wanted to climb down. At the same time, she had to know. She needed answers, and that meant looking again. Memories of Crowstone's marsh mists and will-o'-the-wisps crossed her mind. Perhaps everywhere had its ghosts . . .

"Betty, come down," Fliss begged, but Betty didn't move.

Shakily, she reached out to sweep the ivy aside. She didn't know what to expect, and scary thoughts flashed into her mind. First that the girl would be gone. Second —and this was worse—that the eerie face would have moved closer, like a figure in a nightmare.

But neither of those things happened. The girl's face was still in the same place and hadn't moved.

"What the . . . ?" A glimmer of a thought pushed into Betty's head. With the flat of her hand, she wiped dirt and grime from the window, making a space to peer through. As she did, the truth suddenly became clear, and she felt ridiculously foolish and relieved all at once. A laugh burst out of her. "Of course!"

"What?" Charlie called. "Betty, what's up there?"

"It's a *picture*!" Betty exclaimed, relief making her giddy. "A painting on the wall inside! Not a real person at all."

"A . . . painting?" Fliss repeated. "But it looked . . . it looked just like a person. How could we have been mistaken?"

"Because it looks real." Betty cupped her hands to the glass and peered through the window. All thoughts of ghosts had vanished now, replaced by curiosity. But she couldn't say she wasn't still spooked. "How can this even *be* here?"

Her eyes adjusted to the gloomy space behind the glass. She took another careful step up the ladder, trying to get a better view. Unfortunately, the glass was old and, at some point, had cracked. Ivy had begun to grow through it and along the inside of the glass, partly blocking the view from the outside.

It was easy to see why she and Fliss had mistaken the painting for a real person. Now that Betty had cleared some of the dirt away, she could see its ebony frame. It was a head and shoulders portrait, painted in such detail and color that it captured the girl as well as a photograph would. The girl was pretty, with wavy, dark hair and large eyes that were more real than Betty had ever seen in a painting. The more she stared at the portrait, the more it felt as though it were watching her . . .

She tore her gaze away and squinted around one last time but couldn't make out anything else. Betty clambered down the ladder, jittery with her discovery.

"A painting?" Charlie fumed, shooting an accusing glance at Fliss. "A stupid old *painting?*"

"Thank goodness," said Fliss, her voice weak with relief as Betty stepped off the ladder. "Oh, Betty, the way it was staring . . . I really believed it was a person standing there, even though I knew the house was empty. That's why I thought it was a ghost."

Betty wiped her grimy hands on her skirt. "I thought she was real at first, too. I've never seen a portrait that looks so . . . so *alive*." She stared up at the cottage and the swaying ivy. Its whispered *shush-shush* noises made it seem even more as though the house were speaking its own language.

"But where *is* it?" said Fliss anxiously. "None of us have seen that painting, and yet it's in our house!" She narrowed her eyes, confused. "Do you see why I thought it was in your room, Betty?"

Betty nodded. The layout of the cottage meant that, wherever the painting was, it was certainly near, or next to, her bedroom. "But there are no windows like that inside," she said. "None were overgrown with ivy." And yet the room existed somewhere within the walls of Blackbird Cottage, which could only mean one thing. "There must be a room somewhere that none of us know about," she breathed, as the spine-tingling possibility stole into her mind. "A secret room."

"A *secret* room!" Charlie echoed, not looking quite so peeved now. "Come on, we have to find it—there must be clues!"

Before Betty or Fliss could say anything, Charlie was off. She hopped over the broom she was supposed to be sweeping with and ran around to the back of the house. Betty and Fliss went after her wordlessly. The door to Fliss's "Nest" was open, and a bright stream of sunshine splashed across the tiles, with Oi stretched out in it, sunbathing.

They entered the cottage and raced up the stairs. Charlie headed straight for Betty's room and immediately leaped on to the bed to knock against the wall, her ear pressed flat to it.

"Is there anything?" asked Fliss. "Does it sound hollow?"

Charlie's green eyes widened, the tip of her tongue poking out in concentration. "Not sure. It all sounds solid."

"Maybe it's farther along, in Father's room," said Betty. But deep down, she knew it couldn't be. Her father's room was next to hers and looked out on the front garden. Betty walked to the other bedroom and stood at the door, staring past her father's few belongings. For the first time, she noticed one very obvious difference.

"The windows," she whispered, skidding back to her own room. A wave of dizziness rolled over her. She was unsure whether it was the heat, the excitement, or simply the sloping floors. "There's another window," she said giddily. "In Father's room, on the side of the house. He has *two*."

Fliss frowned at her, not understanding. "So? I knew that. I cleaned them yesterday."

"So this room should have two windows, too." Betty stepped past her, watching as Charlie moved along the wall and continued her knocking. "The bedrooms mirror each other, except Father's has an extra window looking out onto the pony paddock. That means there should be one there." She pointed to her built-in closet. "But instead there's that."

"Betty!" Charlie rapped on the wall next to the wardrobe. "It sounds different here." Her eyes were wide and excited. *"Hollow."*

Betty strode to the closet and opened it, sweeping aside the clothes hanging inside. "You know, I thought this seemed strange," she murmured excitedly. She had known every nook and cranny of the Poacher's Pocket, which made this discovery even more thrilling. A hidden room to explore and a mystery to uncover! It hummed of adventure. "Now it makes sense."

She ran her hands over the back of the wardrobe, feeling paneled wood. She tapped it hard, hearing a distinctive echoing sound. "This is hollow, too. The secret room has to be behind here, I know it! But how do we get through?"

"Betty," Fliss said in a low voice. She hung back, her arms crossed over her chest as though she were about to make the sign of the crow. "Are you sure you really want to?"

Betty whipped around. "Of course we do. There must be a reason that room's there, and I want to know what it is."

"Me too," said Charlie, hovering behind Betty. "Let me see!"

"There's nothing to see yet," said Betty. "It looks like it's been properly sealed up."

"Exactly," said Fliss unhappily. She started to pace, absentmindedly chewing her fingernails. "Properly sealed up! You said it yourself: there must be a reason for it being there, and I'm betting it's not a good one."

"Why not?" Charlie asked. "There might be something exciting behind there, like old family jewels . . . or a skeleton!" She paused, looking equally thrilled and horrified as her imagination ran away with her. "Yep, an old skeleton of someone walled up alive, right next to where Betty sleeps. *Oooh.*"

"Charlie, that's gruesome!" said Fliss.

Betty ignored them, too drawn to the closet—and what might lie behind it—to concentrate on their chatter. Because however sensible she liked to think she was, the idea of a secret place hidden within her new bedroom really was rather exciting and mysterious.

"Can we at the very least wait until Granny and Father are back?" said Fliss. "They'll know what to do."

Charlie rolled her eyes. "Grown-ups never know what to do. They just *pretend* to."

"Doesn't look like we can get in, anyway," said Betty, disappointed. "Not without knocking through the wood." She ran her fingers over the wooden paneling, feeling the grooves and notches. But wait . . . Was it her imagination, or was there a draft coming faintly through the gaps? Her nose twitched. There was a definite musty smell. A smell of things old and forgotten.

"Shall I fetch Father's toolbox?" Charlie asked. "There's a big hammer in there. I reckon one good bash—"

"Charlie!" said Fliss. "We are not letting you loose with a hammer!"

Betty ignored their squabbling. Her fingers suddenly found a notch in the wood that was bigger and different from the rest. Unlike the rough knots and knobbles that appeared in wood naturally, this felt smooth, like it had been hollowed out by hand. She slid her fingers into it and tugged, first one way and then the other. Nothing budged. She pulled harder, gritting her teeth . . . and felt the paneling shift, sliding to one side by a finger width. A hiss of stale air wafted out.

"There's a gap!" she exclaimed. Instantly, her sisters stopped their squabbling. "I think I've found the way in —help me pull it open!" She changed position, making room for Fliss and Charlie to step into the closet beside her. The hangers scraped and rattled on the rail as they jostled for space.

"There's just enough room to slide our fingers through," said Betty. "Grab the edge of the panel, then pull. Ready?"

Charlie nodded eagerly, clearly enjoying being part of the discovery. Fliss looked as though she would rather place her fingers in a mousetrap but went along with it.

"Pull!" said Betty, and the three of them heaved.

There was a moment's resistance as the panel stuck fast, held in place by years of grime and damp. And then it slid to the right with a slithery growl, vanishing out of sight.

"Whoa," said Betty, stumbling back into Fliss. Charlie fell back, too, trampling Betty's toes. They clutched at each other and gazed into the dark, damp-smelling space behind the back of the closet.

"Jumping jackdaws," Betty murmured. "We *found* the secret room."

Chapter Seven

Ivy

"THAT'S CLOSE ENOUGH FOR ME," said Fliss, stepping back. "You found it, congratulations. Now let's get out of here."

"Featherbrain," Charlie said scornfully. "Of *course* we're going in."

The air caught in Betty's throat as she peered into the musty room. Not much more than a cupboard-sized space, it held a small, wooden table and a chair. The floorboards were bare, the walls faded and peeling. Cobwebs hung like old lace from the ceiling. The whole place had clearly been untouched for years. And it made the painting seem even stranger.

A thin beam of light reached through the gaps in the ivy, but the plant was still so thick across the window that the room was bathed in a shimmering, green light. It had the feel of somewhere underwater or perhaps in a forgotten forest overgrown with moss. There were even strands of ivy growing up along the ceiling. They stretched across the room like veins.

"Spooky," breathed Charlie, huddling between Fliss and Betty. "What *is* this place?"

Betty shook her head, mesmerized. It *was* a little spooky, but to her it seemed more magical than anything else. A place forgotten by time. "I don't know. But whatever it is, no one's been in here for a long time."

"It must have been for a person," Fliss said quietly, edging forward again. "Or else why would there be a chair?"

"Maybe it was some sort of temporary hiding place," said Betty. "It's too small to be a bedroom." She squinted through the gloom, then glanced at Charlie. "It's barely big enough for a child to lie down in."

"What if this room *was* for a child?" Charlie asked in a small voice. "A place to lock up naughty children?"

No one said anything. It was a horrible thought.

"Where's the painting?" Fliss said faintly. "There's no sign of it."

"It was facing the window," said Betty. "So it must be on the wall next to us." She held on to the edge of the opening and leaned into the secret room.

Something feathery brushed against her face. Betty jerked back with a gasp.

"What?" Fliss cried.

"Nothing." Betty recovered herself. "Just a cobweb, that's all." She scrubbed it away from her face, her skin crawling, and carefully leaned back into the tiny space again, turning her head.

There. The ebony frame hung on the wall, barely an arm's length away.

"I see the frame. I could probably reach it, but it looks heavy."

"Leave it there," said Fliss. "We shouldn't touch any-thing."

But Betty suddenly felt compelled to see it again and unravel the mystery of this strange room. Why would there be a portrait in here? It seemed completely out of place. Her eyes swept the room, taking in more now that they'd adjusted to the dim light. There was something under the chair, she realized, a sheet of cracked plaster perhaps or maybe crumpled paper.

"There's something over there—papers, I think. I'm going in for a better look."

"Don't," Fliss begged. "Please, Betty. Look at this place! It hasn't been touched for years—the whole thing could collapse around you." She wrinkled her nose. "The floorboards might be rotten. These cobwebs are probably the only thing holding it together."

Betty snorted. "I doubt that. It's probably stronger than it looks. And if that *is* paper, it might tell us when the room was last used."

"Just leave it," Fliss snapped. "We should close up this place and forget we ever saw it. I'm the oldest, and when Granny and Father aren't here, I'm in charge. You're not going in!"

"Watch me." Betty stepped into the room carefully, testing the floor under one foot with the other firmly anchored in the cupboard. There was a slight creak, but it held firm.

"Betty Widdershins, you come back here right now!" Fliss hissed.

Betty had no intention of doing so. "It's safe," she said, reaching out in front of her to clear the way of cobwebs until she stood before the painting. Though it was dark, the light from the window fell directly on the portrait. Now, with no leaves or dirty glass in the way, Betty could see it more clearly.

The girl in the painting gazed back at her. Up close,

she was even prettier than Betty had first realized, with a classical beauty to rival Fliss's. She looked around the same age, too, but was darker than Fliss, with long, wavy hair that was almost as black as the wooden frame. Her rosebud mouth was pink and plump and there was a blush to her skin so lifelike that Betty almost expected the girl to breathe. It was her eyes, however, that were most startling. They were an unusual color, somewhere between blue and green, and again were painted so realistically that Betty felt as though the girl were looking straight at her.

It was easy to see why the portrait had appeared real when glimpsed from outside. It was hung at such a height that the eyes were virtually level with Betty's. The ebony frame and background would have been almost invisible, blending into the dark room perfectly so the face and shoulders were all that could be seen.

Why would it be in here, hidden away like this? There was something not right about it all, Betty thought. The more she looked at the portrait, the stranger it seemed. She moved past it, the sound of her footsteps muffled by the thick layers of dust on the floorboards. Crouching by the chair, Betty reached out for what was underneath it.

She had been right—it was a sheaf of papers. She

leafed through them carefully, half expecting them to be old newspapers, but they appeared to be sketches. Very good ones, of people, animals, and flowers. On one, a faint note had been lightly penciled at the bottom:

Tick Tock Forest — rules
1. Don't fall asleep.
2. Don't speak when the clocks are ticking.
3. Never ask what the time is.

"Three rules?" Betty muttered, increasingly intrigued as she remembered what Miss Pilliwinks had said about Tick Tock Forest being enchanted. How peculiar!

"Betty!" Charlie said impatiently. "What you looking at?"

"Drawings," said Betty. She gathered a couple more of the loose papers, shaking a spider off one of them. There was something written on them in black ink that was neat and swirly. "Looks like some sort of poem."

"Poem?" said Fliss, interested now. "What does it say?"

Betty squinted. The ink was smeared in places, as if water had splashed onto the paper. "It's too dark to read it properly, and it's smudged."

"I want to see," said Charlie, using the momentary distraction to barge past Fliss and into the secret room.

"*Oooh*. It really is creepy in here." She turned and stood in front of the painting, her mouth open slightly. "She *does* look real. Wonder who she was."

Betty tilted one of the drawings to the light. There was a word at the bottom in the same neat, black writing.

"Ivy," she read aloud, tracing it with her finger. There was something unusual about the way it was written. The *v* in the middle had been penned in such a way that it resembled a real ivy leaf, with a pointed tip and two smaller points at the edge of the letter. It was a clever way for the artist to sign their name. "That's the name of whoever drew these pictures. Ivy."

"This one, too," said Charlie. She pointed to the painting, her lips moving silently as she sounded out the word in her head. "There, look, and there. Two places."

At first Betty couldn't see what Charlie meant. Two places? She could see only one *Ivy* painted into the canvas. Then she realized that the second word was worked into the wooden frame. "This must be the painting's title," she said. "Ivy. It's a self-portrait." She stared at the girl in the painting. The faint smile on the figure's lips seemed to confirm what she had said. Her eyes were fixed on Betty's, frozen in time.

Now that Betty looked closer, she saw that even the frame was a work of art. It had been decorated with swirling masses of ivy leaves, which were carved into the black wood.

A light breeze from outside ruffled the ivy at the window, making the green light in the room ripple. *Ivy*, thought Betty. It was everywhere in and around this room. Not just the plant, but *her*, the girl. Hidden away in a shroud of its own green leaves. The strangeness of it settled around Betty like dust. How long had this room waited here like this, undiscovered? And why would a painting this beautiful be hidden in a secret room? Surely the owner hadn't meant to leave something so valuable behind.

"Don't you want to see this, Fliss?" she asked, captivated by the mystery of the room. She felt as though she'd unearthed a treasure chest that had lain undisturbed for decades. "It's like something out of a fairy tale."

"No," Fliss said curtly. "I saw it just fine from the window, and I—"

The sound of something smashing from downstairs made them all freeze.

"What was that?" Charlie hissed.

"There's no one else here," said Betty, the dreamy hold of the room finally breaking. "Unless Father and Granny have come back." But no voices called out, and there was no hum of chatter from downstairs to suggest the girls were no longer alone. The cottage was filled with silence, apart from the *shush-shushing* of the ivy at the window.

"The back door," said Fliss hoarsely. She gazed through the gap at Betty, her dark eyes wide. "We left it wide-open. Anyone could have . . ."

"Come on." Betty took Charlie's hand and they squeezed out of the secret room into her bedroom. Bright sunshine dazzled her eyes, making them water. She turned and closed the closet as quietly as she could before heading to the door where Fliss was waiting, chewing her bottom lip. Together, they moved out of the room and down the stairs, with Fliss in the lead and Charlie behind. Each creaky step on the stairs sounded huge in the stillness.

It was probably something caught in a draft, Betty thought. *That's all. We're all feeling jittery because of what we just found. It has nothing to do with opening up a secret room . . .*

But it wasn't just the room, she knew that. It was the salt lining the entrances, and the silver coins. A thought came back to her, the same thought that had popped into her head when they had first entered Blackbird Cottage. *What might be let out . . .*

They reached the bottom of the stairs and turned to face the kitchen area. There was no sign of anyone or anything broken. Just sunlight streaming over their half-unpacked boxes of belongings and specks of dust glittering in the beams of light. Charlie stepped out from in between her sisters.

"I bet it was Oi," she said. "Maybe he knocked over one of the milk bottles outside—" She stopped, her hand flying to her mouth.

"What?" asked Betty, moving to one side. Now she could see it: shattered glass on the floor just beyond the table and a bent and broken frame next to the pieces. It had been a small, oval mirror that Granny had hung on the wall just last night. Some of the glass remained in the frame, like jagged teeth. The hook was still on the wall . . . so how had the mirror fallen and smashed?

Something moved past the kitchen window, shocking them all. A hooded figure dressed in dark, raggedy clothes rushed swiftly through the garden and along the path. It was Fliss who moved first, sweeping toward the Nest and the open back door with Betty and Charlie on her heels.

"HEY!" Fliss yelled as the fragments of glass crunched under her feet. "Who are you?"

Long, gray hair spilled from the hood as the figure paused and glanced back at them. It was an old woman, Betty realized. The woman's eyes narrowed, skimming over Betty and her sisters one by one. The look in them was so full of anger and loathing that Betty grabbed Charlie and pulled her close.

Finally, Betty found her voice. "What are you doing in our garden?"

The woman didn't answer. She turned on the path and lifted a wrinkled hand. She stared directly at Fliss, one clawlike finger pointing at her. Her mouth moved soundlessly, and the sight of it filled Betty with cold dread. She heard Fliss gasp, saw her make the sign of the crow, and then the woman fled. She slipped farther along the path and through the leafy archway, disappearing into the overgrown garden.

Betty was the first to recover. She took a hesitant step outside, scanning the back garden. The only movements were the lazily swaying flowers and insects buzzing around them, drowsy in the heat. There was no sign of the strange woman. She seemed to have simply vanished. In the warm sunshine, some of the dread Betty had felt melted away, but she was still rattled, her heart pounding from the shock.

"Who *was* that?" Betty muttered. She closed the door and bolted it, then the three of them returned to the kitchen. The door to the Nest had been wide-open . . .

and only one person had been near when the mirror broke. The old woman must have been inside the house. Betty shuddered at the realization. It was a horrible feeling to know that a stranger had wandered into their home.

"Why did she point at Fliss like that?" Charlie asked, her voice trembling.

"She didn't," said Betty, finding it hard to meet her sisters' eyes. She knew it was a lie, but the incident had rattled them all, and Fliss didn't deserve to be singled out like this.

"Yes, she did," Fliss said. Her dark eyes were troubled. "Don't lie, Betty. She looked straight at me as she did it."

"She was probably looking at your dress," Betty protested. "It's such a mess that it's hard *not* to look."

"It didn't seem like that," said Charlie, her voice unusually quiet. "She looked . . . scary. Angry."

"She must have wandered into the wrong house," said Betty. Seeing her sisters' worried faces made her desperate to explain away the strange incident. "Perhaps she was lost or confused—there must be an explanation. But we should ask Father to put up a gate to stop something like this from happening again."

Fliss stared at the broken mirror, giving no indication that she had heard. She glanced at Charlie and gave herself a firm shake. "Watch out for that glass. I'll get the dustpan and sweep it up before Granny gets back."

"I don't understand," Charlie asked, looking confused. "How did it fall off the wall?"

Betty glanced at Fliss. Neither of them spoke, but she knew they were both thinking the same thing. The mirror hadn't fallen. It had been dropped—or thrown—and only the stranger had been downstairs when it had happened. *Seven years' bad luck*, thought Betty. *That's what Granny says about broken mirrors.* This was the last thing they needed.

Fliss fetched the dustpan and brush and knelt to sweep up the mess. She had barely begun when low footsteps sounded on the gravel outside. All three girls froze a second time, their eyes fixed on the kitchen window. A dark shape swept past it, brushing against the overgrown brambles, out of view in seconds.

They all knew that the figure was heading for the back door of the Nest, even before the sharp knocking came.

"Don't answer it," whispered Betty.

"Let's go out the front," said Charlie at the same time.

Fliss said nothing. Instead, she dropped the dustpan and brush, letting them clatter on the tiles, and stood up quickly. Her pretty face was twisted in anger, her dark eyes burning. She snatched up a poker from the nearby fireplace and marched into the Nest, shoulders squared.

"Fliss?" Betty scurried after her, alarmed. "What are you *doing?*"

"Getting rid of her." Fliss's voice was low and flat. She unbolted the back door and threw it open hard, brandishing the poker. *"Leave us alone!"* she roared.

Betty skidded to a halt in time to see Todd cowering on the doorstep, a look of fear and confusion on his face. He had flung up an arm to fend off a blow from the poker, and the three roses that he'd been carrying had dropped onto the path, scattering some of their petals.

"Oh," said Fliss. She was breathing noisily, the poker still in the air. "It's *you.*"

Todd took a step back, eyeing her uncertainly.

"Is this a bad time?"

Chapter Eight

A Curse ... ?

TODD'S GAZE DROPPED to the crimson stain on
Fliss's dress. He gasped.

Fliss's gasp was louder. "Oh," she said again, looking
mortified. She whipped the poker behind her back. "We
were just, um . . ."

"She fell off a ladder," Charlie added helpfully. "Into
some berries."

"I'd hate to see the berries," Todd joked.

Fliss flashed a dazzling smile and leaned against the
doorframe, still managing to look lovely despite her pale
face and ruined dress. She pawed at her short hair, trying
to smooth down the sweaty tufts. She had also managed
to smear soot across her forehead from the poker.

Betty squeezed next to her, staring past Todd into the garden.

"Did you see anyone on your way here?" she asked. "Did you pass someone—an old woman?"

Todd's dark eyebrows knotted together in confusion. "An old woman? No, I didn't see anyone. Why? Have you lost your granny?"

Betty shook her head, impatient. "Not Granny. A stranger. She came into the cottage and was poking around."

Todd's blue eyes widened. "That must have been a shock. Is that why you fell off the ladder?"

"No, there was a . . ." Fliss caught herself. "There was a spider in the ivy and it made me jump. I slipped and fell." She gave Betty a sidelong glance, and Betty gave her the smallest of nods to show that she understood. They would not be speaking to anyone outside the family about the secret room—or what they had found in it —just yet.

"Did she say anything, this woman?" Todd asked.

"Nope," said Charlie. "Well, her lips were moving, but we couldn't hear her. She pointed at Fliss."

"You really didn't see anyone?" Betty asked, feeling an unexpected chill as she remembered the strange woman and the intensity of her stare. "She had long, gray hair and was dressed in dark clothes. Does that sound like anyone in the village?"

Todd shrugged helplessly. "Sorry. It could've been any number of people in Pendlewick. Sounds like she might have come to introduce herself to your granny and you made her jump?"

"No." Fliss frowned. "It wasn't like that. She smashed a mirror and pointed at me. It was like . . . like she was putting a *curse* on me or something."

A curse. The word hung in the air like a bad smell. The Widdershinses were no strangers to curses. Each of the girls had been born under one, a family curse that had prevented them from ever leaving Crowstone and its neighboring islands. If they'd tried to, they would have died at the next sunset. However, with Betty's determination and the help of three magical objects, the sisters had managed to undo the curse in the very place it had all begun: Crowstone Tower. While it seemed unlikely that the Widdershinses would be unlucky enough to be cursed again, Betty knew that luck was not her family's strong point. And she couldn't help agreeing with Fliss: it really had looked like the old woman, with her face so twisted and angry, had been muttering a spell.

Betty waited for Todd to say something, to reassure

Fliss that things like this didn't happen in Pendlewick. But what he said wasn't quite what she was expecting.

"Don't go talking about curses here," he said, lowering his voice. "People don't like it. It's a bit of an unwritten rule that we don't talk about magic."

"Why?" asked Charlie, puzzled. As far as she was concerned, only good things had ever come from the use of magic. Sure, it might have gotten the sisters into several scrapes, but it was magic that had gotten them out of trouble, too.

"Does this have anything to do with what Miss Pilliwinks said?" Betty asked, recalling the shopkeeper's words. "About magic and trouble going hand in hand?" She remembered the story about the Hungry Tree, too, and the history of witches in Pendlewick. The old lady, with her ragged clothes and straggly hair, had certainly looked like a witch.

Todd shrugged and gave a wry smile. "I suppose because, when we talk about something, it makes it seem real. It . . . *invites* it in." He wiped his hand on the back of his neck, looking both hot and sheepish. As his words sank in, Betty became aware that he had been standing in the blistering heat for several minutes and not one of them had invited *him* in.

"Todd, how rude of us," she said, urging Fliss to step back from the door. "We've left you roasting on the doorstep—come in."

"Oh," said Fliss blankly. She shook her head slightly, as though clearing it of her thoughts. "So we have." For the first time, she noticed the crumpled roses outside the back door. "Oh dear. Were they for us?"

"Er, yes." Todd bent down and retrieved the drooping flowers. "They're looking a bit sorry for themselves now, but I brought you each one. As a sort of 'welcome to Pendlewick.'" He passed the two sunny-yellow ones to Betty and Charlie. The third, which was a deep red, he offered to Fliss.

Fliss thanked him as she took it. Betty watched her closely, relieved to see a deep blush creep up her sister's cheeks.

"I'll put them in water," Fliss said, leading the way through the Nest. She stopped abruptly as they reached the kitchen. The shattered pieces of mirror were still scattered over the floor.

"I'll do that," said Betty, picking up the dustpan and brush.

Fliss sidestepped the broken glass and went to the sink. She found a bottle and filled it with water, poking the stems of the roses into it. "I'd offer you a cup of tea, but everyone says my tea is lousy."

Betty gaped. It was true that her sister *was* rather useless in the kitchen, but it was unheard of for Fliss to admit it—especially to a boy she had her eye on. She must still be shaken from the fall and the appearance of the old woman. Or perhaps, Betty thought guiltily, she shouldn't tease her quite so much.

Todd chuckled. "Lucky for you, I make excellent tea. Why don't I put the kettle on? You look like you need to sit down."

Fliss flopped into one of the chairs and fanned herself. "It's too hot for tea."

"Granny says it's never too hot for tea," Charlie pointed out immediately.

"Some water, then." Todd busied himself looking for glasses in the cupboards.

Betty glanced at him gratefully, glad of his attempts to lighten the mood. The glass tinkled as she swept it into the pan. It had gone everywhere, and there were so many pieces she was sure they'd be finding fragments of it for days.

"Make sure you get all the bits," Charlie said anxiously. "I don't want Oi hurting his paws."

"Who's Oi?" Todd asked. He'd lined up four mismatched glasses and flicked the tap on to allow the water to run cold.

"Our cat," said Charlie, rushing on breathlessly. "He's a beast, though. Do you like animals? Want to see my rat?"

"Charlie!" said Betty.

"What?" said Charlie. She grinned at Todd expectantly.

"Er . . ." said Todd.

He was saved from having to reply by the tap, which began to spurt, like something alive and hiccupping. The water stopped and started, shooting out in violent jets that splashed right out of the sink.

"Must be an air bubble in the pipes," said Todd.

The water slowed to a dribble, then a drip. Then it stopped altogether. Todd turned the tap one way then the other, but it seemed to make no difference. There was a horrid gurgling sound and a long green string came spewing out.

"Meddling magpies!" said Fliss, leaping out of her seat. "What *is* that?"

Todd reached out and pulled at the slimy green strand. A length of it slid out of the tap, but there was still more. "It's a *plant*," he said, wrapping it around his hand and tugging again. The strand continued to slither out. "Must be growing in the pipes!"

Betty didn't understand it. They'd been using the water since arriving at the house, and there had been no sign of anything wrong with the pipes. Heck, Fliss had put the roses in water just a few moments ago, and the tap had been fine then. The green strand looked familiar, and already she knew what it was. They had been staring at it all morning. Betty took a step nearer the sink. *How strange . . .*

Todd yanked at the vine and it finally came away from the tap, allowing the water to flow freely. "It's . . . ivy," he said. A look of confusion crossed his face and he shook his hand so the plant fell into the sink.

"Do you think it's been stuck up there a long time?" asked Charlie, peering at the coil of green.

"It can't have been," said Betty. "If it had been sitting in water, the leaves would have gone all slimy."

"Oh!" Fliss exclaimed, pointing. "The water—look!"

Since the water had been running properly, no one had glanced at it. Now Betty saw that the strangeness of the ivy coming out of the tap was only the beginning. The water was running bright green, the color of grass.

"Yuck!" said Charlie. She made a heaving noise. "I ain't drinking *that*."

"It should clear in a moment," Todd said, but even he looked doubtful.

Betty watched the green water trickling down the drain, lapping at the coil of ivy in the sink. If it had been anything else, such as grass or moss, she might not be feeling so spooked. But *ivy?* After everything that had happened with uncovering the secret room, and the painting and drawings . . . the one thing linking them all was ivy: the plant *and* the girl. Granny didn't like ivy, Betty knew that much. One year the girls had brought home yule wreaths they'd made at school, and Bunny had been very strict about not bringing them in the house.

It invites misfortune, she'd said, as she did of so many things. *Never bring it indoors.*

Unlucky Ivy, thought Betty. Who was the girl in the painting, who had left the drawings in the secret room? Was she the one who had left the silver coins and sprinkled salt on the windowsills, too?

"It's clearing now," said Todd, sounding relieved. He filled a glass and held it up to the light at the window. "See?"

The water still had a greenish tinge to it, but it had definitely improved. He tipped it down the sink, then refilled the glass, checking again. Wordlessly, Betty reached past him and took the coil of ivy out of the sink. It was cool and wet in her hand as she walked quickly through the house and threw it out of the back door into some bushes. Instantly, Oi shot out from under them and rewarded her with a filthy look. He shook water droplets off his black coat and stalked away to sulk.

Betty returned to the kitchen, already feeling better. She was being silly. There were always strange goings-on in old places, if you looked hard enough. People left things behind—they'd done it themselves in the Poacher's Pocket. *Blast Granny's superstitions*, she thought crossly. They got under your skin no matter how you tried not to let them.

Even so, none of them made any move to drink the glasses of water Todd had poured. The tap dripped a few times, then was silent.

A moment later, there came the sound of keys in a lock and then the front door swung open. "Yoo-hoo!" called Granny. "Girls?"

"In here, Granny," said Charlie.

"Betty Widdershins," Granny grumbled, stomping toward the kitchen. "I thought I asked you to dust the hallway. There's a cobweb as long as my leg. Or were you planning on hanging the wash on it to dry? You—oh! I didn't know we had a visitor."

Granny had reached the kitchen and was staring at Todd. Father appeared beside her, laden with groceries.

"And who might you be?" he boomed a little too loudly. He moved past Granny to set down the basket he was carrying and offered his large hand to Todd.

"Todd," said Todd, wincing a little as Father shook his hand very firmly indeed. "Todd Berry. I met your daughters yesterday, and I—"

"Felicity!" Granny gasped suddenly, rushing over to her. "What happened?"

"Fell off the ladder," Fliss replied glumly. "Yes, I'm all right, and no, it's not blood."

"Oh, Fliss." Granny shook her head in dismay. "That lovely dress. You look like a raspberry meringue."

Charlie smirked. "A squashed one."

"Thank you, Charlie," Fliss said huffily.

"I came by to ask whether the girls would like me to show them around some more," said Todd.

Fliss peered dismally at the berry stain. "I'm not sure I'm dressed for it."

"No," said Betty quickly. "Get changed. I think you could do with some fresh air. But let's get you cleaned up first—some of those scratches look nasty."

She busied herself swilling some salt water into a bowl

and sent Charlie to find a couple of clean washcloths. It would do Fliss good to get out of the cottage for a little while after the shock of falling off the ladder, but it would also give Betty a chance to do some more investigating. She wanted a proper look through the papers she had found in the secret room—and that would be easier if Fliss wasn't around making a fuss about it. Betty had a feeling that Granny would make a fuss, too, and probably order them all to be destroyed. Already Betty couldn't bear the thought of this. To her, the tiny room was a mystery that had to be solved, an itch she simply had to scratch.

In the jostle of groceries being unpacked by Father (and raided by Charlie) and Granny clucking around Fliss, Betty slipped out of the kitchen unnoticed and went upstairs. For the first time, she realized she had no idea what she'd done with the handful of papers taken from the secret room. In the moments following the crash from downstairs, she must have dropped them, for she found them scattered on her bedroom floor.

Her bedroom. How nice it was to have her own room at last! And how handy, now that it allowed her more privacy to continue her snooping.

Carefully, she collected the papers and placed them

on the bed. Then she opened the closet and slid the panel back in place, sealing off the hidden room. Stale air whispered over her face. She fought the urge to go in and look at the painting again.

Betty leafed through the drawings. They were yellowed with age but beautiful and cleverly done. She lingered over a sketch of Blackbird Cottage from the front, showing the roses around the door in full bloom. Something about the picture niggled her, but she couldn't work out what it was. Betty flicked through detailed drawings of flowers and herbs with notes to accompany them. Then there was sheet music with lyrics to a song: something about witches. The words *Pendlewick* and *Hungry Tree* danced before her eyes, and she felt a hum of anticipation. Would this tell her more about the strange story Miss Pilliwinks had hinted at? Greedily, Betty began to read.

She came in off the road one day
In search of somewhere safe to stay.
She called herself Eliza Bird.
With her arrival, mischief stirred.

It started when she came to harm
While working on the village farm.

Oh, dearie me! How very grim!
A wooden stump replaced the limb.

Out, witch, out!
Be gone from Pendlewick.
Out, witch, out!
Be gone and make it quick.

Eliza swore that from that day
The folk of Pendlewick would pay.
And everywhere Eliza went,
There seemed to be an accident.

A scourge of roaches, rats, and mice
And beds and heads alive with lice.
A sickness here, a stumble there,
Misfortune always in the air.

Out, witch, out!
We will not live in fear.
Out, witch, out!
We'll have no witches here.

The villagers could take no more.
They gathered at Eliza's door

And took her to the village green,
The last place that the witch was seen.

She cursed them with her dying breath
And on the spot she met her death.
The Hungry Tree grew from her bones.
The villagers were turned to stones.

Out, witch, out!
Beware the Hungry Tree.
Out, witch, out!
Eliza's legacy.

Betty glanced over the song again. How gruesome! So Eliza Bird was the mysterious witch with the wooden leg supposedly buried on Pendlewick Green, whose bones, according to Miss Pilliwinks, the Hungry Tree had grown from.

"What a creepy song," she muttered to herself, feeling as though it had been waiting for her to find it, but why? She was almost giddy with the discovery and strangeness of it all. She had been hoping to find out more about the mystery of the room, and Ivy, and instead she'd found this. How curious that it should have been in the room . . . perhaps locked away for its mere mention of magic. She leafed through the papers, eager for further secrets to un-cover. There were more sketches of plants and creatures, a couple of small, sketchy ink drawings. And then something else.

Pages from a diary.

Chapter Nine

The Diary of Ivy Bell

Friday, June 13th

THERE IS SOMETHING WRONG in Pendlewick. I've felt it for weeks now, but Uncle Jem won't listen to me. When I try to talk about it, I am silenced. He reminds me of what could happen and what could go wrong.

We won't stand for any trouble here, they say. *Magic has no place in Pendlewick.*

But how else can I explain what's been going on?

Yesterday, several things happened. I woke to the mysterious sound that has been bothering me since this

116

all began. A *shuffle-shuffle* sound, like someone moving slowly along outside my door. The noise stopped, but I heard it again at the breakfast table. This time it sounded as though there could be a creature trapped under the floorboards trying to nibble its way out. Uncle Jem could not hear it and told me to get my ears checked by Dr. Mangle. So I went to the blasted doctor and had my ears poked and prodded only for her to tell me that they are working perfectly well, and that the noise must be all in my head! She told me to stop reading so much and suggested that books make the imagination "overactive." *Hmph.* I felt like suggesting that *she* should read *more*, for some joy in her life might make her less of an old grouch. (I didn't dare, of course.)

On the way back through the village, I picked up some more pencils and paints from the village store. Miss Pilliwinks and Mrs. Lightwing were as kind as ever. They insisted I take back some more jam for Uncle Jem and gave me a glass of water with a dash of their homemade syrup, because they said I looked very hot. (In truth, I wasn't. I think my face was still red from being cross with Dr. Mangle.) They really are very generous, if a little odd. But it was after I left that things became odder still.

As I crossed the bridge to come back up Bread and

Cheese Hill, I glanced down at the stream as I always do and suddenly felt very thirsty. I wondered if the sugary syrup I'd drunk in the village shop was to blame. By then, it was midday and scorching. I suddenly felt that if I didn't have something cold to drink I might not make it back up the hill in the heat. After crossing, I went down the bank and began scooping up handfuls of water to drink. The crystal-clear stream rushed past, carrying a scatter of red rose petals that looked like a fleet of tiny fairy boats. They swept along and vanished under the bridge, and I wondered if they might have come from one of our very own rose bushes at Blackbird Cottage. I sat back on my knees for a moment, splashing more water on to my wrists and neck.

I wouldn't have noticed anything peculiar if it hadn't been for Verity, the butcher's daughter. As I made my way back up to the path, I noticed her standing by the wall. She had stopped to watch me with that spiteful look of hers. Oh, how annoying to have been spotted by *her*, of all people! It's true that she and I have never been friends, but I've felt she's been waiting to catch me out ever since that day last year when she spotted me leaving Tick Tock Forest and ran straight to Uncle Jem to snitch.

But today, as I stared back at her, her face changed and went beyond its usual sneer. There was something else, something I couldn't quite work out. I had the odd sense that I'd been caught doing something wrong. Certainly, it wasn't polite to drink out of a stream like a stray dog, but it wasn't forbidden, either—unlike entering Tick Tock Forest. The memory of how angry Uncle Jem had been, even when I explained I'd only gone in there to sketch some woodland toadstools, made my temper flare even now. She had gotten me into such trouble.

"All right, Verity?" I said sharply. She didn't answer. She looked from me to the stream, and back again. Then she turned away and ran across the bridge as fast as her legs would carry her. I checked my clothes, wondering if I'd muddied them, but they were clean. I glanced down at the water to make sure I'd left nothing in case Verity accused me of littering and I *almost* missed it.

The stream was flowing in the wrong direction.

It was impossible, but it was true. I blinked and blinked and even pinched myself, but my eyes were not lying. For a moment, I doubted myself: was I mixing things up? Had the water always flowed this way? *No*, I thought with a sudden chill. *Of course it hasn't.* The stream had always run *down* from the direction of Bread and Cheese Hill and towards the village, not away from it. So how—and when—had it changed direction?

With a jolt, the image of the rose petals on the water

flashed in my mind. They had been traveling in the right direction—I'd seen them whoosh past and vanish under the bridge. Which meant that, at some point after that, the water must have changed direction without my noticing . . . when I was drinking it or splashing it over my skin. As if to back up my thoughts, I caught sight of the petals now traveling the opposite way, back in the direction they'd come from. One by one they dipped and were pulled under the water by some unseen current.

Verity had noticed. That's why her expression had changed from scornful to . . . fearful. I understand now. Somehow, Verity thought *I* had made this happen.

I backed away from the stream, keeping my eyes on it until the hedges hid it from view. Then I turned and fled up the hill back home, feeling the cold water from the stream sloshing in my stomach like poison. Twice I stopped and looked back, for I heard a faint shuffling noise and thought it was the sound of someone behind me on the path. But as soon as my footsteps stopped, so did the sound. I began to wonder if Dr. Mangle was right —was it all in my head?

When I reached Blackbird Cottage, I was shaken, and only then realized I had forgotten my key. Uncle Jem keeps a spare one under a flowerpot, but as I neared it I heard something from the back of the house. I made my way through the gardens and found Uncle Jem tending to the vegetable patch, turning over soil and pulling weeds. Our cat, Tibbles, was snoozing contentedly between the strawberry plants with her back legs in the air and her paws covering her face. The sight of her and my uncle calmed me a little. His fluffy beard and the hair poking out from under his cap matched the white fur on Tibbles's tummy perfectly. They go together like strawberries and cream.

The moment he looked up at me, Uncle Jem knew something was wrong.

"What is it?" he asked, setting down his trowel.

I hadn't planned to tell him what had happened by the stream. I didn't want to worry him, and besides, I knew what he would say. But his warm, brown eyes were so kind that before I knew it the truth came spilling out. He listened without saying anything, his craggy, old face grave.

"Sometimes," he said when I'd finished, "our eyes can play tricks on us. For instance, when we're watching a wheel spinning very fast, it can appear to be turning the opposite way. Or when we glance at a clock and think we've seen it ticking backwards. That sort of thing."

I considered his words. I wanted to believe him very badly, but there was one thing that stopped me. *Verity.*

"It wasn't like that," I whispered, sinking down on to the little wooden stool my uncle used in the garden. "It wasn't a trick of the mind."

Uncle Jem's eyes were on me, questioning. "If you say that's what you saw, then I believe you. But tell me now, did anyone else see?"

It was a question I had been dreading.

"No, Uncle." I couldn't look at him. The lie stuck in my throat like a thorn. "No one else saw."

"Good." He patted my hand, relief lighting up his face. "I'll go and make a pot of tea."

I stayed where I was, not wanting tea but company. I listened to the tap of his walking stick on the path and the shuffle of his feet and thought of the other sound. Now that I compared them, it wasn't like a person shuffling along, after all. So what *was* it?

Tibbles rolled onto her front and watched as Uncle vanished into the house. On a cooler day, she might have followed and mewed at him for a saucer of milk, but today it was too hot even for Tibbles to move. She blinked lazily and yawned, watching a spider weaving a web above her.

"You're squashing those strawberries," I scolded her half-heartedly, reaching down to tickle her chin.

My voice sounded loud in the quiet garden, like an unwanted guest. Trees whispered and bees hummed. Somewhere, a cricket chirped. I noticed a peacock butterfly on a branch next to me, flexing its wings. It was rust-colored with bright blue circles ringed in black, giving it the appearance of having eyes. I shuddered. Normally, I enjoyed seeing butterflies, but today I felt too anxious. After the strange sound that had followed me up the hill, the eye shapes only added to the feeling of being watched.

Another sound disturbed the peace. I looked away from the butterfly. Tibbles had gotten to her feet and was leaning over the path, her plump tummy heaving and churning. I sighed, knowing what was coming: a hairball. At least this time it was outside and not on one of the rugs indoors, I thought, getting up to fill a bucket with water so I could wash it away.

But what came out of Tibbles was not a hairball or even vomit.

It was a frog. A large green one that was very much alive. I froze, staring at it. Poor Tibbles stared, too, as bewildered as I was. She didn't even chase it when the creature gave a cheerful *ribbit!* and hopped away into the bushes.

How was this possible? Cats don't swallow their prey whole and alive—yet that frog didn't have a mark on it. And Tibbles had been peacefully snoozing in the garden, something she wouldn't have done with a live frog wriggling in her belly. It was another thing that made no sense.

I was still unsettled when Uncle Jem returned. He was out of breath and red-faced, and the tea tray wobbled in his hands as he rested it on the low wall.

"Now then," he puffed. "Let's have a nice cup of tea and we'll say no more about odd things and streams flowing the wrong way. You know how people talk around here. How they're afraid of what happened . . . before."

I nodded, uncomfortable as my thoughts returned to Verity. She sure as heck won't keep what she saw to herself, I know that much.

Any mention of strange or unnatural things isn't welcome in Pendlewick. The witches might be long gone, but no one forgets. Some even say there have always been witches here, and always will be. That spells are bubbling away under the surface. And so people are always ready to suspect another Eliza Bird or Rosa Ripples working dark magic—and look at what happened to them. Besides, there's only one other person I'd want to tell and I don't dare to write his name here. Even though I'd rather be filling these pages with thoughts of him instead of the other odd things that have been happening. But there will be time for that, I'm sure.

Uncle Jem is calling me for supper now.

I haven't told him about the frog.

Chapter Ten

Nettle Soup

THE DIARY ENTRY FINISHED THERE. Betty looked through the papers and found another entry. From the date written at the top, she could see this had been written less than a week after the one she'd just read. She settled into a more comfortable position, preparing to read it, but felt a pang of guilt. Diaries were private, secret thoughts. Fliss got huffy if Betty or Charlie dared to sneak a look at her love poems. A diary was even worse. And here she was, about to delve into the secrets of a stranger.

But it's not like I knew Ivy Bell, Betty reasoned with herself. *Whoever she was—or is—surely she would have taken these things with her if they were that important?* And truth be told, Betty was curious. About the secret room, about the painting, and about the strange things they'd found in Blackbird Cottage. Perhaps Ivy's diary would help her answer some of the questions she had. Her eyes lingered on the strange part about the frog. Then again . . . perhaps not. Maybe Ivy's diary wasn't to be trusted. For all Betty knew, she could have been inventing the strange happenings out of boredom, or perhaps, as the doctor suggested, the girl had an overactive imagination.

"What you doing?"

Betty's eyes shot up, and she hurriedly tucked everything behind her back before realizing it was Charlie. "Oh, it's you." She gestured to the papers. "I was just looking through these."

"Anything interesting?" Charlie asked, chewing the end of one of her pigtails. "Ooh," she said suddenly, before Betty could answer. Her green eyes lit up as she put a finger in her mouth and wiggled. "Another wobbly tooth!"

"You still haven't gotten rid of Peg," Betty teased with a smile, feeling lighter now. "Who gives an old tooth a name and carries it around for months, anyway? Strange child!"

"I told you," said Charlie determinedly, patting the pocket where she kept Peg, "I want to see the tooth fairy, and she ain't having Peg until she shows herself." She looked concerned all of a sudden. "Will the tooth fairy know where to find me now that we've moved?"

"The tooth fairy can find you anywhere," Betty promised.

Reassured, Charlie sat down next to her and pointed at the papers. "Is that a poem?"

"It's a song," said Betty, gathering it up and slipping it behind some of the drawings. She didn't want Charlie reading it and having nightmares. "About a witch who lived in Pendlewick. The one with the wooden leg."

"Why would it be in our house?" Charlie asked.

"That's what I'm trying to figure out."

"Are you going to tell Granny and Father about it?"

"No," said Betty. "Not yet, anyway. You know what Granny's like. She'd make Father brick that room up and burn all these papers before I have a chance to look at them properly. Let's keep it our secret for now."

Charlie nodded solemnly, but her eyes sparkled. There were few things she enjoyed more than being included in Betty's and Fliss's secrets.

"What about the old woman?" she asked. "We should tell about her, shouldn't we?"

"Yes," Betty replied. It might earn them a scolding from Granny and Father about not keeping the back door closed, but they needed to know. "We can't have strangers walking in here like that." She gave one of Charlie's pigtails a playful tug. "Why did you come looking for me, anyway?"

"Oh," said Charlie, "that's what I came up here to tell you. Granny says we're to bathe"—she wrinkled her nose—"and get dressed in our smartest things because Miss Tiddlywinks and Mrs. Lightwing have invited us to supper this evening." She giggled. "She said she couldn't think of an excuse not to go. She's so cross!"

"I bet she is." Two things Granny found tiresome were making polite conversation with strangers and being on her best behavior. Back in Crowstone, the customers in the Poacher's Pocket were used to her quick temper and plain speaking. They hadn't dared complain when she banged down their glasses and slopped beer everywhere. But of course the Widdershinses were not in Crowstone anymore.

Betty wasn't too pleased about it, either. She was itching to read the next part of Ivy's diary—if the whole thing wasn't nonsense, it might explain the hidden room. For now, though, it would have to wait.

"They could have waited until we'd settled in a bit," Granny muttered as they began walking down Bread and Cheese Hill. Overhead the sky was the color of marigolds as the sun slipped lower over Pendlewick. "We only arrived yesterday."

"Stop grumbling, Granny," Fliss scolded, slipping her arm through Betty's as they walked along the lane in the warm evening sunshine. "It's nice to be invited somewhere, isn't it? They probably thought they were being helpful by having us over for supper. It's one less thing for us to take care of." She'd recovered from her shock now, no doubt helped by her afternoon stroll with Todd. Her hair was neatly combed and she wore a pale pink dress that was the exact shade of her cheeks. The only signs of Fliss having fallen off the ladder were the cuts and bruises on her arms.

"Mmm," said Granny. "Charlie, will you stop kicking the dirt up like that? It's going all over your nice dress."

"Don't like dresses." Charlie scowled down at her yellow dress but did as she was told.

"But you look so sweet," said Fliss. "Like a little buttercup!"

"It's itching me," Charlie said, fidgeting, but at the same time Betty detected a slight smirk on her little sister's face and had a feeling she might be up to something. The suspicion was confirmed when Charlie reached up to her collar and pretended to scratch, but Betty caught sight of a telltale movement in her hair.

"Charlie!" she whispered. "Tell me you *didn't* bring Hoppit!"

Charlie grinned up at her wickedly. "Yep."

"But . . . but we told you to leave him at home!" Betty hissed. "You can't bring a rat to a dinner party."

"Can." Charlie stuck her tongue out and skipped ahead to Father, where she knew Betty wouldn't question her further, and slipped her hand sweetly into his. Betty felt her upper lip get even sweatier in the humid evening. The last thing the Widdershinses needed was an invisible rat creating mischief when they were trying to fit in and make a good impression.

"Here we are," said Granny, as they came to the bottom of the hill. "Foxglove Cottage."

"How lovely," said Fliss, admiring the tiny thatched house. "And it's surrounded by foxgloves, just like its name."

Betty agreed. It was a pretty place. The cottage had white walls, neat hedges, and a bright red door with a black iron knocker shaped like a piece of knotted cord. She hoped that one day Blackbird Cottage would look as lovely as this.

She stood back as Father knocked and stared back down the path toward the center of the village. From here, she could see the start of the bridge over the stream and Ivy's diary entry crept into her mind. Had the water really flowed the wrong way? Or had Ivy been mistaken? For the first time, Betty wondered how long ago it was that Ivy and her uncle had lived at Blackbird Cottage. Perhaps it was more recently than Betty had thought, for Ivy had mentioned Miss Pilliwinks and Mrs. Lightwing in her diary, after all.

Betty turned back as the red door swung open. Miss Pilliwinks beamed her picket-fence smile and beckoned them in. She looked younger than she had when Betty had first seen her at the village store. Betty wondered if it was down to the peachy sunset, for even her hair seemed less gray and more copper in color.

"Welcome, welcome!" she said. "You're right on time. Come in and make yourselves at home."

She swept them down a carpeted hall and toward a door that was not quite closed. Like Blackbird Cottage, the kitchen appeared to be at the back, for Betty could hear the sounds of crockery being set out and the smell of something peculiar cooking. As they approached the door, she became aware that there was a tapping noise coming from the other side of it, rather like a clock. But as Miss Pilliwinks showed them inside the room, the sound stopped.

It was large and well lit, full of little knickknacks and

pressed flowers that had been framed and hung on the walls. A dining table had been set with seven places. At the front of the room, by the window, a woman stood up and came forward to greet them. She appeared older than Miss Pilliwinks, with her gray hair pinned up on her head. She didn't have glasses or the magnified eyes, but the hawkish nose was the same. Her eyes were a dark greenish gray and rather stern, but with a kindly twinkle. She reminded Betty of a schoolteacher she once had.

"This is my sister, Mrs. Lightwing," said Miss Pilliwinks, nodding and blinking fast behind her owl glasses. She seemed younger still in the presence of her sister, and again Betty wondered if it was the soft lamplight in the room.

"How nice to meet you all," said Mrs. Lightwing, her piercing gaze sweeping over them. Her voice was low and quiet, the voice of someone used to being listened to.

One by one Father introduced them all politely. Betty waited for Mrs. Lightwing to say, "Oh, call me Doris," or whatever her name was, but she didn't.

"A spinning wheel," Charlie exclaimed suddenly, wandering away.

Betty peered around Granny. Sure enough, Charlie was right. A wooden spinning wheel the color of straw was in front of the window. This must have been the tapping noise she had heard before they'd come into the room. Betty stared at the silver spindle, thinking of curses and pricked fingers. "Don't touch, Charlie," she warned, as her little sister went closer.

"I've never seen a real one before," said Charlie, fascinated. "Does it work?"

Mrs. Lightwing smiled, her eyes crinkling. "Yes, child. I was just spinning some nettle thread when you arrived."

"Nettle thread?" Charlie asked doubtfully, shrinking back. She had been badly stung when she'd fallen into a nettle patch when she was younger and had been afraid of them ever since. "Like *stinging* nettles? Don't you get stung?"

"Never. But it takes some practice," said Mrs. Lightwing. "Let me show you." She sat down at the stool and reached into a basket next to her. She took a pinch of silvery-looking fibers so fine that they looked like strands of fair hair. Then she began working the pedal with her foot, and the wheel started to turn. Her fingers moved quickly, twisting the fibers onto a piece of cord that ran along through the machine and collected on a spool. "Like that, see?"

"Why do you use nettles?" asked Fliss.

"You can spin thread with lots of things," said Mrs. Lightwing. "Plant fibers, sheep's wool. Even hair." She set down the thread and stood up, brushing a loose fiber from her skirt. "But nettles make excellent cord. They're plentiful and strong. Delicious, too."

"You eat them?" Charlie squeaked.

"Yes." Mrs. Lightwing smiled again and glanced at her sister. "In fact, nettle soup is what we're having for supper. Isn't it, Miss Pilliwinks?"

Another rattle sounded from the kitchen. Betty wondered who was in there if both the sisters were in the dining room with the Widdershinses. Perhaps they had a cook helping them, but it was Miss Pilliwinks who excused herself and returned with a large steaming pot and a platter of crusty bread.

"Please sit down," she said.

One by one they took their seats as the nettle soup was ladled into bowls. It was bright green with swirls of cream running through it. Betty glanced sideways at Charlie, who was making no effort to hide her disgust and was sneaking crumbs of bread up to her collar for Hoppit. Cautiously, Betty lifted a spoonful to her lips. It was surprisingly tasty, and she suddenly realized how hungry she was.

The meal passed in a blur of chat, during which Granny and Father spoke about their previous home in Crowstone and asked questions about Pendlewick.

"The stone circle by the pond on the village green," Father asked, tearing off more bread. "How long has it been there?"

"Over a century," Mrs. Lightwing replied, taking a dainty sip of soup. "Before the time of anyone living in Pendlewick now, of course. It's said that each stone was a person, a villager, and that they were cursed by a witch."

At the mention of witches, Betty's spoon paused halfway between her bowl and her mouth.

"Eliza was her name," Miss Pilliwinks added. "Eliza Bird."

Words from the old song that had been in the secret room went through Betty's head.

She called herself Eliza Bird.
With her arrival, mischief stirred . . .

"A nasty piece of work, she was," said Mrs. Lightwing. "Wherever she went, people got sick. Hens stopped laying eggs; crops rotted in the fields. More than once she was heard wishing bad luck on people."

Eliza swore that from that day
The folk of Pendlewick would pay . . .

"You said she had a wooden leg," said Betty.

Miss Pilliwinks nodded. "She'd had an accident down at the farm. Trod on an old, rusty blade. The wound became infected, and so . . . *chop!*" She sliced down with her butter knife. "Off it came, just below the knee."

"How dreadful," said Fliss.

"There was a suspicion that she'd hidden the blade herself," said Mrs. Lightwing, "for the farmer, after they had an argument about money. But somehow she forgot where she'd left it and injured herself."

Miss Pilliwinks nodded. "Serves her right."

"And the stones?" Father asked.

Mrs. Lightwing put down her soup spoon and steepled her fingers. "Well, legend has it that eventually the villagers had had enough of Eliza and her wicked ways. A crowd of them gathered and went to Eliza's house, accusing her of witchcraft. They held a trial on the village green. Eliza was put in the stocks—"

"The very ones opposite the village shop," Miss Pilliwinks put in.

"—and questioned for hours. When she still wouldn't confess, they floated her in the pond."

"Floated her?" asked Charlie, puzzled. "Like a duck?"

"Oh, no, dearie!" Miss Pilliwinks tittered. "That's

what they did to suspected witches back in those days. They were dunked in water to see if they were innocent or guilty. If they were guilty, they floated. If they were innocent, they drowned."

"But that's not fair!" Betty blurted out angrily. "And it makes no sense. What if they could swim?"

"No one can swim with their thumbs tied to their toes," Mrs. Lightwing said with a shrug. "In any case, Eliza didn't sink. She floated."

"Perhaps it was her wooden leg," said Granny.

"This *is* just a story, isn't it?" Father interrupted with a worried glance at Charlie.

"Oh, probably," said Miss Pilliwinks. "Most of it, anyway. You know how villagers like to gossip. No doubt the story has been embellished over the years." She winked at Charlie. "So don't you go having nightmares, dearie."

"She was found guilty and hanged on the green," said Mrs. Lightwing. "So the story goes," she added quickly, glancing at Father. "But before she died she muttered a curse and turned the crowd of villagers into stone. There they remain to this day. It's said that whoever can correctly count the number of stones in the circle will be able to undo the spell on them."

"I bet I could," said Charlie at once.

Miss Pilliwinks smiled. "It's been tried many times,

but it's harder than people think. No one has ever managed to count the stones and find the same number twice."

"This soup is delicious," said Father in a bright voice that suggested it was time to change the subject. "What's the recipe?"

"Oh, that's a family secret, I'm afraid," said Mrs. Lightwing, tapping her hawkish nose with a smile.

Betty nudged Charlie under the table. "You haven't touched your soup," she whispered. "Try some."

Charlie shook her head stubbornly, her pigtails swishing. There was a naughty look on her face, and suddenly Betty spotted what her little sister was staring at. Charlie's napkin was moving slowly across the table by itself, with a small round shape underneath it. *Hoppit!*

For the first time, Betty came very close to wishing that they didn't have the magical nesting dolls, for Charlie seemed to think they were toys and she was getting too fond of using them for her own amusement.

Betty nudged her little sister hard with her elbow. *Pick him up*, she mouthed, afraid one of the adults would see. Luckily, they seemed engrossed in a conversation about Granny's horseshoes and other lucky charms, but Betty realized it was only a matter of time before one of them noticed. She knew Charlie was just bored and messing around, but at that moment, with Granny and Father both looking happier and more relaxed than they ever had in Crowstone, Betty wanted more than anything for the Widdershinses to belong in Pendlewick. She was determined that nothing should ruin their fresh start. Especially not a mischievous little sister and an invisible, three-legged rat . . . who was now wandering too far from Charlie and in the direction of Miss Pilliwinks. Even Charlie was looking alarmed now.

Betty lunged for the napkin, managing to scoop up the rat just before he bumped against their host's hand. Unfortunately, in leaning across the table, she managed to tip up her own bowl of soup. It sloshed all over her front and onto the white tablecloth, making a big green mess.

"Oh, I'm sorry," Betty blurted, dabbing herself with the napkin. Under the cover of the tablecloth she passed a wriggling Hoppit back to Charlie with a warning glance, then gestured to her dress. "I need to rinse this before it stains. Is there a sink nearby?"

"In the kitchen," said Miss Pilliwinks cheerfully, not seeming to mind the mess Betty had made of her table. "Just down the hall."

Betty shot her a grateful smile, then left the dining room and headed toward the back of the cottage, where she had heard the sounds of crockery earlier. It could have been worse, she thought. Spilled soup was nothing compared to an invisible rodent.

Like the dining room, the hall was covered in lots of little picture frames containing dried and pressed flowers, each one labeled in squiggled pencil. As Betty reached the kitchen door, she stopped dead and stared at one of the frames. Not all of them were flowers, after all.

This one was a butterfly, with rust-colored wings and blue spots shaped like eyes. It was a peacock butterfly, like the one Ivy had mentioned in her diary. A silver pin pierced the middle of the creature, holding it in place. It was strange, Betty thought, that she should see it so soon after reading the diary. But then, she supposed, if it hadn't been for the diary, she wouldn't have given the butterfly a second glance. They were probably everywhere—she just hadn't noticed.

Betty went into the kitchen, scraping at the stain on her clothes. A sludgy piece of nettle came away under her fingernail. She'd been right about the cook, for there was a woman hunched over the sink, scrubbing at a large black pot. She had her back to the door and was so intent on her work that she didn't hear Betty approaching.

"Excuse me?" Betty said softly, not wanting to startle her. "I spilled some soup. Could I please have something to . . ."

The woman glanced at Betty and froze. Their eyes locked, both widening at the same time. Betty recognized her instantly and felt a spike of dread.

"*You!*" she whispered.

For it was the old woman who had been in Blackbird Cottage.

Chapter Eleven

The Sleepwalker

THE BLACK POT SLIPPED THROUGH the old la-
dy's fingers and fell into the sink with a splash. It sent
up a wave of soapy water that drenched her apron and ran
down the cupboards to drip on the floor.

Betty stared at the old woman, afraid and confused.
Could she be mistaken? She took in the woman's straggly, gray hair, the stoop of her back, and the wrinkled,
milky eyes with their strangely intense stare. It *was* her.
But why had Miss Pilliwinks and Mrs. Lightwing's cook
been in the Widdershinses' new house and broken the
mirror? And most importantly, why had she pointed at
Fliss in such a way?

Betty took a step back. One quick shout and Father

143

and Granny would come running, but as Betty opened her mouth to yell, the woman lunged at her and clamped her hand over it, stifling her cry. Betty tasted soapsuds, surprised by the strength in the wrinkled, old hand. The woman was not as frail as she appeared.

Betty seized the hand, realizing at the same moment that the old lady's head was shaking from side to side, her lips moving soundlessly.

Betty stared into her eyes, frozen with fear. *Was she cursing Betty, too?*

The thought cut into her, making her brave. She twisted out of the old lady's grasp and backed away, her chest heaving with shaky breaths. She could hear it now: a low whispering coming from the woman's lips.

"No, no, no," she whispered, her eyes still wide and fixed on Betty's. She shook her head and seemed to be trying to say something, but what it was Betty couldn't tell.

Betty stared back at her, disturbed. She could still shout out now: one word and the others would come. She drew a breath, but something about the woman's expression cut off the cry in Betty's throat. Was there a trace of fear? And at the same time a small and selfish part of her whispered: *Don't make a scene; don't upset things more than you already have. Just get away, far away, from this strange, old woman—now.* All the same, she decided to give her a warning, too.

"I'll keep quiet for now," she whispered fiercely. "But if you ever show up like that again, I'll know exactly where to find you." She paused. "What were you doing in our house, anyway?"

The old lady stared back at her, saying nothing.

Betty stiffened, her confusion thickening. She was beginning to wonder if the woman was crazy, or playing some kind of trick. Either way, Betty had had enough.

"I don't know what you wanted, but you stay away from us," she hissed. "Do you hear me? You stay *away* from our house and my family."

Unsettled, Betty turned to leave the kitchen, but the woman reached out to her again. This time there was a damp cloth in her hand. She motioned to Betty's dress.

"I'll do it," Betty muttered, but the woman persisted and began firmly but gently dabbing it on the soup splashes on Betty's dress.

"It should all come out now." The words were like cobwebs and dust, whispered so softly that Betty wondered if she'd imagined them.

Betty inspected the damp patch. She could see no sign of the green stain at all.

"Looks like it's out already," she said stiffly. Her skin

crawled, hating being this close to the old woman. She couldn't work out what it was, but something about her felt . . . *wrong*. Something didn't fit.

The woman gave a strange little smile, one that didn't meet her eyes.

Uneasy, Betty turned and hurried out of the kitchen, eager to get back to the low chatter of the dining room. As she entered the hall, a small movement caught her attention and she found herself glancing at the framed peacock butterfly she'd noticed before. She blinked. She could have sworn that the wings had moved, but now it was completely still.

Of course it's still, she told herself. *The poor thing is dead! What's gotten into you, Betty Widdershins?*

Of course, she knew what—the old woman. She couldn't forget the look of rage on her face in those moments at Blackbird Cottage. Perhaps she *should* say something to Granny and Father? And yet now that she was away from her, Betty began to doubt herself. The woman had certainly frightened them that day, but did it mean she deserved to get into trouble? It could all be a silly misunderstanding. Betty thought of the woman's old, chapped hands, which were a little like Granny's. If she said something now, it might even cost the old woman her job. Or worse, Betty could get labeled a trouble-maker, and their nice, new start could turn sour before it had even properly begun.

Mrs. Lightwing was standing by the dining-room door when Betty went in.

"There you are," she said, taking her seat again. "We were wondering what happened to you."

"Got the stain out," Betty mumbled, sitting down. "And then I was looking at the pressed flowers and the butterfly." She felt a little better now and was beginning to wish she'd had more time to enjoy exploring Foxglove Cottage with its intriguing knickknacks.

She nudged Charlie, who was idly stirring her un-touched soup with one hand and wobbling her tooth with the other. Charlie put the spoon down again and picked at a piece of bread. There was, thankfully, no sign of Hoppit causing any further mischief and Betty guessed he must be asleep in one of Charlie's pockets.

"Your cook helped me, actually," Betty said, wondering if she might be able to find out more about the mysterious woman. "I'm not sure what she used, but it did the trick."

"Oh, yes." Mrs. Lightwing smiled faintly. "Miss Webb has been very useful, hasn't she?"

Miss Pilliwinks glanced up from her bowl, nodding. There was a smear of soup on her chin, making her look faintly ridiculous. "Very useful. Although"—she lowered her voice—"she sometimes acts a little strangely, so please let us know if she says or does anything that concerns you."

Like wandering into people's houses? Betty thought. Instead, she said, "What do you mean, 'strange'?"

"Well," said Miss Pilliwinks, "she is quite fond of going near the Hungry Tree, even though everyone knows to keep away. And she has a habit of talking nonsense to people. Fortunately, she's harmless. Most of the villagers know not to take any notice of her."

"It sounds like she's lucky to have you," said Father.

"Doesn't sound like anyone else would have *her*," Granny added drily.

Betty relaxed a little, glad she hadn't made a scene in the kitchen. It seemed as though Miss Webb wasn't anything to be afraid of, however troubled she might be.

"Are you expecting a visit from the tooth fairy, child?" Mrs. Lightwing asked, fixing her huge eyes on Charlie. "You've been wobbling that tooth all evening."

"Not yet," said Charlie gloomily. "It's not loose enough. But I still have my last tooth, Peg."

"Charlie Widdershins, don't you dare," Granny began,

but Charlie had already produced Peg from her pocket. "Where are your manners?"

"Oops," said Charlie, losing her grip. The tooth dropped into the cold soup with a little *plip*. Betty and Fliss exchanged embarrassed glances. Charlie looked equally horrified and began scooping through it with her spoon. "Oh no! PEG!"

Miss Pilliwinks gave a tinkling laugh. "Charming! Don't you worry, dearie. We'll fish that out and rinse it off for you." She rose and began collecting the dishes. "Now, who's for dessert? We have homemade honey cake."

"Does that have nettles in it, too?" Charlie asked distractedly, one eye still on the soup containing her lost tooth.

"If it did, I'd have said so, dearie," Miss Pilliwinks answered, patting Charlie on the head. "However, little girls who don't eat their supper don't usually get dessert in this house." She looked at Granny expectantly.

Bunny waved a hand. "It's fine. She normally eats everything—"

But Charlie never got to eat any of the honey cake, and neither did Betty. For it was at that moment that Betty began to feel very peculiar.

"Oh," she said, creasing up in pain. "Ooh, my tummy

hurts." She pushed her chair back and stood up. "I'm so sorry, but I think I need to go home. I'm not feeling well."

"Goodness," said Mrs. Lightwing, her gravelly voice full of concern. "I do hope it's nothing serious." Miss Pilliwinks hovered by her side, nodding vigorously.

"Oh dear," she said, placing the dishes back on the table and wringing her hands. "Oh dearie me, indeed."

"I'll come with you, Betty," said Charlie, clearly bristling at being called a little girl.

Between groans and gritted teeth, Betty thanked Miss Pilliwinks and Mrs. Lightwing and set off up the hill, with Charlie trotting beside her in concern.

"Are you all right, Betty?" she asked, rubbing her sister's back. "I'm glad *I* never ate that soup."

"It can't have been the soup, Charlie." Betty leaned against a low wall, clutching at her tummy. "Everyone had it except you." She fumbled with a button at her neck, her fingers slippery with sweat. Her skin burned, like she had a temperature. The evening was still so warm and the sky not yet completely dark, though stars glittered in it.

She staggered onward and was perhaps halfway to the cottage when she had to stop again. "Oh, jumping jackdaws. I'm going to be sick!"

She leaned over and heaved into a scrubby area of bushes, her stomach emptying of the thick, green soup.

Soon there was nothing left, only a sour taste in her mouth. Afterward, she felt a little better. The pain left her tummy and her legs felt a little stronger, but she still felt feverish. "Shall we go back?" she asked, realizing as she said it that she didn't want to.

"Nah." Charlie wrinkled her nose. "Let's go home. I don't think Miss Periwinkle likes me, anyway, now that I wouldn't eat her soup. She patted my head too hard, and she pulled my hair when she did it."

"It must have been an accident," said Betty, thinking of how concerned the two women were. "Perhaps your hair got caught on a ring she was wearing. They seem like nice old ladies. Anyway, what were you doing with that rat of yours? We're supposed to be making a good impression, remember?"

"It was just a bit of fun." Charlie shrugged, licking her lips wistfully. "Do you think they might send some honey cake back home for us with Granny?"

Betty didn't answer. She didn't care about honey cake; the thought of eating anything else at that moment was quite unbearable.

"It wouldn't have hurt Fliss to come with us," Betty grumbled as they reached the front door of the cottage. "She barely even looked at me when I said I didn't feel well." Normally, Fliss was the one who fussed if someone was ill. Perhaps she was still feeling shaky herself after her fall from the ladder.

They stepped into the darkened cottage, almost tripping over Oi, who shot past their ankles to get out.

"Ooh," said Charlie, crouching down on the tiles. "Look, a little frog! Oi must have brought it in."

"It's alive?" Betty asked in surprise, but already she could see the frog hopping over the kitchen floor.

Charlie scooped up the creature and carried it through the Nest to release it out the back door. Betty climbed the stairs and sank into bed, exhausted. Her forehead had begun to burn. She pushed her face into the cool pillow, trying to press away feverish thoughts of frogs and nettles and butterflies. At some point, Charlie came in and settled next to her, whispering softly.

"Betty, I forgot Peg."

Betty stirred, trying to find a cool place on the pillow.

"I'm sure Miss Pilliwinks will look after Peg," she mumbled. "Is Granny home?"

"Not yet," said Charlie. "But, Betty, what if they throw Peg away with the soup?"

Betty didn't answer. Right now, she didn't care about Charlie's silly tooth or anything else except her burning, throbbing head and the need to make it stop. She slid deeper into a restless sleep where everything around her melted away.

She awoke to a darkened room dappled with moonlight. What time was it? The sky outside the window was deepest blue, pricked with stars. Charlie was fast asleep next to her, sprawled out with her mouth wide open and Hoppit nestled under her chin. Betty frowned, spying the nesting dolls on the bedside table. Charlie must have been messing with them while Betty slept.

Betty sat up. The room felt airless, and her mouth was dry. She desperately wanted a drink of water. She put a hand to her forehead, finding it clammy but cool. Whatever temperature she'd had, it had broken. She slid her legs over the side of the bed and stood up.

What was that?

Her ears had caught a sound. She listened. A snuffle from Charlie and, across the landing, a snore from Father's room. So he and Granny and Fliss *had* returned while she'd been asleep. But neither of these sounds was what she'd heard.

She took a step toward the door, then paused. There it was again. A low whispering. The ivy on the outside of the house?

With a jolt, she saw that the closet door was open. Just a crack, but Betty was sure it had been closed when she'd left the room earlier that evening after getting ready. She took a step toward it, hand out to push it closed—then froze.

The whispering was coming from *inside*.

The sweat on Betty's face turned colder still. She pulled the door open a tiny bit more, allowing a chink of moonlight into the dark space. Her fingers trembled. The panel at the back of the closet was open, revealing the hidden room. The whispering trickled out, a jumble of words that Betty couldn't quite string together.

Someone was in there—but who?

Thoughts of Miss Webb crept into her mind. Could the strange old woman have followed them home? But she pushed this notion aside. Granny would have locked up—there was no way someone could have sneaked into the house a second time. And would the old woman dare after Betty's warning?

Betty hesitated, afraid and not sure what to do. If she went to get Father, it meant leaving Charlie alone with whoever—or whatever—was only footsteps away in the secret room. If she woke Charlie, then they would be heard.

For a moment, everything fell completely still and silent, like the house was waiting to pounce. It was then that Betty caught a snatch of the whispered words, and this time it was enough to understand them.

> *"Out, witch, out!*
> *Be gone from Pendlewick.*
> *Out, witch, out!*
> *Be gone and make it quick."*

Betty clapped a hand over her mouth. She knew that voice . . . but it couldn't be, could it? Shakily, she pulled the closet door wider. It opened without a sound. She stepped inside, breathing in the familiar stale air, and peered into the secret room. The whispering was louder now, and she could see a figure standing motionless in the middle of the darkness. She wore a flowing white nightgown and her short, choppy hair stuck up in tufts as if she'd gotten out of bed in a hurry. And though Betty couldn't see her face clearly, she knew now that she had been right.

"*Fliss?*" she whispered in amazement. "What are you doing in here?"

Fliss didn't reply or even seem to have heard.

"Fliss?" Betty repeated, stepping closer to her sister. She strained to see in the darkness, then glimpsed her sister's face and gasped.

Fliss's eyes were glassy and staring. It was clear that she didn't see Betty, and Betty knew instantly what she was looking at.

The painting.

But was she really seeing it? Or was she sleepwalking? Betty crept closer, hesitating. Fliss continued to whisper, only it was the same part of the song Betty had found in the room. The chorus, over and over again.

> *"Out, witch, out!*
> *Be gone from Pendlewick.*
> *Out, witch, out!*
> *Be gone and make it quick."*

"Fliss, please," Betty whispered, touching her arm lightly. "Come out of here." Her heart was thumping now, making her breathless. The sight of her sister—who hadn't wanted to put a foot inside the hidden room before —now gazing at the eerie painting and whispering, *chanting*, about witches was filling her with fear.

She had never known Fliss to sleepwalk before, if that's what this was. But the way she was staring and whispering did not feel as though her sister were in a dream. And with an icy realization, Betty remembered that she alone had read the song—and she hadn't told either of her sisters about it. So how did Fliss know the words?

"Come on, Fliss," she said gently, taking her sister's hand. "Come with me. Back to bed now."

Again, Fliss gave no sign that she had heard Betty, for her gaze remained fixed on the painting. Betty glanced at it, her skin crawling. In a shaft of moonlight, Ivy's eyes gleamed back at her, more lifelike than ever. Betty tugged Fliss's hand more firmly.

"Come on," she said again, and this time Fliss followed her through the opening and into Betty's room. The whispering became muttering.

"Fliss," Betty whispered. "Please stop that."

But the muttering continued, all the way down the stairs and through the kitchen. They passed Granny, fast asleep and smelling faintly of tobacco, on her fold-out bed. It was only when Betty led Fliss into the Nest that the whispered words finally stopped and her sister obediently slid into the sheets and closed her eyes as though she had never been out of her bed.

Betty watched her, making sure she really was asleep. Then she got herself a glass of water and drank it, trying not to think of the green water and ivy that had come out of the tap before. Returning to bed, she firmly closed the closet door and wedged a chair against it.

Are you doing that to stop anyone from going in? asked the little voice inside her head. *Or to stop something from getting out?*

Either way, Betty had a horrible feeling it was already too late. The one thing she did know was that she needed to find out exactly what had happened to Ivy Bell. As much as Betty told herself that she was being ridiculous, she couldn't help feeling that the girl's presence still lingered. That she had some strange hold over Blackbird Cottage.

Checking that Charlie was still asleep, Betty reached under the corner of the mattress and pulled out the papers. She wasn't sure why she had hidden them, exactly. Partly because she knew Granny wouldn't be happy with Ivy's talk of strange goings-on in their new home, and partly, if Betty was really honest, because she wanted to keep the discovery to herself for now. Fliss had been disturbed by the secret room, and Betty wondered if it might be best to hide the mention of witches from Charlie until she knew more.

Looking through the papers, she found the next part of the diary. Then she lit a candle and began to read in the flickering light.

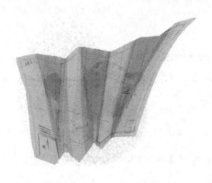

Chapter Twelve

The Diary of Ivy Bell

Thursday, June 19th

I AM NOT IMAGINING IT. More things have happened, and it's getting worse. Because now other people are noticing.

I woke to that sound again. The shuffling sound that haunts me. As soon as I decide it sounds like one thing, I begin to wonder if it sounds like something else. Sometimes it's so bad that I stick my fingers in my ears hard enough to make them ache. Only then does the noise stop.

Uncle Jem is losing patience with me. When I mention the sound now, his eyes glaze over and it's as though he is not even listening. So I try not to talk about it at all. Before school, I helped him hang some clean clothes out to dry in the garden. We both saw Tibbles throw up not one but *two* live frogs, which hopped away to the pond. I told Uncle then about the other frog a few days ago. His explanation is that now that Tibbles is so old and has bad teeth, she can't chew properly—but I don't see how she could have even caught them. I have no other explanation, though. At least not one I can say aloud.

What happened at school made me even more glad that I am leaving there forever in three weeks. Of course, that hateful little sneak Verity has told people about what happened at the stream, just like she told people about me going into Tick Tock Forest. No one has said anything to me, but I've seen them whispering, and Magda overheard and told Verity how silly she sounded.

Magda's a good friend. I feel bad lying to her, telling her that what Verity says isn't true. Because it *is*. We both saw it. What I do know is that *I* didn't make the water flow the wrong way, no matter how it appeared. But with the other things that are happening, it will be hard to convince anyone else.

I could almost have forgotten about the stream and the frogs this afternoon. The weather has been so warm that Mr. Travis suggested we take our art lesson outside on the village green. It was wonderful to be out of the stuffy schoolroom—I felt like one of the poor trapped insects buzzing at the windows before it's released. We set up our easels in a shady spot at a safe distance from the Hungry Tree and the stone circle, and Mr. Travis told us we could paint or draw whatever we liked, as long as it was something we could see. He really is the best art teacher anyone could ask for, even though he hardly seems old enough to be one.

I wanted to paint the reflections on the surface of the pond, for the light was so pretty, but we're not really supposed to pay much attention to the Hungry Tree and the standing stones or the pond. I remember someone wrote a story about them once and got into trouble for it. How can we be expected not to be interested in them, though? We've grown up hearing the stories and songs of Eliza Bird and Rosa Ripples and warned of what might happen to us if we wander down the witches' path. It's hard to look at that green pond without thinking of Rosa Ripples, the second Pendlewick witch, and the story of what happened to her. Parts of the song drifted back to me then, the song everyone knows but no one is supposed to sing:

Rosa Ripples, maiden fair,
Bonny face and golden hair.

Once a girl so good and plain,
Prettiness had made her vain.

From dumpy duckling to a swan,
Knobbly knees and pimples gone.
Why the reason for this switch?
Rosa Ripples was a witch . . .

I hadn't realized I was whispering it to myself until Magda elbowed me and gave me a warning look. I shook myself out of the daydream.

In the end, I decided to paint Mr. Travis. His dark skin and handsome looks make him a good subject for a portrait. Of course, the person I really wanted to paint was . . . No. I mustn't write his name. If Uncle found this diary, he would be so cross! He often tells me I've no time for sweethearts. I opened my paintbox, filled my water jar, and set to work. The strokes of my paintbrush swirling colors, the summery day . . . before long my mind drifted back to the song:

Piece by piece and day by day,
She magicked all her flaws away.
She gave them to the village folk
And wore their beauty like a cloak.

But with each thing that Rosa stole
It left a scar upon her soul.
The more she posed and preened with pride,
The uglier she was inside . . .

The next thing I knew, Magda was tugging one arm
and Mr. Travis the other. Both were speaking to me gently, pulling me out of a soft haze.

"Ivy," Magda said. "Can you hear me? Please stop!"

I realized I was standing next to the pond, just a footstep away. My shoes were beside me on the grass, my skin
was sweaty, and my arms felt hot and prickly from the
force of the sun. I had no recollection of how I came to be
standing there.

"What am I doing here?" I asked. "How did my shoes
come off?"

"You took them off yourself," said Magda. Her troubled eyes searched mine. "Don't you remember? You did
it just now." She nodded at the pond. "We called and
called you, but you couldn't seem to hear us. And then
all of a sudden you stopped and took your shoes off, and
it looked as though you were about to step into the water."

My head throbbed with the heat of the sun. I felt
groggy, like I'd been asleep. How long had I been standing

here? And then I realized what Magda had said. "What do you mean, I stopped? Stopped what?"

"Walking," said Mr. Travis. He was watching me intently, as fearful as Magda. "Around and around the pond."

I shook my head, wincing as it throbbed even harder. "Walking . . . around and around?" I heard the confusion and panic in my own voice.

"You did," Magda whispered. "And what's even stranger is you walked around it backward, without once looking at where you were going." She took her hand off my arm and lowered her eyes. "You went around it three times."

"I don't understand. I can't remember doing that. I don't remember how I got here. One minute I was painting . . . the next I was here."

"Come on," Mr. Travis said. His voice was kind, like his dark brown eyes. Yet I could hear the worry and see it. "Perhaps you've had too much sun. It can do strange things."

I picked up my shoes and allowed him to lead me back to the group. They were watching me with their mouths hanging open. Like I was something hooked out of the pond that had been put in a jar for them to gawp at.

Mr. Travis told us to pack up our things as the church

bell struck three. I was glad to, but when I turned to my easel, there was another shock in store. For there on the paper was a painting I didn't remember doing. It was not of Mr. Travis, as I had planned. It was a picture of the pond with the sunlight on its surface and the twisted root of the Hungry Tree reaching into the water. Beyond it were the standing stones. Out of habit, I began counting them. Counted them again. The numbers didn't add up, of course.

"Who painted this?" I asked. My voice was so dry, it wasn't much more than a rasp.

"You did," Magda said quietly, emptying her jar of paint water onto the grass. "Who else could have painted something like that?"

She was right, of course. I'm always careful not to seem bigheaded about my artwork, but everyone says I'm the best in the class—in the school, even. But how could I have painted something this good, this quickly, and still had time to circle the pond three times? It made no sense.

I peered closer at the water in the painting. There was something in it that I hadn't seen at first, something only just noticeable within the green, murky water. A face. A fair-haired, pretty girl. I stared. Who *was* that? Certainly not me, though I'd been close enough to see my own re-flection. Odder still, there was no one on the edge of the pond looking in. It gave the eerie appearance of someone *in* the pond gazing *out*. And all of Pendlewick knew there was one person whose name was linked with the pond on the village green: *Rosa Ripples*. The final part of her song whispered in my head.

> *There never was a girl more fond*
> *Of gazing in the village pond.*
> *Smiling down with deep affection,*
> *Worshipping her own reflection.*

> *One day Rosa failed to see*
> *A movement from the Hungry Tree.*
> *With a mighty splash, she fell*
> *And after that? No more to tell . . .*

What had happened to me? How had I managed to paint a picture without any memory of doing it, and how had I ended up beside the water? And why was this haunting song tormenting me? I glanced around at the faces of my classmates. Some of them were smirking; others were curious. A few were afraid. Had any of them noticed the face in the painting? I picked up a large, flat brush and swirled it in green paint, then dragged it over the face again and again until she was gone.

It might have ended there. I might have convinced them that it was all a daring prank to liven up a sleepy afternoon or that I'd simply had a funny turn in the intense, prickling heat. But then the butterflies came.

It was on the walk back to the schoolhouse that I noticed them. A few at first, five or six fluttering around us before circling me. Then more. People stopped, stared, and murmured as the numbers grew. Ten, fifty, a hundred. Two hundred perhaps. Swooping around me again and again. All of them identical: brown with blue spots on their wings that looked like eyes watching me. *Peacock butterflies.* Settling on me, settling on the path, and forcing me to stop in case I stepped on them.

I held my breath, trying to shake them off, hating the feel of their tiny legs crawling on my skin and their papery wings skimming my cheeks.

Then all of a sudden, they shot into the air and clustered together to make a shape. There were gasps and cries. People froze, pointing up. There was no denying that the creatures had formed a word: the word everyone knew and feared.

Witch.

Chapter Thirteen

Wicked Spells

OVER THE NEXT COUPLE OF DAYS, Granny kept the girls and Father busy. Slowly, the little cottage was transformed by coats of fresh paint. The gardens became neater and prettier, and everything soon had a place.

Three days after Fliss's sleepwalking, Betty woke and went downstairs to a quiet house. She found Granny in the kitchen, hanging curtains up while balanced dangerously on a stool. Her pipe dangled from her lips and smoke puffed around her.

"Granny, get down from there!" Betty scolded. "I'll do that."

Granny did as she was told, brushing ash from her chest. "Have you seen my pipe?"

Betty snickered. "You're smoking it, Granny."

Granny gave an impatient tut. "I'm not a twit, Betty. This is my old one. I'm talking about my new one."

"Nope." Betty clambered up on the stool, rubbing her eyes. She was tired and her mind was as foggy as Granny's tobacco smoke. Not surprisingly, she hadn't slept well since finding Fliss in the secret room, and then Ivy's diary and the strange songs about Eliza Bird and Rosa Ripples kept playing in Betty's head.

Fliss remembered nothing of her little nighttime wander and insisted that Betty must have been mistaken as a result of the strange, feverish sickness she'd had. In fact, this combined with the golden sunshine streaming into the pretty cottage was starting to make Betty wonder if she'd dreamed the whole thing. There was also a possibility that Ivy's diary, with its fantastical descriptions, was affecting her more than she cared to admit. To her relief (and disappointment), there were no more diary entries within the cluster of papers, and thanks to another restless night with dreams of ponds and frogs, Betty had decided that even if she discovered more, she wouldn't read them.

"There's porridge for breakfast," Granny said, heaping

a dollop into a bowl without waiting to be asked. "After you've eaten that, wash the breakfast dishes, and then I need you and Charlie to take Fliss's lunch to her over at Peckahen Farm. There's a list with a few other chores for you and Charlie, too."

"Couldn't she have taken her own lunch?" Betty grumbled, hopping down from the stool. She had forgotten that today was Fliss and Father's first day working over at the farm. It would be strange not to have her older sister around.

"She forgot," said Granny, rolling her eyes. "She's been half in a daydream ever since that boy came knocking."

"Fliss is always in a daydream," Betty muttered. It was true, but Fliss had been noticeably more scatterbrained than usual, floating around in a daze. *She must have it bad for Todd*, Betty thought.

She ate a spoonful of porridge and glanced out of the window. Beyond the garden, she could see Charlie in the distance, swinging underneath the hawthorn tree. Once again, the sky was blue and cloudless, but at some point it had rained in the night, for the garden path glistened with moisture. A frog hopped across it in the direction of the pond, bringing Betty's thoughts back to the diary and the secret room.

"Granny," she began, "have you ever lived anywhere with a secret passage . . . or a hidden room?"

"No," said Granny. "I always wanted to, though." She chuckled mischievously. "When your father and his cousin Clarissa played together as children, I told them the Poacher's Pocket had a secret passage. They spent hours looking for it and never found a thing!"

Betty couldn't help grinning. "Why didn't you ever tell Fliss and Charlie and me that?" she asked. Even if it hadn't been real, it would have been fun to believe.

Granny sighed, the laughter leaving her eyes. "I'm not really sure. You forget things as you get older. Like how to have fun, I suppose. You know how it was at the Poacher's Pocket—work, work, work."

It was true. Granny had had a lot to deal with. All of them had been forced to work, and there had been other things to worry about—not least the family curse. There hadn't been much time for fun.

"Why did places have those sorts of hidden rooms?" Betty asked casually. "Were they to hide smugglers and stolen goods?"

"Sometimes, yes," said Granny. "They were also made to shelter persecuted people, such as those suspected of witchcraft."

Betty felt a spoonful of porridge stick in her throat. "W-witches?" she asked after gulping it down.

"Mmm," said Granny, distracted as she polished her boots. "People called them 'witch holes' or 'crook holes,' depending on who they were being used to hide."

Witch holes. Betty stirred her porridge. Was this what the secret room upstairs was? She thought of the creepy songs. There were only two witches mentioned in it— Eliza Bird and Rosa Ripples. There was no mention of Ivy Bell, and from what Ivy had written, it seemed she hadn't been dabbling in magic or understood the things that were happening to her. Betty hoped that the strange goings-on had come to nothing. As much as Ivy's diary had unnerved her, she couldn't help feel a little protective toward the girl.

"Right," said Granny, pulling on her boots and then draining a cup of tea. "I'm off. Wish me luck."

"Off where?"

"The Sugar Loaf," said Granny. "I'm doing a trial run in the tearooms, mustn't be late." She stamped down the hall and winked back at Betty over her shoulder. "If it goes well, you'll never want for ice cream again. They have almost every flavor, you know."

"Hopefully not whiskey flavor," Betty muttered as

the front door slammed, leaving her alone in the cottage. Only then did she realize she hadn't wished Granny luck. She washed the dishes quickly, uncomfortable in the silence of the house, then grabbed Fliss's lunch and went outside, glad to escape into the gardens, where the smell of rain still hung in the air.

"Charlie?" she yelled. "Come on, we're going out."

She followed the path farther down as Charlie leaped off the swing and came racing back to the walled garden, her wild hair flying behind her.

"We're going to the farm," Betty explained, turning and shooing her little sister back up the path toward the cottage.

"To get chickens?" Charlie asked hopefully.

Betty shook her head and playfully swatted her. "You and your chickens."

They had just reached the path around the side of the cottage when Oi slunk out of the bushes and looked up at Charlie with a mournful yowl.

"What is it?" Charlie cooed. "Poor Oi. Is it too warm for you? Oh no—he's going to be sick!"

But he wasn't sick, not exactly. And while Betty had somehow known what was going to happen, she still froze as a slimy green frog came tumbling out of the cat's mouth.

"Jumping jackdaws," Charlie breathed. "Is that . . . *alive?*"

"Yes," Betty whispered. She felt cold and nauseous and afraid. She couldn't pretend anymore. No matter how much she wished for everything to be normal in their new house and in Pendlewick, there was no denying it. There was something wrong at Blackbird Cottage. Whatever had happened to Ivy Bell was starting again. "It's happening to us," she whispered, hardly realizing she'd said it out loud.

"What is?" Charlie frowned, holding out a gentle hand to Oi. He hissed at her and skulked off into the bushes. The frog stayed on the path, watching them with eyes like black beads.

"Whatever happened before."

Peckahen Farm was hot and smelly. The walk there should have taken around twenty minutes, but Betty had made it in fifteen, practically dragging Charlie behind her through the winding lanes in her rush to find Fliss. They arrived drenched in sweat, and Betty's hair was wilder than a haystack.

"Don't be silly, Betty," Fliss said irritably once they'd tracked her to a barn next to the farm shop. She hefted another crate of strawberries onto a stack and wiped her hands on a cloth. "He obviously gobbled up the frog without chewing and it didn't agree with him. I bet it happens all the time."

"You don't think it's strange?" Betty argued, following Fliss into the barn. "When Ivy Bell, who lived in our house, wrote about the *exact* same thing in her diary?"

"I think it sounds like a thing cats do." Fliss sat down on an empty crate and took an enormous bite of her sandwich.

"But they *don't*," said Betty. "And even without that, what about the other stuff?" She lowered her voice. They were alone in the barn, but she could hear people next door in the farm shop buying goods. Just out of earshot, Charlie was leaning over a stone wall to fuss over some piglets, where she'd been since they arrived. In the distance, Father and Todd were in the fields, shifting a trough.

"You don't think it's odd that we found all those things hidden in a secret room and that the diary mentions Ivy walking around the pond without knowing she was doing it? And then you get up and walk through the house in the middle of the night without even realizing it?"

"I told you, I don't sleepwalk." Fliss picked a crust off the bread and popped it into her mouth. "Granny said so, too. Besides, you had a fever. Everyone knows people have strange dreams when they're not well. We'd only just found that room, for crow's sake—it must have been on your mind."

"But, Fliss," Betty began, "I really don't think I dreamed it. It was too vivid. I *touched* you. And then there was that witchy song—"

"Exactly," Fliss cut in, gazing past Betty to the fields. "You were the one who found the song, not me. I'm telling you, it was a dream."

"There's something else," Betty blurted out, desperate to hold her sister's attention when it was clearly wandering off to Todd. "I should have told you before. The night we had dinner with Miss Pilliwinks and Mrs. Lightwing, I . . . I saw the old woman who came into the cottage. The one who pointed at you."

Fliss lowered her sandwich, frowning. "Where?"

"She's their cook," said Betty. "I saw her when I went into the kitchen."

"You *what*? Why didn't you say anything? You should have called Father or Granny—"

"Perhaps because I was too busy trying not to throw up at the time," Betty retorted, also irritable now. *And because you didn't care enough to come home with me.* She was still peeved about this, as well as the way Fliss was dismissing her worries about everything going on with

is the only farm in Pendlewick. This is where . . . where it happened. She didn't lose her leg here, though. She cut herself and the wound became infected. So the story goes, anyway."

He examined the cut, gently prodding it. A trickle of blood oozed from it and dripped to the ground. Betty looked away, queasy, and saw that Charlie had come over and was staring at Todd's foot.

"Yuck. Does it hurt?"

"A little." Todd winced. When he spoke next, he looked Charlie in the eye, his voice lower, more serious. "Don't go telling anyone I cut myself, though."

"Why not?" asked Charlie. She sat down next to Betty, reeking of the pigsty. Betty wrinkled her nose.

"Every time there's an accident—especially here or near the green—people start talking."

"About what?" Betty asked, even though she had a good idea what Todd was going to say.

"Witches." Todd kept his voice quiet. "Some say Eliza buried things in the dirt after a fight about pay. Ill wishes."

Charlie's eyes widened. "What's an ill wish?"

"A wicked spell," Todd explained. "Wishing bad luck on a person. The story goes that Eliza enchanted things— old blades, rusty nails, and such—to do worse than just cause a cut. And that she accidently stepped on one of the ill wishes herself."

Betty nodded. "That's what Miss Pilliwinks told us, too."

"If people find out I cut myself in the fields, they'll start saying it's something Eliza left from years ago," said Todd. "So it's best not to mention it."

"Even after all this time?" Betty asked. Pendlewick folk appeared so cheerful and breezy that it seemed odd they would link an accident now to a witch from a century ago.

"It's silly, I know," said Todd, forcing a little laugh. It didn't quite meet his eyes.

"Silly," Betty echoed, but her mind was working fast now, trying to unpick the knots of these peculiar Pendlewick mysteries and why they continued to have such a hold.

And everywhere Eliza went,
There seemed to be an accident . . .

Could there be another reason why Todd was so superstitious about it, something closer to home?

"I was wondering about another thing," Betty added quickly. "You said one of your cousins had an accident—"

"The one called Wags," Charlie put in.

"Did that happen here on the farm, too?'"

Todd shook his head. "That was something . . . different."

There was a beat of silence in the barn. Somewhere outside a duck quacked indignantly, as though it were telling someone off. Betty waited, wondering if she had asked one question too many. Perhaps Todd found his cousin's accident too upsetting to talk about and she had stirred up uncomfortable memories. But then he took a breath and began to speak in a rush.

"We say it was an accident, but the truth is no one really knows what happened to him. There wasn't a mark on him when he was found, not that we could see. Whatever went on"—Todd tapped his head—"it happened in there. No one's ever managed to get to the bottom of it." His mouth twisted bitterly. "But everyone knows it was something to do with Ivy Bell."

Betty went very still. "Ivy B-Bell?"

"She lived in your house until two years ago," Todd said shortly. He pulled a piece of hay loose from the bale and shredded it, not meeting her eyes. "She'd been acting strangely for some time. Kept talking about the Pendlewick witches, Eliza Bird and another girl, Rosa Ripples. Weird things were happening around her. Animals and creatures doing odd things. Someone said they saw her make the stream flow backward. I never believed it at first—I thought it was just stupid gossip. But then one day on the green, she got up and began walking backward around the pond, like she was in a dream." He shuddered. "Her entire class witnessed it. That was when the rumors really started."

"That she was a witch?" Betty whispered.

Todd nodded. "People got really afraid, then. There was talk of driving her out, her and her uncle Jem. But she must have found out about it and decided to run away before they could get to her because she vanished a few days later."

"What about her uncle?" asked Betty, excited to have Todd's account, especially as it confirmed what had been written by Ivy herself. "Did he leave, too? And where does Wags come into it?"

"Wags was the last person to see her." Todd's eyes flashed with anger. "They were seen together by the stones on the green the night she vanished. Wags was always fond of her, you see. She'd looked after him and Scally sometimes. It would have been easy for her to lure him there. He'd grown up trusting her."

"What did she do to him?" Charlie asked.

"Like I said, no one knows," Todd said curtly. "But it must have been a spell. When he didn't come home for supper, we went out looking, and that's where he was found. Alone." He paused. "Since then, he's never said a word nor grown an inch. As for her uncle, he stayed for a while after Ivy vanished, but eventually he left, too. Moved to a town on the other side of Tick Tock Forest."

Todd flicked away the piece of hay he'd been playing with. "I suppose he didn't want to be reminded of what she'd done."

Betty swallowed as Todd's words went around in her head.

"So you knew her," she said. "Do *you* believe she was a witch?"

"Yes," he said softly. "I knew Ivy. And whatever was going on, there was magic involved." He blinked, giving her a hard look. "You know, you ask a lot of questions."

Betty shrugged and lowered her gaze. She had to ask questions if she was going to discover what was bubbling away in this little village, but perhaps she had said too much. "I'm just curious."

"So was Ivy," said Todd with a frown. "You should be careful what you talk about in Pendlewick. You don't want people getting suspicious."

Betty chanced a look at him and found his blue eyes were trained on her. There was a glazed look to them that made her a little uneasy. "Suspicious of what?"

"There's a saying that there will always be witches in Pendlewick," said Todd slowly. "You don't want the finger pointing at you. Magic always leads to trouble, and we don't want any trouble here."

"No," Betty said quietly, spooked by the familiarity of his words. "No, I expect you've had enough of that." She got up just as Fliss returned to the barn with a bowl of soapy water and a soft cloth in her hand. "Right. Well, we'd better get going."

"Do we have to?" Charlie asked, glancing longingly at the pigsty again. "Mrs. Heckapen said I could help her feed the piglets in a little while."

"Maybe tomorrow," said Betty. "We have chores to do for Granny."

"See you at dinner, Fliss," Charlie said a little mournfully.

"See you," Fliss echoed, barely looking up from the bowl of water as she tended to Todd's foot.

Betty frowned. It was unlike Fliss not to say a proper goodbye. She and Charlie left the stifling barn and stepped out into the blazing afternoon sun, waving to Father as they passed the field along the dirt track that led away from Peckahen Farm.

"Meddling magpies," Charlie moaned. "I'm melting, Betty. Do we *really* have to do chores? Can we at least get an ice cream on the way home?"

"There's no time for that," Betty said in a low voice. "And the chores will have to wait, too. There's something more important we need to do."

"What?" asked Charlie, looking at her strangely.

Betty took a deep breath. "Charlie, listen to me. I think . . . I think something's going on in Pendlewick. Something with magic . . . and witches."

"You mean like what you said earlier?" Charlie asked. "About things happening again that had happened before?"

"Yes. Because . . ." Betty hesitated. There was something about speaking fears aloud. It made them stronger, more real, but she couldn't ignore the coincidences any longer. "Because this time I'm scared that Fliss could be in danger."

Charlie looked up at her gravely. "What are we going to do?"

"We're going to investigate." Betty swallowed a lump in her throat. Her little sister's words, and complete trust, were like a hug. Already she felt stronger, more determined.

"If someone *is* messing around with magic in Pendlewick, then they've got a shock coming. Because us Widdershinses have a bit of magic up our sleeves, too."

Chapter Fourteen

The Ill Wish

THERE WERE FOUR FROGS HOPPING around the kitchen when Betty and Charlie arrived back at Blackbird Cottage. A fifth frog had been cornered by Oi next to the pantry.

"Oh no," said Charlie, shooing a furious Oi out of the way. She bent down for a closer look at the frog and her eyes filled with tears. "It's belly up—I think he killed it!' She scooped it up gently and turned it over. "Oh, wait— it was playing dead!"

"We need to get them out," said Betty. She felt repulsed at the sight of the squirming, hopping creatures. It had sounded crazy when Ivy had described it in her diary, but it wasn't crazy. It was magic—the kind that only led to bad things — and she wanted the frogs gone. "Make sure Oi's shut out, too. At least if he throws up any more, they can hop off to the pond."

Together, they managed to rid the kitchen of frogs, giving them a chance to escape down the garden path.

"Good thing Fliss isn't here," said Charlie, nudging Oi out the back door. "She wouldn't like all these frogs."

When they went upstairs, there was one more in the bedroom, resting on Betty's bed.

"Ugh," she said in disgust. "Right on my pillow!"

"How did it get all the way up here?" Charlie wondered.

"It didn't." Betty pointed at a furry patch on the bed. "Oi must have slunk up here for a nap and threw it up on my bed." She chased the frog around the bedroom, finding that every time she made a lunge for it, it slipped out of her grasp. "Help me catch it, Charlie!"

While Charlie scampered after the frog, Betty spied her wooden nesting dolls on the dressing table. They were the reason she'd come upstairs. She felt giddy and panicky as she grabbed them. Whatever was going on at Blackbird Cottage felt dark and scary, and right now she needed to arm herself with magic of a good kind.

Charlie pounced, brushing against some clothes that were hanging over the bedpost. A dress slipped to the floor and landed in a heap on the frog. "Got it." Charlie slid one hand under to cup the frog, flinging the garment aside with the other. It landed at Betty's feet. Something small and green tumbled out of the dress and rolled just under the bed.

"What was that?" Betty's nose twitched as a smell wafted up. She knelt down and peered under the bed. Another whiff caught her nose, something so peculiar she couldn't place it at all. Betty reached out and took the little green item, feeling a crumbly texture under her fingers. For a moment, she was afraid it might be yet another frog—a dead one, shriveled up and dried out—and she shuddered in revulsion. But it wasn't a frog.

It was a tiny bunch of twigs and herbs not much larger than Betty's thumb, bound tightly with thin string. Some of the herbs were dried and others had been fresh but were now wilting in the intense heat. Betty lifted the bundle to her nose and sniffed carefully. Her stomach clenched in a familiar way. Her eyes went to the dress on the floor.

"That's what I wore to dinner the other night," she whispered, understanding dawning. "To Miss Pilliwinks and Mrs. Lightwing's house. And this was caught up in it." She grabbed the dress, looking it over. There, just above a faint soup splash, was a pocket. She recalled the chapped hands dabbing at her dress, and the feeling she'd had at the time of things being wrong. It made sense now. She felt sick, only this time it was with shock. "It was *her.* That's how she did it."

"How who did what?" asked Charlie, grappling with the squirming frog.

"Miss Webb," said Betty. "Their cook. It was *her,* Charlie. The old woman who broke into the house. And that night, when I went to the kitchen, she must have put a bad spell on me with *this.*"

Charlie eyed the little bundle fearfully. "Perhaps you shouldn't touch it."

"It's already done what it was supposed to." Betty's fist clenched in anger, and she felt the little herb parcel fall apart in her fingers. "This is what made me sick the other night. She made that happen, I just know it. It's like what Todd talked about—an . . . an ill wish." She remembered now what the strange old lady had said: *It should all come out now.*

"She wasn't talking about the stain," Betty realized. "She was talking about the soup! She must have poked this into my pocket while she was wiping my dress. She knew I'd recognized her and wanted me out of the house in case I told on her!"

It was all starting to make sense now: the old woman

had cast a spell on Betty and had put a spell—or curse—on Fliss, too. That must be why Fliss had been acting so strangely, so uncaring toward her. She wasn't just lovestruck—she was bewitched!

"There *is* a witch in Pendlewick, all right," said Betty, her eyes lingering on the spell bundle. Now that it had come apart, it looked innocent, like a handful of something Granny might throw in a stew. Betty knew what it had done, but would anyone else believe her? "This is proof, but it's not enough. She *did* do something to Fliss that day when we saw her in the garden."

Charlie bit her lip. "When she pointed at her?"

Betty nodded. "And if I'm going to put a stop to it, then I need to find out exactly what she's up to." She pocketed the nesting dolls and went rushing down the stairs with Charlie behind. Together, they released the last frog and the ill-wish bundle into the garden, with Betty stamping the sickly smelling herbs into the dirt, wanting to be rid of it.

Stepping back into the kitchen, Betty parted the two halves of the outermost nesting doll. "I'll need to use these," she began, then paused. A twitching brown nose had appeared in Charlie's collar as the magic of the dolls was undone.

Charlie frowned. "What about me? I'm coming, too."

"Charlie, you need to stay here. It's not safe for you to come with me—she's already put spells on me and Fliss. I can't risk anything happening to you as well."

Charlie shook her head obstinately, reaching up to tickle the rat's chin. "I'm coming with you. Anyway," she added, "we'll be invisible, won't we?" She glanced around the kitchen uncertainly. Betty felt a pang of guilt. Of *course* Charlie wouldn't want to stay here alone, in this cottage of secret rooms, spluttering taps, and thrown-up frogs. There was no guarantee she'd be any safer here than she would be with Betty.

"You're right." Betty relented, hoping she wouldn't regret it. "I can't leave you here on your own. But Hoppit has to stay behind."

Charlie pouted but knew better than to argue, especially after her recent rat-related mischief. She ran upstairs, presumably to hide Hoppit in the little doll's house that was, unbeknown to Granny, his secret home.

When she returned, Betty plucked a hair from Charlie's head and put it into the third doll next to Hoppit's whisker. She then pulled one of her own frizzy brown hairs out and placed it carefully in the second largest nesting doll before stacking the dolls inside one another. Standing in front of the kitchen window, she twisted the two halves of the outer doll so that they were perfectly aligned. Her reflection in the glass vanished instantly. She turned to Charlie and smiled faintly. They might be invisible to anyone else, but they could still see each other.

"Come on, let's go," she said. Together, they slipped out the back door, and Betty locked it. "We'll go through the back gardens," she said. "The kitchen window at Foxglove Cottage looks out over them, just like ours. If Miss Webb's there, we can spy on her and see what she's up to. We've got to prove she's behind all this strange magic —the way Fliss has been acting and Oi with those frogs."

They needed evidence and this was the perfect way to search for it without drawing any attention to themselves.

They passed the pond, now alive with the ribbiting of frogs, and headed down the path. The end of the garden was still an overgrown mass of brambles and fruit trees, yellow and parched from the summer heat.

"Let's go through the meadow," said Betty. "It's less overgrown."

"What about through there?" Charlie pointed past the gate to what appeared to be a leafy tunnel that ran along the back gardens.

It wasn't a lane, exactly. More like a walkway that was half-hidden under a canopy of greenery, and it was so wild that, even without the invisibility of the dolls, Betty was sure they wouldn't have been seen.

"Someone's been along here," she said, pointing to the grass. "Look, it's all trampled down." She remembered the way the old woman had vanished so suddenly. Could it have been Miss Webb, who had used it to access Blackbird Cottage? "This probably wasn't a good idea," she muttered as the leafy tunnel narrowed. "If anyone comes along the opposite way, there's not much room at all—they might not see us, but they'd feel us, all right."

"Just keep going," said Charlie, swatting bugs away from her face. "We must be nearly there now—look. There's a gate."

"There's Lark Cottage," said Betty. This gate was barely visible through the weeds; it was clear no one had used it in a long time. "Foxglove Cottage is the next one along."

They hurried on in silence, thoughts of Ivy's diary and Eliza Bird weighing on Betty's mind as heavily as the summer heat. She couldn't let anything bad happen to Fliss—she had to stop that old witch, whatever she was up to.

The next gate they saw was bright red, and the area around it neatly tended.

"Same color as the front door," Charlie whispered.

Betty nodded, reaching for the latch and praying it wasn't bolted from the other side. The latch lifted, and she gently pushed the gate, holding her breath. Even invisibility wouldn't prevent a telltale creak, but they entered the garden soundlessly and easily. She urged Charlie through into a long cottage garden. It was similar to the garden at Blackbird Cottage, with taller fruit trees at the back and row upon row of plants set out in neat sections: flowers, herbs, and vegetables. The only area that looked vaguely wild was a large area of stinging nettles, but as she recalled the green soup and the silvery thread on the spinning wheel, Betty suspected the nettle patch was exactly as Mrs. Lightwing intended.

They followed a winding path through the garden until they reached the pretty cottage. It was such a bright day that the inside of the house appeared dark, and Betty wished that the door had been open to allow them a glimpse inside. She wondered if they might have wasted their time. With Miss Pilliwinks and Mrs. Lightwing at work in the village store, it was their best chance of catching Miss Webb up to something. Only now she realized with disappointment that she had no idea what the old woman's working hours were. Perhaps she only came by in the evenings, and only if her employers needed extra help. Still, she and Charlie were here now, and Betty was determined to find out something that could help her stop whatever was happening to Fliss.

Laundry flapped on a line, partly hiding the kitchen window. Betty ducked under it and, feeling bold thanks to her invisibility, stepped up onto a low drainpipe for a better view.

"See anything?" Charlie whispered, looking anxious.

Betty shook her head, cupping her hands to the glass. For a moment, she thought the kitchen was empty, but then she realized with a jolt that someone was standing by the counter. Betty wobbled in alarm, grabbing the sill to steady herself. It was Miss Webb! She was stooped over something, working intently. Betty could hardly tear her eyes away from her. It was one thing to have a bad feeling about somebody, but quite another to find out that feeling was right. Betty glanced around the rest of the room, heart racing. There was a large basket next to the sink, filled with freshly cut nettles. On the stove, a pot of peeled potatoes sat in water, ready to be boiled.

It just looked like any other kitchen. There was nothing to suggest any wrongdoing here, yet Betty knew different. However innocent the old woman appeared, no one else could have planted the spell bundle in her clothes . . . and no one else had been skulking around their garden, muttering curses and pointing fingers.

The problem was, Betty couldn't see anything much from where she was. She had to get inside somehow. Her tummy flipped at the thought of it. *Just a peek*, she told herself. *Just a better look at what she's doing in there. But how?*

Maybe they could draw her out. Betty stepped down from the pipe. She considered knocking on the back door, but that would only make Miss Webb suspicious. She brushed against the clothesline, and it gave her an idea. Quickly, she pulled off several items, scattering them around the garden. Then she darted back to Charlie, and the two of them waited just beside the back door. Minutes passed with the sun blazing down on their shoulders.

"Betty," Charlie whispered. "It's so hot. Can't we wait in the shade?"

"No," Betty whispered back. "I have to get a look inside, so we need to be ready or we might not make it to the door in time." Her neck itched with sweat and her hair began to frizz uncontrollably. Surely Miss Webb should have looked up by now?

"Stay here," she told Charlie, creeping back to the window. She stepped up onto the drainpipe and bit back a shriek. Miss Webb's face loomed behind the glass, staring straight at her.

She can't see me, Betty reminded herself. *I'm safe, I'm hidden.* But still her breath caught in terror to know she was face-to-face with a witch. The woman's face twisted in annoyance, her old, milky eyes narrowed and suspicious. Betty jumped again to avoid the water flowing out of the drainpipe as Miss Webb used the sink. Carefully, she stepped down, urging Charlie back. Any moment now . . .

A key scraped in the lock and the red door opened. Miss Webb marched outside, clearly flustered as she began gathering up the dropped clothes.

"Doesn't make sense," she muttered, pinning a pair of baggy stockings back on the line. "There's hardly a breath of wind!"

Betty slipped her hand into Charlie's and tugged her through the open back door into the cool kitchen. The simple idea had worked like a charm, but they had to be quick!

They had barely taken two steps when Betty heard Charlie gasp in pain. At the very same moment, a sharp sting sliced into the soles of both her feet. She bit her lip to stop herself crying out, but her eyes watered in agony. Had she stepped on broken glass?

"Betty!" Charlie whimpered, her eyes full of tears. "My feet! They're hurting, like I've cut them, or I've been stung . . ."

Betty's eyes went to the basket of nettles. She took another step and felt another sharp pain like the pricking of a pin. *Stung*...

"Oh no," she whispered, as she realized too late that they had made a dreadful mistake. "Charlie, I think there's a spell on the cottage! We have to get out—"

It was at that moment the kettle on the stove began to whistle, quickly rising to a high-pitched shrill. Betty stared at it in horrified amazement. How was it boiling when there was no flame beneath it? Steam billowed from its spout and the scream became a voice, a horrid shriek that sounded remarkably like a person.

"Intruders! Intruders in the kitchen!" it screamed. *"Get them out, get them out!"*

"Run, Charlie," Betty said urgently, but already she saw that Miss Webb had heard the shrieking kettle and rushed back to the kitchen doorway, barring their exit.

They were trapped.

Chapter Fifteen

Hubble, Bubble, Trouble

BETTY SQUEEZED CHARLIE'S HAND, nodding in the direction of the hallway.

Front door, she mouthed. *Go!*

Charlie shook her head, tears running down her face. A whimper escaped her lips, which Betty hoped was disguised by the screaming of the kettle. She could tell Charlie, with her fear of nettles, was too afraid and in pain to take another step.

Miss Webb remained frozen in the doorway, her eyes flashing around the kitchen, seeing nothing but the kettle. She looked both alarmed and suspicious. Locking the door behind her, she pocketed the key and stepped into the kitchen. Betty felt a lump of dread hardening in her throat. Now the front door was their only option.

Miss Webb dumped the clothes in her arms on the table before taking the kettle off the stove and resting it on a chopping board. The kettle quieted instantly, but continued to let out angry little puffs of steam as if in warning to the intruders.

Betty just had time to take one silent, painful step out of the way as Miss Webb grabbed a broom by the door and rushed into the hallway. The sound of her footsteps pounded the floor as she first entered the dining room, then took her search upstairs. A peculiar sound drifted down through the ceiling. A *swish-swish-swish* and muttered words. Betty stiffened. Was this another spell?

"Charlie, listen to me," Betty whispered frantically. How could she ever have thought she would get away with spying on a witch, and with her little sister in tow? "You have to go out the front door and run all the way home. Every footstep is going to hurt as long as we're in this house, but you have to be brave and not make a sound, understand?"

Charlie looked up at her, her large green eyes watery and red-rimmed. "B-but where will you be?" she asked, her voice trembling.

"I'm going to stay here," said Betty, gritting her teeth at another sting. "I need to keep looking. Just for a few minutes."

"But, Betty, what if she catches you?"

"She won't. I'll be careful," said Betty. "For the cottage to have these enchantments on it, she *must* be hiding something. And I might not get another chance to find out what."

Betty gave her sister a quick hug. "Now go. Wait for me in our garden."

Charlie gulped, gritted her teeth, and took a tentative step toward the hall.

"Oh, Betty, I can't! It hurts!"

"You *have* to!"

With a last teary glance at her sister, Charlie set off again, sniffling as doors from above slammed. At least the kettle had shut up now, Betty thought grimly, but no sooner had it entered her head than another voice cut through the silence.

"Intruder! Intruder in the hall! Get her out, get her out!" it trilled in a wickedly triumphant voice. Betty stared down the hall, consumed by panic as footsteps sounded on the upstairs landing. This was all going so wrong! Charlie was halfway across the hall, her hand reaching for the door and her shoulders shaking with silent sobs. Above her

on the wall, surrounded by all the pressed flowers, was a cuckoo clock. But instead of *cuckooing* the hour, the horrid little wooden bird with a spiteful beak and beady eyes was snitching on them.

Even though Betty's stinging feet burned, a cold dread settled over her. Her gaze dropped to the framed peacock butterfly she had seen before. Her dread deepened as the wings twitched slightly, and the eyes on them winked, as though watching her.

The whole house is enchanted.

She stared, hardly daring to breathe, as Charlie unlatched the front door and slipped out, closing it silently behind her. Betty gave a silent, relieved sigh. For a moment, she'd been afraid that the house might keep Charlie trapped. Miss Webb was coming down the stairs now, drawn by the cries of the cuckoo clock. She paused in the hall, then hurried into the sitting room. Betty could hear her skirts rustling as she swept past furniture, no doubt peering behind curtains and under tables.

With Charlie safely out of the house, Betty felt a little braver, but it did nothing to lessen the stinging in her feet. Where to look first? Could she make it upstairs now that the witch had come down? She took a painful step toward the hall, then hesitated and looked back as the kettle let out another angry spurt of steam. Her eyes rested on the counter, next to where she had first seen Miss Webb hunched over the sink. There was something hidden under a tea towel. She drew closer, each step a fresh rash of stings, and lifted the fabric. She had thought the housekeeper had been preparing vegetables or kneading bread, but what lay on the counter was neither. At first Betty thought it was a bunch of rags, but a closer look made her tummy somersault.

Three little figures lay in a row. They appeared to have been made from straw, like the corn dollies Betty remembered seeing at a little stall in Crowstone on market day. Her eyes went immediately to the middle figure. A cloud of wild, woolen brown hair stood out from its head. It was unmistakably her.

The smallest doll had two brown pigtails, and in its open mouth sat a tiny white tooth—the tooth Charlie had dropped into her soup.

"Peg," Betty whispered in disbelief. Disturbingly, both this and the Betty doll had a twist of twine around their heads, covering their eyes like tiny blindfolds.

It was the largest figure that scared her the most, though. It had short dark hair and a tiny, pink, sewn-on mouth. *Fliss*. Unlike the other two dolls, this one wasn't blindfolded, but it had been tightly bound from feet to chin with a strand of ivy. There were other things woven into it, too: sprigs of a green plant with gray-green leaves. Betty was sure it was one of the herbs that had been in the spell bundle she'd found in her dress pocket. She now wished she'd looked more closely before she'd crushed it. The only one she knew for sure was the ivy.

Ivy. It seemed to have had a hold on them ever since they'd moved to Pendlewick. Could this horrid little doll be the reason why? Had Miss Webb been weaving Fliss into a spell from the moment they'd arrived? Were the other figures blindfolded to try and stop them from seeing what was going on? The plants looked springy, newly picked. Like the dolls had only recently been made.

Footsteps in the hall spurred Betty into action. She stuffed the three dolls into her pocket, where they vanished into the invisible folds of her clothes. This was the proof she needed that the old lady was using magic against the Widdershins sisters—perhaps by getting them away from Miss Webb, it might weaken the spell. In any case, Betty knew she needed to show Granny. Granny, who with all her superstitions and wisdom, would know what to do. Ignoring the shooting pains in her feet, she grabbed a few items of clean wash from the table and arranged them under the tea towel.

And with no time to spare, for Miss Webb appeared in the doorway, still with the broom in her hand. She glanced around the kitchen, breathing heavily. Betty kept as still as a stone, but inside her heart was pounding like she'd run a race, threatening to give her away at any moment.

"One of their little tricks?" Miss Webb murmured, her eyes sweeping the room. "Or something else?"

Betty stiffened. One of *whose* little tricks? What happened next caught her off guard. The housekeeper stepped into the kitchen, briskly sweeping with the broom and chanting in a low voice:

> "*Magic broom, trusty broom,*
> *Sweep intruders from this room!*"

A peculiar sensation took hold of Betty, as though she were being propelled—or swept—by an unseen force toward the back door. She bit back a gasp of surprise as she lost her balance and was pushed forward, staggering into a cupboard door.

Miss Webb stopped sweeping and turned sharply, her eyes wide and darting as she tried to work out where the sound had come from. Somehow Betty managed to remain absolutely still, even though her stinging feet were throbbing. There could be no more slipups now. She had to get out of this cottage of tangled spells before the housekeeper discovered her.

Miss Webb gave the broom another firm sweep over the tiles, muttering the same little spell. But this time Betty was ready for her, and she clung on to the handle of the cupboard, refusing to be moved. The sweeping continued, pushing against her like a strong wind and making her dizzy. It finally stopped when Miss Webb placed the broom down. Her face was still a mask of suspicion, and evidently not satisfied, she began checking the larger cupboards, opening each one and looking into it. Betty edged silently away, creeping to the hallway door.

The housekeeper paused by the tea towel and looked under it. Her face fell, and Betty felt a twinge of satisfaction as she dropped the towel on the counter.

Not so clever now, are you? she thought savagely, then flinched as the kettle gave another loud warning toot.

They both jumped at the sound of the front door swinging open, and then Mrs. Lightwing strode down the hallway to the kitchen, eyes flashing wildly. To Betty's surprise, she turned on Miss Webb, her hawkish face full of suspicion.

"What have you been doing?" Mrs. Lightwing demanded.

"N-nothing." The housekeeper wrung her hands, but there was a stubborn note in her voice. She gestured to the pot of potatoes and the basket of nettles. "I've been getting on with the things you asked."

Mrs. Lightwing's eyes narrowed. Betty sagged with relief at the sight of her. It was so good to see someone else and not be trapped with the witch alone! How tempting it was to reveal then and there what she'd discovered—but she couldn't, of course. To do so would mean making herself suddenly visible, and Todd's warning was still ringing in her ears. Any hint of magic would place Betty right alongside the real witch.

"Have you been up to your little tricks again?" Mrs. Lightwing asked in a low voice that suddenly sounded rather dangerous. She advanced into the kitchen, leaving the door to the hall clear. "Did you invite someone in?"

Tricks? Betty frowned. It was the same word Miss Webb had used earlier. Would the housekeeper enchant her employer, the way she had the kettle and the cuckoo clock? Or would she save her spells and talk her way out of trouble?

"I-I didn't . . ." Miss Webb began, looking panicked. "I didn't let anyone in! But the kettle and the cuckoo clock . . ."

"Yes," Mrs. Lightwing said coolly. "The silver bell in

the shop jangled and alerted us that something was going on."

The silver bell? So it *wasn't* just an old one as Miss Pilliwinks had said, thought Betty, as a horrible suspicion crept over her. A suspicion she desperately hoped wasn't true—but Mrs. Lightwing hadn't seemed at all shocked by Miss Webb's mention of the enchanted kettle or the cuckoo clock. And the way she had spoken about the silver bell suggested that that was far from ordinary, too . . .

Using the exchange between the two women to cover her tracks, Betty began to edge away to the hallway. Each footstep seared her with fresh stings. Normally, when using the dolls, she felt bolder and braver. There had been times when she'd used her invisibility to frighten people who were up to no good—but those had been people who'd feared magic. Miss Webb possessed magic of her own. Magic that might undo the power of the nesting dolls.

Betty glanced up at the cuckoo clock on the wall, taking a deep breath. It was sure to go off the second she crossed into the hall, but if she was to get out of there she had no choice. The instant her foot touched down, the little wooden door opened and out flew the cuckoo, just as it had with Charlie.

"Intruder! Intruder in the hall! Get her out, get her out!"

Betty fled along the hall as fast as she could. The pain in her feet was unbearable, each step bringing tears to her eyes. She took hold of the latch and lifted it, but just then a shadow appeared on the other side of the glass. Betty barely had time to step out of the way before the door opened and Miss Pilliwinks stepped into the cottage, smiling toothily. The door swung shut, and before Betty's horrified eyes, Miss Pilliwinks lifted her hand and snapped her fingers. There was a loud click as the door was locked with an unseen bolt.

Betty took a step back, knowing it was hopeless. Her breath was coming in quick, frightened gasps now, giving her away. She turned slowly, finding herself face-to-face with Mrs. Lightwing. Her suspicions had been confirmed. There was not one witch at Foxglove Cottage. There were three.

"Well, well," Mrs. Lightwing murmured, a smile curving her thin lips. "Hubble, bubble, someone's in trouble."

Chapter Sixteen

Cobwebs

MRS. LIGHTWING'S HAND REACHED OUT, snatching at the air. Betty tried to creep away silently, but fear made her clumsy. She was halfway down the hall when her shoulder knocked into the framed peacock butterfly. It came to life behind the frame, fluttering and beating its wings against the glass.

Betty backed away, pressing against the spindles of the staircase. She was shaking. How would she get out now? The only two exits were barred, and Mrs. Lightwing didn't seem in the least bit afraid that an invisible intruder was in her house. Her eyes were burning with anger, ready to deal out punishment. Perhaps it was Betty's terror, but Mrs. Lightwing didn't look quite so old or much like a teacher now. She looked younger, and capable, and mean. She came a step closer, her outstretched arm swiping through the air. In another step, she would reach Betty.

The cuckoo clock continued its cries of *"Intruder!"* the shrill sound ringing in Betty's ears.

"I-I tried using the broom," Miss Webb said, appearing in the kitchen doorway, wringing her hands. "But it didn't work."

"Splendid," said Mrs. Lightwing. "We don't *want* to sweep her out. We want to catch her!" She lunged toward the stairs, and in that instant Betty felt her legs kick into life. There was only one place to go—up. She ducked out of Mrs. Lightwing's grasp and fled, taking the steps two at a time. Now there was no being quiet, for her footsteps pounded for all to hear. Even if she had moved silently, the stairs would have given her away, for creaking voices rose up from underneath her in the same eerie chant:

"Intruder! Intruder on the stairs! Get her out . . ."

Betty reached the landing. There was a large window with a low sill next to a small cabinet displaying trinkets and a large vase of peacock feathers. *More eyes.* From somewhere nearby, she became aware of a sound she had heard before. A *shuffle-shuffle-shuffle.*

Three doors surrounded her, all of them closed. There

was barely any time to think through her choices, for Mrs. Lightwing was rushing up the stairs now, her skirts rustling. Miss Pilliwinks was right behind her, her horrid teeth bared in a chuckle. Betty knew she had only one chance to get away—and whatever these witches had up their sleeves, she still had invisibility on her side. She had to use it. She flung open a door to fool them into thinking she'd gone through it. Instead, she waited on the landing until Mrs. Lightwing neared the top of the stairs.

Then she seized the vase of feathers and threw it as hard as she could. There was a scream and a sickening thud as it hit Mrs. Lightwing. She toppled down the stairs, landing at the bottom in a heap with Miss Pilliwinks crumpled beneath her. The vase smashed to bits, the sound ringing in Betty's ears. Betty ran to the window. It was open a little way, and directly below was a springy-looking hedge. For a moment, she considered jumping, but it seemed a long way down.

"Don't let her get away!" Lightwing shrieked, prompting Betty to bolt through the door she had opened. Instantly, the cry of *"Intruder!"* began, but Betty could hardly hear it over the *shuffle-shuffle* noise, which had grown so loud it was almost deafening. It came from a spinning wheel in the center of the room. Betty watched for a second, mesmerized and horrified. The pedal was tapping up and down of its own accord, weaving a thread of silvery white. It was not the one she had seen in the dining room on the evening they'd been invited over. This one was larger and ancient looking. There was something evil about it, and its spiteful spindle glinted like a knife. Betty glanced around the rest of the room. More silver threads hung in glittering veils that stretched from floor to ceiling. Betty recognized them instantly.

Cobwebs. Thousands of them, as thick as blankets in some places, but not a spider in sight. The silvery cobweb threads were coming from the spinning wheel.

What is this room? She backed away, but not before she noticed there were objects caught in the webs. Little things, the kind that could easily get lost: a pendant, a pipe, and a child's windup doll with glassy, accusing eyes. Betty realized with horror that it was this that was calling *"Intruder!"* in a screeching voice as its eyes swiveled toward her. There were hundreds of objects all over the room, most so thickly cocooned with web that it was impossible to see what they were. Instinctively, Betty knew that whatever spell was being worked here, it wasn't a good one. There was no way she was setting another foot into the room. She feared that if she did, she wouldn't get out again.

She spun back to the landing, dreading what might be hidden behind the other doors. By now, Miss Webb had arrived at the bottom of the stairs, where Mrs. Lightwing and Miss Pilliwinks still lay groaning.

"After her!" Lightwing spat, and Miss Webb clambered over her.

Out of time and out of choices, Betty leaped onto the low sill and pushed the window open wider. She didn't want to look down — it seemed so far — but she knew she must, to try to aim for the springy hedge. She gulped, shaking with fear. But her fear of getting caught was worse.

Betty jumped, her tummy flipping like a pancake as she fell. Her elbow scraped brick as she hit the bush, which was even springier than she'd imagined. It gave her a huge bounce and she rolled off, landing on the grass with a mighty smack. She heard a loud crack as the nesting dolls in her pocket hit the ground.

Almost sobbing, she scrambled to her feet and fled down the garden path toward the overgrown walkway she had taken with Charlie. Her hand fumbled in her pocket for the nesting dolls. Already she knew something was wrong: they were rattling and loose. *Too many pieces.*

"Please," she whispered to herself. "*Please* don't be broken!" But as her fingers found the pieces, she realized that while the dolls hadn't broken, the outer doll had come apart in her pocket with the force of the fall.

She was no longer invisible.

Betty staggered through the gate with one fearful glance back. It should have been a beautiful sight, a country garden in summer bloom, but her eyes went only to the window she had leaped from.

Miss Webb stood at the window, her face white and pinched. Her gaze was fixed on Betty. Now she knew *exactly* who had been in Foxglove Cottage—and that Betty had uncovered the witches' dark secret.

Chapter Seventeen

The Splintered Broomstick

BETTY RAN AS FAST AS SHE COULD over the dry, uneven ground. She pushed aside low-hanging brambles, fighting them as they snagged in her hair. The overgrown tunnel of greenery was no longer a friend, but an enemy trying to slow her down. Her stinging feet hurt with every step. She could feel them blistering and swelling in her shoes.

She reached the gate to Blackbird Cottage and stumbled up the path. Her eyes were leaking tears, both from the pain and shock of what she had learned.

"Charlie?" she croaked, trying to get herself under control. "Where are you?"

Her little sister stepped out from behind a bush, her face grubby and tearstained.

"Oh, Charlie!" Betty flung herself at her, hugging her tight. "I'm sorry. I should never have taken you to that awful place!"

Charlie returned the hug just as fiercely, sniffling. "I was so afraid," she whispered. "I thought . . . I was beginning to think you wouldn't come back."

"So was I." Another hot tear spilled down Betty's face. She looked back anxiously. Miss Webb must have told Mrs. Lightwing and Miss Pilliwinks by now that it was Betty who had sneaked into their home. How long before the witches came after them? She gazed at the windows of the cottage, wishing they'd never swept away the salt. Someone had put it there for good reason, for protection. To keep bad things out. To keep the *witches* out.

"Charlie, we can't stay here. It's not safe." Betty urged her sister to the path leading around the side of the house. Her thoughts were whirling, panicked. She needed to tell Granny and Father everything . . . but the farm was too far, too long and dangerous of a walk. She couldn't risk it. "We have to go and get Granny—she's the closest."

"Why isn't it safe? She couldn't see us—"

"That's just it! She did! She *did* see me. Oh, Charlie, I messed up. The dolls . . ." Betty took them out of her pocket, twisting them uselessly back together again. For all the good it would do them now. "They chased me upstairs. I had to jump from a window and the dolls came apart as I landed . . ."

Charlie gulped. *"They?"*

Betty nodded, her voice trembling. "It's not just the housekeeper. It's all of them: her *and* Miss Pilliwinks and Mrs. Lightwing."

"All of them?" Charlie repeated fearfully.

"There are three witches in that house, and now they'll know I'm onto them. It won't be long before they come for me. They'll want to shut me up, make sure I can't tell anyone else."

From somewhere within the bushes, there was a familiar retching noise, and then a frog hopped past them in the direction of the pond.

"Come on," said Betty. "We have to go now."

"But, Betty, my feet!" Charlie whimpered. "They're so sore. I looked for dog leaves to help with the stings, but I ain't found a single one!"

"I know." Betty smiled faintly at her sister's mistake but didn't correct her. "Mine are sore, too, but we can't stay here. Maybe we'll come across some dock leaves on the way into the village." She took Charlie's hand. "And when we pass Foxglove Cottage we need to stay *quiet.*"

They left by the front garden, passing no one on Bread and Cheese Hill. The heat had baked everything into a sleepy silence, as though summer had cast a spell over the village. The cobwebbed room was fresh in Betty's mind. All those little objects, all of them once belonging to someone. How had they gotten there, and what could they mean? She remembered what Granny had said when she'd first given the nesting dolls to Betty:

"Take something of yours, something small enough to fit inside . . . something personal."

The dolls' magic only worked with an object that had a strong link to a person. Like a hair, a tooth, or a treasured trinket. Betty had an awful feeling that the items caught in the cobwebs were being used in a similar way. But how, exactly? From what Todd said, the folk of Pendlewick were afraid of magic, but how would they react if they knew it was real and there were actual witches living among them? And as for Lightwing and Pilliwinks . . . Betty remembered that first day in the shop.

"Magic and trouble go hand in hand," Miss Pilliwinks had said.

Yes, thought Betty, understanding suddenly. *Because it was the Widdershinses' magic that found you out.* If it hadn't been for the nesting dolls, she would never have dared set foot in the house and wouldn't have made all those grim discoveries. All the while, the bigger question ticked over in her head like a clock that was running out of time. What were the straw figures made by Miss Webb being used for, and why was Fliss in particular being targeted?

"Betty?" Charlie whispered. "You still haven't told me what's going on."

"Quiet," Betty said, snappier than she'd normally be. "Don't breathe a word."

They were almost outside Foxglove Cottage now. Though they remained invisible, Betty crept as silently as she could, unable to take her eyes off the house. She'd half expected to hear echoing cackles and spells being chanted, but the only sounds from the little cottage were birds nesting and tweeting in the hedges.

Of course, thought Betty, recalling her first sight of Blackbird Cottage. Real witches didn't live in tumbledown, neglected places. That would give them away too easily. No, they lived in postcard-pretty, little cottages, so that no one suspected a thing until it was too late.

Only when they had reached the bridge and crossed the stream did Betty let go of the breath she'd been holding. She released Charlie's hand as they approached the busier part of the village, feeling safer now even as they passed the post office. But it didn't stop her feeling of dread from growing as she glanced across the village green to the Hungry Tree and the stone circle. More than ever, it seemed possible that the tree really had grown from Eliza Bird's wooden leg. Maybe it wasn't just an old story, after all.

"Down here." Betty ducked into a narrow street that reeked of fish. In a locked side entrance to a fishmonger's, she twisted the dolls in her pocket to make herself and Charlie visible once more. Then they strode out in the direction of the Sugar Loaf.

"Granny must have gotten the job," said Charlie. "She's been there a long time."

But when they reached the Sugar Loaf, Granny was nowhere to be found. Betty and Charlie traipsed from room to room through the rabbit warren of neat, little tables. Charlie sniffed the air longingly, eyeing up cakes and ice creams that customers had ordered. Eventually, Betty asked the red-cheeked woman behind the counter, who had been so friendly to them before.

"Bunny Widdershins?" The woman's expression soured immediately, and a cross look came into her eyes. "No, she did *not* get the job."

"Er . . . oh." Betty's stomach squirmed unpleasantly. What on earth had Granny done to earn such a withering look? "Any idea where we can find her?"

The woman's eyes narrowed. "Last I saw she was heading in the direction of the pub. That was two hours ago."

Two hours? The squirming sensation worsened as Betty hurried Charlie out of the door.

"No free ice creams for us, then," Charlie said gloomily, prodding her tummy.

"I think we've got bigger problems than that," muttered Betty as she marched toward the Splintered Broomstick, heat rising in her cheeks. A wall of smoky, ale-scented air hit her as she swung open the door and went in. Breathing deeply, she closed her eyes. Just for those few seconds, it almost, *almost* felt like she was back at the Poacher's Pocket. Tears sprang into her eyes for the second time that day, and she squeezed them away fiercely. This was no time to feel homesick or sentimental.

"Oi!" said a griping voice from a dark corner. "No kids in 'ere. Clear awf!"

A round, balding man waddled toward them, gritting teeth that looked like a row of falling dominoes—a set that was missing a few. He glowered at them, his upper lip shiny with sweat, and jabbed a black fingernail at a sign that read: UNACCOMPANIED CHILDREN WILL BE COOKED AND SERVED AS PIES.

Betty stood her ground, her own temper flaring. In a place where witches were working their spells, children being cooked and eaten didn't seem so impossible. No doubt the sign was meant as a joke, but she wasn't in the mood.

For one thing, being asked to leave a pub after growing up in one felt like an insult—not that she expected the man to know this. And two, she'd just spotted Granny over the man's shoulder.

"Excuse me," she said coldly. "Our granny is over there, so there won't be any pies today." His mouth dropped open as she swept past him with a gleeful Charlie right behind.

"You told him, Betty," she said in a loud whisper. "Grumpy old boot. Who's he think he is, anyway?"

"The landlord, probably," Betty replied, remembering the name Todd had given them on their first day in Pendlewick. "Brutus Crabbe."

"He looks like he had bees for breakfast," Charlie replied.

"And wasps for lunch," Betty said. They passed under a broomstick that was hanging from above, broken into two pieces. It was an unpleasant reminder of the enchanted broom Miss Webb had tried to sweep her out with.

Granny was sitting in a dark corner at a sticky table. At first Betty thought the row of empty whiskey glasses—plus the half-empty one in her hand—were her only company, but she quickly saw that, behind a wooden partition, a hairy old man was sitting next to her, staring into his beer intently and nodding at something her grandmother had said.

"Granny!" Betty said sharply. "What are you doing in here?"

The hairy man jumped and let out a snort. He wasn't listening or gazing into his beer as Betty had first thought. He was in a drunken sleep. His head nodded again and flopped onto Granny's shoulder.

"Having a drink," Granny said, raising her glass in Betty's direction. "Making friends."

"A drink?" Betty fumed, pointing to the empty glasses. "Thirsty, were you?"

"Stop making a fuss." Granny patted the seat next to her. "And don't tell your father I was in here."

"I won't need to," Betty snapped, refusing to sit. She needed Granny to be clearheaded, to listen, but already Betty saw the chances of this were slim. "One look at you and he'll see you're pickled."

"Don't mince your words, Betty," Granny mumbled, having the good grace to look ashamed. "Not that you ever have."

"I won't," said Betty. She was annoyed and worried

and afraid all at once. She needed Granny to believe what she was about to tell her. She needed help, but it was clear Granny was in no fit state to put up a fight—especially a magical one. She looked as though she wouldn't be able to fight her way out of a candy wrapper. "What happened at the Sugar Loaf?"

Granny hiccupped sadly. "I didn't get the job."

"I gathered that. But why not? The woman there didn't seem very pleased when I mentioned your name."

Granny's face darkened. "Something about some ash in the ice cream."

"Ash?" Betty demanded.

"Oh, *Granny*," Charlie said reproachfully. "You weren't smoking over the ice cream, were you?"

"It was only a quick puff," Granny said. "Two at the most."

"You didn't!" Betty exclaimed.

"She shouldn't have left me on my own," Granny protested. "Busiest time of day and she kept disappearing and leaving it all to me, the lazy so-and-so!"

"She was probably testing you," Betty said crossly. "To see how you'd cope."

"Well, I got flustered. And when I get flustered, I smoke. *That's* how I cope. Now stop nagging me."

"Fine." Betty swallowed down her annoyance. The

truth was, it was hard to imagine Granny doing anything but pulling pints. The thought of her serving cakes and being nice to customers in a fancy tea shop seemed as unlikely as her sweeping chimneys. "I didn't come here to nag you, anyway. We need your help."

Granny gave a sleepy blink. "Go on."

"It's . . . it's Fliss," Betty began. "She's in trouble."

Granny sat up straighter, her eyes sharpening. She gave the old man asleep on her shoulder a shove, sending him slumping the other way. "Trouble? Is this about that lad who's been sniffing around her?"

"Why would he *sniff* her?" Charlie asked. "Does he like her perfume?"

"They've been sniffing around each other, if you ask me," said Betty. "And no, Granny. It has nothing to do with Todd." She looked around hesitantly. She knew only too well that pubs were always full of pricked ears and prying eyes, but at the same time, she couldn't think of anywhere else to have this talk. The cottage certainly didn't feel safe.

"Spit it out, then," said Granny, impatient. "What's she done?"

"She hasn't done anything," Betty said in a low voice. "But something's being done to her—and all of us." She took the three straw figures out of her pocket, keeping them half-hidden in the folds of her skirt. "Look, Granny. I-I found these in Foxglove Cottage today."

Granny frowned at Betty's lap. "Foxglove . . . ?"

"Where Miss Pilliwinks and Mrs. Lightwing live," said Betty.

"Mrs. Frightening, more like," Charlie added darkly.

"They're supposed to be us," said Betty. She pointed at the blindfolded eyes on the Betty and Charlie dolls and the binding around Fliss. "They're trying to bewitch Fliss and they don't want the rest of us to see."

She gulped, thinking of Fliss in the secret room in the dead of night. The glazed look in her sister's eyes and the muttering of a song she'd never heard. *Bewitched.* Betty hadn't allowed herself to think it until now, but she knew it was true. "And the worst thing is, I think it's working. Granny, we've got to do something before it's too late!"

Chapter Eighteen

Clear Awf!

GRANNY GAVE ANOTHER HICCUP. "Bewitch Fliss? Who's trying to bewitch her? If this is one of your games, Betty—"

"It's not," Charlie whispered, glancing around cautiously. "It's *real*, Granny. There are witches in Pendlewick. Wicked ones."

"I think I prefer the imaginary rat game," Granny muttered.

"This isn't a game!" Betty's voice was sharp, earning her a curious glance from a couple of men playing a card game at a table nearby. She fought to remain calm and keep her voice hushed. "Things have happened in this village before, bad things. Now everyone is afraid of magic—they don't even like speaking about it. But what they don't realize is that it's all around them."

Granny lifted a gray eyebrow, going slightly cross-eyed in the process. "And what *is* going on?"

"I . . ." Betty faltered. "I haven't worked that out yet. But I know it's something bad."

She shuddered, thinking of the room of webs and the tiny objects caught up in them. The spinning wheel and its *shuffle-shuffle-shuffle* . . . She took a deep breath and the words spilled out in a jumble: the kettle and clock, the nettle stings in the enchanted house. "There's more, too. We haven't told you everything about Blackbird Cottage. There's a secret room—a crook hole. We found things belonging to the girl who lived there before—Ivy Bell. A painting of her and a diary."

"Go on," Granny said thoughtfully.

Betty felt a glimmer of hope. If anyone would believe them, it was Granny, with her superstitions and lucky charms. But however stern and formidable Bunny Widdershins was, could she be a match for real witches with cunning, dangerous magic?

"There *are* witches in Pendlewick," Betty went on, keeping her voice low. "And I think they've been here a long time. But I don't think Ivy was one of them. She was scared and confused. She didn't understand the things that were happening to her."

Quickly, she told Granny of the diary, of the frogs, the cloud of butterflies, and the stream running backward. "It's them, Granny. We've seen it with our own eyes— Charlie and me. It's Pilliwinks and Lightwing, and their housekeeper, too—Miss Webb. She was the one making these dolls."

Granny was silent for a moment, staring at the straw figures. Finally, Betty thought, it seemed her grandmother was listening.

"Has it occurred to you that they're a gift?" Granny asked.

Betty looked at her blankly.

"She's probably made them for Charlie, to amuse her," said Granny. "Look at all those little details. She must've thought you'd love them . . ." Her expression clouded. "And you're telling me the two of you have been snooping around their house, swiping things? What's gotten into you?"

Betty gazed at the straw figures, then at her grandmother. She didn't like the expression in the old woman's eyes. The glazed look she wore now had nothing to do with whiskey, Betty was sure of it. With a chill, she realized it was very much like the look Fliss had worn when Betty had found her alone in the secret room.

"What's gotten into *us*?" Betty said desperately. "What's gotten into *you*? Why can't you see what's going on?"

"Please listen, Granny," Charlie begged, pulling anxiously on a pigtail. "Oi's throwing up frogs, we got snitched on by a talking kettle, and our feet are stung to bits by nettles!" She bent down, about to pull off her shoes, but Granny stopped her.

"Enough!" she tutted. "Thrown-up frogs! Talking nettles and stinging kettles! You girls are either trying to play a trick on me, or you've frightened yourselves silly by listening to too many stories—"

"But they aren't just stories," Betty began, stung by her grandmother's dismissal. "You're normally the first person to be worried by things like that—you never even liked going past the crossroads in Crowstone!"

"And you're normally the first person to tell me off for listening to superstitious nonsense," Granny shot back. "Every place has its stories. You know that better than anyone. Why, in Crowstone it was Sorsha, the sorceress on the marshes escaping the prison tower." She wagged a finger. "Now I don't doubt that *something* happened up there, but I certainly don't believe she summoned imps off the marshes to help her escape, do you?"

"No." Betty clenched her teeth. She knew exactly what had gone on in the tower, but it was something she could never tell Granny. "But the point is—"

"Just as I don't believe for a second in a hungry tree that gobbles things up," Granny continued. "Or that a bunch of standing stones were once people. They're stories and nothing more. Made up to frighten children or to make the time pass quicker at work."

"But . . . but you thought the cottage was spooky, too," Betty stammered. "With the salt on the windowsills and the coins in the corners. How can you believe in that and your horseshoes, but not in this?"

"Because one's about luck and the other's about magic," Granny said. She glanced around herself uncomfortably, then began stuffing her pipe with tobacco. "And maybe those girls the villagers whisper about—those *witches* —were messing around with things they shouldn't have been, trying to make trouble for others. It sounds like they got what they deserved. After all, magic and trouble go hand in hand."

An icy shudder went over Betty's skin. *Magic and trouble go hand in hand* . . . These were the exact words

Miss Pilliwinks had said on their first day in the village shop. Words repeated by Todd . . . and now Granny. It was too late, Betty thought, watching as Granny fiddled with her pipe. An image flashed into her mind, then, of a similar pipe caught in the giant cobweb in Foxglove Cottage. A pipe very like the one Granny had lost . . . only Betty had been too terrified to register it at the time. But now, hearing Bunny utter those words and thinking back to all the tiny, easily lost things, Betty felt a creeping terror slide over her. What if the witches' enchantment went further than Fliss? What if it reached to others in the village, to keep them dazed and unsuspecting . . .

Too late.

"All right, Granny." Betty swallowed a hard lump in her throat. "We must have made a mistake." She ignored a confused look from Charlie and began to back away. "You're right. We frightened ourselves by listening to too many stories. We'll go home now. We've still got chores to do." Granny wasn't listening, and if Betty's suspicions were correct, then no one else in the village would listen, either. They were all deep under a spell, just like Fliss. Betty and Charlie were on their own.

Granny nodded. "Good girls. No more nonsense." She rummaged in her purse, raking over the unfamiliar coins. "But while you're here, fetch me another whiskey." She raised her empty glass and nodded at the girl behind the counter. Betty whipped the glass out of her fingers and began to shake her head at the girl, but Granny's next words made her stop.

"Make it a large one, Magda."

Magda? Betty stared at the girl in shock. She looked about the same age as Fliss. Could this be the same Magda whom Ivy had written about in her diary? She was the right age, but that was the only clue Betty had to go on.

She went to the bar and put Granny's empty glasses on it. Charlie stood beside her, helping herself to a handful of nuts in a bowl. The girl took a fresh glass and measured a nip of whiskey into it and was about to add another, but Betty caught her eye and mouthed, *"Small."* Magda gave the slightest of nods and put the whiskey bottle down.

Betty handed over the change Granny had given her and watched Magda carefully. She looked hot, tired, and fed up—not that Betty blamed her, with a landlord like Brutus Crabbe—but she was attractive: dark featured with brown skin and tightly curled, black hair. Betty badly wanted to ask her about Ivy Bell and what had happened after the art lesson on the village green, but there was simply no way she could blurt out questions like this to a stranger. Even if she did, Magda was unlikely to answer.

But as it happened, Magda was the one with a question.

"Where's your sister, then? Working?"

Betty let the words sink in. On the surface, they were pleasant enough, but there was an edge to the girl's voice that told her something was bubbling underneath.

"Fliss? Yes, she's over at Peckahen Farm." She paused. "Do you know her?"

The girl shrugged. "I've seen her." She hesitated. "With Todd."

Betty narrowed her eyes. Was Magda jealous? Did *she* like Todd? "Todd's been kind to us since we arrived, showing us around," she said. "And yes, he and Fliss have taken a liking to each other. Is there something wrong with that?"

Magda stared back at her. "He always did like a pretty face. But your sister's isn't the only one."

"What do you mean?" Betty asked, confused.

"There was a girl before," said Magda, collecting dirty glasses off the bar. "But she fooled him, just like she fooled everyone else. Her beauty hid what was inside and . . . and the badness."

"You mean . . . ?"

"She even *looks* like Ivy, your sister. The dark hair and those big eyes."

Ivy.

Magda's voice had dropped to a whisper. There was sadness in her eyes, as though she couldn't quite believe her friend had become one of the village legends.

Ivy's words floated back to Betty from the past: *Magda's a good friend. I feel bad lying to her . . .*

The truth swirled around Betty as two things clicked into place. The sweetheart Ivy had been too careful to name in her diary entry had been *Todd*. Which explained why, when he'd visited them at Blackbird Cottage for the first time, he hadn't knocked at the front door. He had come straight around the back . . . because it was something he was used to doing. With Ivy.

"Yes," said Magda, biting her lip. "Ivy. He was hers first."

Betty took the whiskey glass with shaking fingers and passed it to Granny.

"Come on, Charlie," she said, preparing to leave, but Charlie was staring at something on the wall.

"Betty, look."

"We need to go," said Betty, but Charlie remained where she was.

"Wait." She pointed. "Look at this."

Something in Charlie's voice caught Betty's attention. She moved to her sister's side. There, on the wall next to a poster for Speckled Pig ale, was a framed photograph. It was black-and-white, faded with age, and showed a crowd gathered in front of the Splintered Broomstick on its opening day, according to the caption.

Charlie pressed a grubby finger to the glass, where two figures stood side by side. Though they were tiny and faded and dressed in an old-fashioned way, there was something very familiar about them.

"It's them, isn't it?" Charlie whispered. "Pilliwinks and Lightwing!"

Betty peered closer, brushing dust from the glass, and felt a chill brush her skin. She would have assumed the figures in the photograph were older relatives who bore a close resemblance. A *very* close resemblance. But her discoveries at Foxglove Cottage left her doubting this. Surely it couldn't *really* be the two witches?

"It can't be," she murmured, at the same time remembering how confused she had been about Miss Pilliwinks's age when she first met her. How she'd seemed older, then inexplicably younger. "*Can* it?"

She was jolted from her questions by something kicking off at the table nearby. The two men who'd been playing cards stood up abruptly, fists raised. Both were roaring about money and cheating, and fistfuls of cards were scattering around them. Betty just had time to grab Charlie and dart out of their way before they went sprawling across Granny's table, knocking her whiskey all over her.

"RIGHT!" she boomed. "You two, OUT!" Seizing one by the ear and the other by the collar, Granny marched the two of them straight past an astonished Brutus Crabbe and launched them out onto the street. Then she stomped back in, her nostrils flaring, and stopped in front of Crabbe.

"You owe me a whiskey."

"I can do better than that," said Crabbe, looking Granny up and down in admiration. "Want a job?"

Granny assessed the pub shrewdly. "When do I start?"

"Now," said Crabbe, shooting a sly look at Betty and Charlie. "Only thing is," he continued as Granny bustled behind the bar and began rearranging bottles, "with your granny busy, I'm afraid that means you're unsupervised. So for you two that means pie or—"

"Don't worry." Betty had no reason to stay. Her head was swimming with the unexplained photograph, Granny's glazed looks, and what she had learned about Ivy—and Todd. "We're clearing *awf*!"

She and Charlie emerged into the fresh air and sunshine, dazzlingly bright after the darkness of the Splintered Broomstick. The streets were busy with people passing through and full of cheerful chatter. On the green, Betty spotted Scally and Wags kicking a ball to each other. Everything looked peaceful and ordinary—but it wasn't.

"Betty?" asked Charlie. "Why didn't Granny listen to us?"

"Because she couldn't," Betty whispered. "She's under their spell, like everyone else in Pendlewick." Saying the words out loud filled her with dread, but she clung to hope. The sight of Granny chucking out the misbehaving customers had been a comforting, familiar one. "She's still in there, Charlie. She's still Granny. We just have to break the enchantment over her somehow."

"But what if they put a spell on us, too?" Charlie asked, her eyes wide.

"I think they've already tried," said Betty, as a thought flashed through her head. "The nettle soup—that must have been how it started. Everyone ate it except us!"

"Everyone except me, you mean," said Charlie. "You ate it."

"Yes, but then I was sick," said Betty. "They meant for me to eat it, but Miss Webb put that charm in my pocket. Thank goodness you were clever enough not to eat that soup, Charlie!"

Charlie snorted. "Well, I knew eating nettles was a

bad idea." She looked worried suddenly. "But we all ate Miss Pilliwinks's jam!"

Betty nodded. "Maybe that wasn't so heavily enchanted," she said. "Perhaps the jam was something small to start off with, to get us to trust them." *To think they were nice, kind old ladies.* "It was after the nettle soup that things really started happening, and whatever they're up to, it's Fliss they want," she said. "It was Fliss who Miss Webb pointed at, and the Fliss straw doll that's trapped. As for the rest of us, they just don't want anyone to notice what's happening. The question is, why?"

"You told Granny you don't think Ivy was a witch," said Charlie.

"No," said Betty. She was wondering now about other similarities between Ivy and Fliss, apart from their looks. Why had they been targeted? "But if we find out what happened to her, we can try and stop it from happening to Fliss."

"What if we don't figure it out in time?" Charlie's voice was small and worried.

Betty gazed across the green at the village store. So quaint, so ordinary. So perfectly disguised. "Then we take Brutus Crabbe's advice and clear off."

Charlie gave her a questioning look.

"Miss Webb saw me. They'll know we're onto them. But if they can't find Fliss, then there's a chance we can save her," Betty explained. "If we run and get her the heck out of Pendlewick."

They reached the stream sweaty and breathless. There was no time to gaze into the bubbles, no time to dip their feet into the cool water. Even Charlie didn't ask to stop. Instead, Betty headed for the church, searching for the headstone with the broken-winged angel and the stained-glass window she'd committed to memory on that first day in Pendlewick.

I'm sorry, Ivy, she said silently, for she was certain now that it *had* been Ivy who had left the salt and coins in their cottage in a bid to protect herself. *We should never have touched those coins.*

Locating the gap in the wall, she scraped out the moss she'd poked in to hide the coins. It had dried out in the summer heat and crumbled in her fingers.

"You looking for that money?" Charlie asked, handing her a pointy twig.

Betty glanced at her, eyebrows raised. She thought she and Granny had been discreet when it came to the silver coins they'd found in the cottage, but evidently little escaped Charlie's nosy eyes and ears. "How did you know? I didn't think you'd noticed."

Charlie gave her a scornful look. "I knew." She shrugged. "I just didn't care."

Betty dug out one of the coins but succeeded only in jamming the rest of them farther into the crack.

"I can only get this one," she said, feeling suddenly hopeless with the weight and worry of it all. Why was she even bothering to retrieve them? The coins hadn't protected Ivy. Perhaps it was that they were simply another part of the puzzle, but Betty felt they were important. Another link to this strange missing girl she had somehow grown to care for.

"I guess one will have to do," she said, standing up and brushing moss crumbs from the coin. It flashed silver in her hand, like a sharp spindle on a spinning wheel.

Chapter Nineteen

Poison

BETTY PACED HER RAPIDLY DARKENING bedroom, gripped with worry. Outside, the sky was a pink smudge as nighttime fell over Pendlewick, but she wasn't tired. And even if she had been, she was too afraid to sleep. The cottage wasn't safe, nor was sleeping. Sleep meant not noticing. Sleep meant not hearing. *Sleep meant danger.* Was this how Ivy Bell had spent her final nights in this house, in this room, even? Too afraid to close her eyes and wishing away the hours until daylight?

"Betty, sit down," Charlie whispered. "You're making Hoppit nervous."

"Sorry, Charlie." Betty paused by the bed, where her little sister was fussing over her rat.

Her gaze strayed to the window. Earlier, she and Charlie had shaken lines of salt along every ledge and every doorway. Now, as she paced, her fingers kept creeping to her pocket to touch the silver coin. It didn't seem as though it would be much good on its own, but somehow knowing it had belonged to Ivy made her feel less alone.

Downstairs, crockery rattled in the kitchen as Father washed the dinner things, and then Granny's voice drifted through the cottage as she hollered at Fliss about wet towels on the floor.

Betty snapped to attention. It was the signal she'd been waiting for: a chance to catch Fliss in a good mood and, most importantly, alone.

"Stay here," she told Charlie. "I'm going to speak to Fliss."

She hurried downstairs and through the cottage. In the kitchen, Granny was making tea and chattering with Father. On the surface, everything might have seemed normal, but the hazy expressions in her family's eyes told a different story. Betty shuddered, following a trail of wet footprints to the Nest. The door was open a little, and Fliss was inside, combing out her wet hair and humming to herself. There was a red petal stuck to her shoulder and the air was heavily scented with roses.

Betty went in, noticing with alarm that the back door

to the garden was wide-open. Oi sat on the path, glaring in, but too lazy to move in the still, warm night. Quickly, she went over and closed the door, bolting the latch against the leafy dark spaces, trying not to think about who might be out there. Watching and waiting.

"Leave it open." Fliss turned around, annoyed. "I like the smell of the garden wafting in."

"The gnats will get in, too," said Betty, thinking quickly. "You don't want to get bitten and covered in red lumps."

Fliss blinked, then her eyes settled into the faint, glazed look once more. She placed the comb down and began fiddling with a vase of flowers she'd picked from the garden.

Betty swallowed, gathering her courage. She had to persuade Fliss to listen to her, to see sense before it was too late. She took the straw figures out of her pocket and pushed them toward her sister.

"What are they?" Fliss asked, barely glancing at them before turning to the mirror.

"Us," Betty said quietly. "They're supposed to be us. It's a spell, Fliss, and you're in danger. We all are."

"A spell," Fliss repeated blankly. She leaned closer to the mirror, muttering crossly. "That *can't* be a pimple!"

"Fliss, please!" Betty insisted, thrusting the dolls

closer. "Listen to me! These dolls . . . they're evil. It's Pilliwinks and Lightwing and that housekeeper of theirs—Miss Webb. They made these, and they're out to get you." A note of pleading entered her voice. "Something bad is going to happen. It's happening already."

"You could be right," Fliss complained. "I *never* get pimples!"

"This isn't a joke," Betty said desperately.

Fliss sighed, finally turning to her. "Then why do you sound so silly? Really, Betty, I thought you were the practical one." She plucked a daisy from the vase and held it to her nose, gazing dreamily out of the window.

"Please, Fliss, you have to listen to me!"

Fliss picked off the daisy petals one by one, whispering under her breath. "He loves me . . . he loves me not. He loves me . . ."

"*Fliss!*" Betty begged. "I'm not making this up—there were all sorts of things in the witches' cottage. Enchanted objects set up to trap us. They mean us harm. They mean *you* harm. We have to leave Pendlewick—"

"Leave?" Fliss snorted. "I'm not leaving Todd. He loves me not . . ."

"Fliss," Betty said gently. "There's something you should know about Todd. He . . . he was Ivy's boyfriend before she disappeared."

Fliss's fingers paused. She stared hard at the daisy and spoke in a cold voice. "So what? Ivy's gone."

"You live in her house. You look similar . . ." Betty faltered. "I think maybe you remind him of her—"

"Todd likes *me*."

"You barely know each other."

"I know enough." Fliss began pulling petals again. "He loves me . . ."

"Stop it!" Betty snapped, knocking the daisy from her sister's hand. "I'm trying to save you—"

"I don't *need* you to save me!" Fliss hissed, rounding on her. Her eyes were wild with the haunting, faraway look that didn't belong in them. "The only reason you're saying those things about Todd is because you're jealous. Didn't anyone ever tell you that jealousy is ugly, Betty?"

Betty took a sharp breath and turned away to hide the tears in her eyes. "I'm not jealous," she whispered.

It was true that in the past she had envied her sister. Her easy charm, not to mention the fact that Fliss had always seemed to be their father's favorite, had stung. But right now jealousy was the furthest thing from Betty's mind. All she wanted was to protect her family, but she could see that already the magic had sunk its claws in deep. "I just want to help you."

Fliss laughed, and it was a cruel, sarcastic sound that

Betty didn't recognize. "Betty Widdershins to the rescue," she said mockingly. "Well, not this time, thank you." Before Betty could say anything more, her sister marched to the door and stood there expectantly, holding it wide. Crushed and choking back tears, Betty left.

It's not her, she told herself as she crept back up the stairs. *It's not really Fliss. It's the spell taking hold of her.*

"She didn't listen, did she?" Charlie said in a small, sleepy voice.

Not trusting herself to speak, Betty shook her head and sank down on the bed next to her younger sister. They lay together in silence as Betty blinked back more tears. Eventually, Charlie's breathing deepened as she fell asleep.

Betty got up from the bed and picked up the pile of Ivy's papers from the hiding place under the mattress and shuffled through them. There had to be something she'd missed, something that would persuade Fliss to listen—but in her heart she knew it was hopeless. Nothing was going to convince her sister to listen, let alone leave Pendlewick. Betty's only hope now was to figure out what had happened to Ivy. Perhaps there was something in the secret room she had missed, some vital piece of the puzzle.

The secret room . . . She thought of Granny's blank face

and complete lack of reaction when Betty had told her about it. That wasn't like Bunny at all. The Granny Betty knew would have had the place bricked up in a jiffy. Instead, she hadn't even mentioned it or shown any interest in seeing it. The realization sent ripples of fear over Betty's skin—just how far under the witches' spell was Granny? And would it deepen the longer it went on?

Lighting the nub of a candle, Betty approached the closet and glanced back at Charlie. She was still asleep, but there was movement in her hair where Hoppit was fidgeting. Quietly, Betty opened the door and slid back the secret panel. It moved with little sound this time, and she stepped into the dark space. The flickering candlelight threw spooky shadows across the walls, turning Betty's own shadow into a monster. She put the candle down on the tiny table and sat on the very edge of the dusty chair, trying not to touch the cobwebs.

Still holding the drawings, Betty let her eyes drift around the room, searching for some hidden nook she might have missed: a loose floorboard, another scrap of paper, or even a message scribbled on the walls. Nothing. She lowered her gaze to the papers in her hands, looking through them in the dim light. She came across the drawing of Blackbird Cottage from the front, remembering the strange feeling she'd had before, like she was missing something. She knew what it was now: that Todd had arrived at the back door instead of at the front. So why was the feeling still there? What was Betty missing now?

She leafed through the pages, squinting at the scribbled notes. She hadn't paid much attention to them before, for the writing was faded and seemed only to label the plants, a few of which Betty recognized. One, a drawing of tiny white flowers, was labeled *Queen's lace. Also known as tickle fingers, frilly mischief, or star flower,* Ivy had written. *Protection against evil magic and witches. Can cause nosebleeds and sickness.* On the same sheet of paper was another sketch of more white flowers, which at first appeared the same, but then Betty saw these were labeled *Demon's dice. Also known as specter's lantern or the gravedigger. Poison—deadly. Can cause illness even through touch. Causes sickness, confusion, and death.*

Betty's heart began to thump hard and her eyes darted from one sketch to the other. There had been tiny white flowers in the bunch of herbs she had found in her pocket, the spell bundle that had made her sick. She began to feel ill now, for the two plants looked very similar. Both plants could make a person sick, but only one was deadly. Had Miss Webb made a mistake and used queen's lace, when she had, in fact, meant to use demon's dice? Had she really meant not just to make Betty sick . . . but to *kill* her?

Her hands shook as she went through the other drawings and paintings. Her breath was coming quicker now, making the candlelight flicker. So Ivy hadn't just been sketching for the fun of it. She had been trying to protect herself and her home. *Juniper, mugwort, mistlefeather.* More protection against wicked magic. Betty went through them all. And then her racing heart skipped a beat as one of the sheets slipped to the floor and turned over, revealing a page of drawings she hadn't seen before. This time it wasn't plants, but other household objects that might, at a quick glance, have looked like everyday things sketched by a bored teenager but were, according to Ivy, ways to keep evil away. A broomstick crossing a doorway; a glass bottle crammed with sharp things such as pins, thorns, and broken glass; a stack of silver coins . . .

Coins made from real silver will blacken in the presence of evil magic, Ivy had written. Betty slid her hand into her pocket, touching the piece of silver.

"Not protection, then," Betty whispered. "But a warning."

She hugged the drawings tightly to her chest, wishing there were a way to look back into the past. But there was nothing, only the sketches and notes of a frightened girl whose portrait hung on the wall.

"What happened to you?" Betty murmured, lifting

the candle. She got up and went closer to the painting. "What did they do to you, Ivy Bell? Where did you go?"

Ivy stared back at her from the portrait, her lips slightly parted as though she wanted to tell her secrets. Betty stiffened as she caught sight of something for the first time. A single teardrop rolling down Ivy's cheek. Had it been there before? Betty was certain it hadn't. It must be a trick of the light, surely? Or else a leak in the roof . . .

She lifted the candle higher and reached with her other hand to touch the painting, expecting to find a drip of moisture. The surface was dry. The teardrop was painted into the canvas. The hairs on the back of Betty's neck stood up. She could not have missed this detail, however small. She had studied the picture carefully and she knew, without a doubt, that the teardrop had not been there before. The painting had changed.

Almost hypnotized, Betty put the candle down and lifted the portrait from the wall. The frame was heavy and cool in her hands, and cobwebs stretched away from it like old lace. Her fingers brushed against paper. Something was taped to the back: an envelope.

Betty pulled it away from the frame and removed a single sheet of paper. A few brief lines had been scrawled on it in a hurry.

To whoever finds this,

If you are reading my letter, then perhaps there's hope for me yet and that ▓▓▓▓▓ and ▓▓▓▓▓ can be defeated. I have tried many times to write this and found that their names cannot be recorded. Each time I try, the paper scorches and the words become unreadable. That is the power of their magic.

I do not know what's going to become of me, but I know I have narrowly escaped the same fate as Eliza Bird and Rosa Ripples — for now, at least. I'm not a witch, though they have made it look as if I am. <u>They</u> are the witches, but they didn't quite succeed this time. The painting is not only evidence, but now linked to my life — or what is left of it. Therefore, I beg you, do not destroy it. It must be preserved at any cost.

I must go. They are searching for me.

Ivy

Betty reread the letter again and again, her thoughts swimming with Ivy's words. *They are searching for me* . . .

Her fingers traced the scorch marks. Ivy had tried

254

to write two names, not three. It made sense that those names were Pilliwinks and Lightwing. Perhaps Ivy hadn't identified Miss Webb as one of them. But if Ivy had narrowly escaped, as she had written, then where *was* she? Could Pilliwinks and Lightwing—and Webb—have caught up with her at last?

Unexpectedly, Betty's fingers found a clip on the back of the frame. She pulled at it, wondering if something else might be hidden inside. Instead, the frame came neatly apart, leaving the canvas free. Betty grappled with it, but was unable to stop pieces of the wood falling. They made a clunk as they hit the bare floorboards. She heard Charlie stir in the bedroom.

"Betty?" she murmured sleepily.

Betty emerged from the closet, clutching Ivy's papers and the painting, which had curled up in her hand. "It's all right. I'm here," she whispered. "Go back to sleep."

"Is it breakfast time?"

"No." Betty scanned the room as Charlie snuffled and turned over. Where could she hide the painting? Under the mattress? Too obvious. Behind another picture? It had to go somewhere, but the secret room was no longer safe now that she'd told Granny about it. Even if Bunny hadn't been that interested, Betty couldn't risk it. One too many whiskeys and Granny might blurt something out to the wrong person down at the Splintered Broomstick—if she hadn't already.

Betty's eyes rested on her maps, finding the thin tube containing the map of Pendlewick given to her by Father. It would have to do for now. She unfastened the lid and slid the painting inside. There had to be somewhere outside Pendlewick that she could hide it.

She had just sealed the lid in place when a sound from downstairs carried up through the silent house. Charlie sat up in bed, wide-awake.

"Was that . . . ?"

Betty nodded. "A door."

The word stuck in her throat. Somewhere in the house a door had just closed.

Chapter Twenty

Pins and Needles

"I THINK SOMEONE'S IN THE HOUSE," Betty hissed, terrified. Ivy's letter echoed in her head: *They are searching for me.* Would the witches be searching for Betty, now, too? They knew she was onto them, knew she had been in their house and stolen the straw figures. The danger was closer than ever, and they needed all the help they could get. "Go and wake Father—quick!"

Charlie was out of bed in a flash, moving soundlessly across the room to the landing. Betty followed her as far as the stairs, waiting at the top. Her ears strained in the silence of the house. Was something creaking—a footstep? Or was it her imagination? She felt sick with fear at the thought of Granny and Fliss downstairs. Were they still asleep, or had they been silenced? The thought spurred her on, down the stairs.

She realized too late that she was still clutching the map case containing Ivy's portrait but didn't dare put it down. The tube was hard and could probably deliver a hefty whack if necessary, but Betty knew she needed another weapon. She slung the map case over her shoulder and grabbed the first thing she saw: Granny's horseshoe, hanging in its new place above the front door. It felt heavy and solid in her hand.

A presence behind her almost made her cry out.

"Charlie! Where's Father?"

"He won't wake up." Charlie's face was pinched and white. "His eyes were open, but it was like he couldn't hear me—"

"Enchanted," whispered Betty. She should have known it was pointless, but Charlie wasn't finished.

"Betty, it was Fliss. I saw her, from Father's window. She's outside!"

Betty went cold. "Outside?" She lowered the horseshoe. She hadn't considered that the door could have been closed by someone on the way *out* of the house. But why would Fliss be leaving the cottage in the middle of the night?

"She's walking down the hill," Charlie said, her teeth beginning to chatter. "Let's get Granny."

If we can wake her, Betty thought, her fear building.

They crept into the kitchen, where Granny was fast asleep on her pull-out bed. Betty stood guard with the horseshoe raised while Charlie tried to rouse their grandmother, but it was no use.

"Granny, please," Charlie whispered. "Wake up!"

Bunny's eyes flicked open, but she wore the same glazed expression Betty had seen previously. Only now it was worse, more vacant than ever.

"It's no good," said Betty, horrified to see her beloved grandmother like this. "She's properly bewitched, like Father. We have to go after Fliss!"

At the same time, she knew that bringing Fliss back to the cottage wasn't safe. Nothing had protected Ivy: neither her talismans nor her notes about plants and their supposed magical properties. Betty's head felt fuzzy with panic and all she could think of was her sister slipping silently down the dark lane, away from them.

It was Charlie who sharpened her thoughts. She shoved a jumble of clothes into Betty's arms, then tugged on some of her own that she'd dragged out of a pile of laundry.

Betty looked at her blankly.

"Well, we can't go after her in our nightclothes, can we?" Charlie said fiercely, wrestling her arm into a sleeve. "I'll get the nesting dolls. You get something of Fliss's."

"The dolls . . . ?"

"They can't get her if they can't see her."

Betty wasn't sure that was true anymore, but it might give them a better chance. Spurred into action, she shrugged out of her night wear and into her clothes. She rushed into Fliss's room. The sight of the bedclothes thrown back and empty was like a slap in the face. She swept her hands over them. The sheets held the faintest trace of warmth and rosewater perfume. She pulled a short, dark hair from her sister's comb and wrapped it carefully in a handkerchief. Returning to the kitchen, she tugged on her boots as Charlie arrived, armed with the dolls.

She looked so small and so young, with her buttons done up the wrong way and her hair all over the place. Again, Betty felt a crippling doubt. She had dragged Charlie into danger once already. Could she really do it again? Then she saw Charlie's determined little face and knew that she had as much right as Betty did to save their sister.

"Let's go," said Betty.

They left through the front door and slipped into the moonlit night. The roses hanging over the doorway were heavy and sweet in the airless night, like a part of Fliss had remained at Blackbird Cottage. *Like Ivy*, Betty thought, with a shiver, eyes adjusting to the velvety darkness.

"We need to hurry," she said, grappling with the nesting dolls. Her own hair was already safely inside the second doll. She popped Fliss's hair into the third doll, along with Charlie's, then thought better of it and slipped Fliss's back into the handkerchief and pocketed it. Until she knew where Fliss was heading—and with whom—it was safer not to make her invisible. If the witches suspected other magic was at play, then it might endanger Fliss further. Twisting the dolls into place, she checked her reflection in a nearby window. It was gone.

She quickened her pace. "Stay with me. And if I tell you to run, you run!"

Charlie gave a solemn nod, saying nothing. Their footsteps were loud, scuffling on the dirt road. Bewildered nighttime creatures were startled, running across their path. A fox, a badger, a hedgehog.

"Where is she?" Charlie said breathlessly. "Surely she couldn't have gone that far?"

It was when they reached the stream that Betty saw further evidence of enchantment.

"Look," she gasped, pointing at the water. "It's flowing backwards, up the hill." *Just like in Ivy's diary.* She glanced at Foxglove Cottage, holding Charlie's hand tightly. At first it seemed there were no signs of life from within. It appeared the same as any other sleepy, little cottage. Then Charlie gripped her hand so hard that Betty winced.

"The *chimney*," Charlie breathed.

Betty looked up and almost tripped over her own foot in shock. Thick, green smoke was pouring out. She thought of witches' brew and frogs' legs in cauldrons. What were they cooking up in there? Had they lured Fliss inside their cottage to work their dark magic on her? Was it already too late?

Then Charlie gasped. "There!"

A figure was visible on the other side of the bridge, just vanishing around the corner where the blacksmith was. Betty glimpsed short, dark hair. It had to be Fliss. She tugged Charlie across the bridge, feeling something bumping against her back as she moved.

"What did you bring that for?" Charlie asked, as she, too, noticed the map case.

"It has Ivy's painting inside," said Betty. "We have to

keep it safe." *Even though it's hopeless now*, she thought silently. *They got her. The witches got Ivy, just like they've almost got Fliss . . .*

She forced the thought from her mind. It wasn't over yet, and Betty wasn't going to give up. Ivy hadn't had sisters to fight for her, but Fliss did. And fighting was one thing Betty knew how to do.

They passed the funeral parlor and the blacksmith's, then the village store, where the street opened out. By now Betty had guessed where Fliss was heading. She stared across the moonlit Pendlewick Green, toward the pond. There was no sign of the witches—or anyone else. Quickly, Betty fumbled with the nesting dolls and added Fliss's hair into the third, along with Charlie's. Now all three of them were invisible.

Fliss was halfway across the grass, gliding slowly and gracefully like a dancer in a dream. The surface of the pond was as flat as a mirror, barely showing a ripple. Fliss stepped closer to the water's edge, and for an awful moment Betty was afraid she'd topple in. A shout lodged in her throat, but then Fliss turned and began walking backward around the pond.

"Just like Ivy," Betty murmured, the shout threatening to give way to a sob. "It's all happening as it did before."

"We have to wake her up, Betty," Charlie said, her little voice choked. "Why is she doing this?"

"I don't know," said Betty desperately. "And I don't know how to break the spell."

A sharp sound pealed out then, cutting across the silent village. Betty whipped around before realizing it was the church clock chiming the hour. *Midnight.* The witching hour. She was turning back when she caught a movement in an upstairs window of the Splintered Broomstick. It was too far away to make out a face, but she knew it must be Brutus Crabbe, peering out onto the green. She tensed. Why would he be looking out there at the precise moment her sister was walking around the pond?

He can't see her, Betty reminded herself. *He can't see any of us.* If he had . . .

If he had, then Fliss would have immediately been suspected as a witch. Ivy's words floated back to her, settling like a heavy cloak.

I'm not a witch, though they have made it look as if I am.

The pond loomed closer as Betty and Charlie hurried toward it. They paused opposite the circle of stones, waiting for Fliss to pass them.

"What do we do?" Charlie whispered, her eyes wide at the eerie sight of their older sister behaving in such a way. "Do we grab her as she goes past?"

"No," said Betty. "Not yet. I think she's going to circle the pond three times, like Ivy did."

"Then what?" Charlie asked, keeping her voice low and her eyes on Fliss. "Then do we grab her?"

Betty didn't answer. She remembered how useless words had been when Fliss had been wandering, enchanted, around the house. How useless they'd been earlier that evening when she'd tried to warn Fliss of the danger she was in. How did you help someone who didn't know they needed saving or want to be saved?

"Fliss," she called softly, desperately, before she knew what she was doing. "Felicity Widdershins. Listen to me."

If Fliss heard, she never showed it. Her face remained like a mask, her eyes glassy.

But *someone* had heard.

A figure moved in the shadows, stepping away from the trunk of the Hungry Tree. Long, gray hair spilled out of a dark hood, and a quiet voice drifted toward them, rooting Betty to the ground.

"She can't hear you."

Betty pressed her fingers to her mouth in horror, recognizing her at once.

Miss Webb pushed the hood back, revealing her face. Her lips were stretched into a gruesome grin, her eerie eyes darting across the pond as she tried to locate where

Betty's voice had come from. She shook her head slowly, stepping away from the tree. "You shouldn't have followed her."

"I'll always follow her," said Betty, her voice trembling. "She's my sister." She darted toward Fliss, fear making her bold but clumsy. She tried to take her sister's hand, but Fliss slid out of her grasp, muttering under her breath as she continued on her bewitched path.

"Out, witch, out . . . be gone from Pendlewick . . ."

Miss Webb paused. "You might have a little magic, but she's already in deep."

"Betty," Charlie whispered. "Look behind her—the tree's moving!"

At first Betty thought Charlie was mistaken, but a black shape just behind Miss Webb's head began to yawn and stretch. It was a hole in the bark, widening like a mouth. A daring, heart-stopping idea came to her. If the tree really *did* eat things, she wondered how it would like the taste of a *real* witch.

"Charlie," she said in a voice that was so low she barely heard it herself. "Stay right here. Keep your eyes on Fliss."

Charlie nodded and Betty crept across the grass, watching the witch beneath the tree. Miss Webb's eyes darted this way and that, waiting for them to give themselves away. The knot in the wood continued to stretch behind her. Betty's toes nudged a pebble as she passed the standing stones. She stooped to pick it up.

"You can still save yourselves," Miss Webb went on, her face twisted, revealing a flash of teeth. "It's not too late to turn back."

Betty stepped closer, her heart thumping so loudly she was sure that, any second, it would give her away. She just needed a moment's distraction . . .

She threw the stone in her hand. It whizzed past the witch and thumped in the grass behind her, sounding just like a footstep. Miss Webb turned toward it, and Betty pounced. She reached out with both arms and shoved the woman as hard as she could into the yawning bark of the Hungry Tree. Her head flashed full of fairy tales: spinning wheels and children pushing witches into ovens. At the same time, a whispering voice reached her ears, but there was no time to work out where the sound was coming from. All her focus was on the old hag in front of her.

The woman toppled backward, her thin body light and bony under Betty's strong hands. "What are you doing?" she cried, as her arm plunged into the black hole in the tree.

"Evening things up," Betty hissed in her ear. "With you gone, that leaves two witches to deal with!"

But to her horror, the black hole did not close around the old woman as Betty had hoped it would. Instead, Miss Webb stumbled and lost her balance, sliding down to land in a heap on the ground.

"I'm not . . ." she wheezed, her hand flying to her throat. "I'm not a . . ." Her lips stretched over her teeth again, and a strange thought occurred to Betty. It looked as though the old woman wasn't grinning after all. Her teeth were bared like an animal in pain. She coughed, and small slivers of silver came away in her fingers. Betty recoiled in shock—what *were* they? Strands of spider's web, perhaps? One of the silver things fell into a scuffed patch of dirt.

It was a shiny silver pin.

"I'm not . . . a witch!" the old woman croaked, spitting out another pin and what looked like two needles. "I'm not one of them!"

"Yes, you are," Betty hissed. "Your poor old lady act doesn't fool me. You cursed my sister that day outside our house, and you're trying to take her. Just like you took Ivy Bell!"

Miss Webb shook her head and there was a desperate look in her eyes. It was so convincing that Betty almost doubted herself, but she couldn't afford to listen. It was a trick—it had to be.

"You don't understand," the old woman whispered, pulling herself to her feet. "I *am* Ivy Bell!"

Chapter Twenty-One

In the Company of Witches

"YOU CAN'T BE HER," said Betty, stunned. "You're lying! Ivy Bell only vanished two years ago, when she was . . ."

"Sixteen," the old woman finished. "Yes, I was." She stood by the tree, making no attempt to come closer.

"But you . . . you're *old*!" Charlie exclaimed, startling Betty. Her attention had been so locked on Miss Webb and her bizarre claim that she hadn't even noticed her younger sister approach.

Miss Webb gestured down at herself, staring at her hands. "Yes. This is what they did to me."

Betty stood rigid as the words washed over her. None of it made any sense, and yet the look on the old lady's face was so desperate that she suddenly found herself wondering if it *could* be true. But Betty didn't trust her.

"Why?" she demanded. "Why would they make you old? To turn you into one of them?"

"You don't understand."

"No," Betty said coldly, "I don't. But I know you tried to poison me. I found that spell bundle that you stuffed in my pocket! You tried to kill me, but you muddled up the plants. All you did was make me sick. Horribly sick."

The old woman blinked, nodding slowly. "I put the spell bundle there, yes. I didn't want to, but I had to. It was the only thing I could think of to . . ." She broke off, coughing and wincing, her hands flying to her throat. From her mouth, she pulled out something dark and spiky, and threw it down on the ground. Betty and Charlie watched in horror. It appeared to be a short stem of something thorny.

"Betty?" Charlie whispered. "What's happening to her?"

"Same thing that always happens," Miss Webb muttered. "Whenever I try to tell their secrets."

"You mean the pins and the brambles . . ." The question hovered on Betty's lips. She remembered how the old lady had struggled to speak that night in Foxglove

Cottage, when Betty encountered her in the kitchen. Was it possible that she was telling the truth?

"Yes. It's their way of keeping my mouth shut." The wrinkled lips formed a hard line. "But not anymore." She looked straight at Betty. "I didn't muddle anything up, and I never tried to poison you. I had to make you sick—it was all I could think of to save you."

"To *save* me?"

"From falling under their spell."

"The nettle soup," Betty said slowly. "I was right. That's why I was able to see what's been happening to Fliss—"

"And me," Charlie pointed out. "I wouldn't eat it."

The old woman gave Charlie a faint smile. "No. You trusted your instincts. I knew you'd be safe, at least at the start. But the rest of your family ate the soup."

"I did eat it," Betty said quietly. "I almost fell under their spell with Granny and Father and Fliss."

"And *I* trusted my in stinks," Charlie said, looking pleased with herself. "Eating nettles is always a bad idea."

"I knew Charlie would be all right," the old woman explained, turning to Betty. "I could hear through the door that she wouldn't touch the soup. But it wasn't enough. There had to be one other person who could see what was going on."

"Why just the two of us, though?" asked Betty. A lump came to her throat as she thought of Granny's glassy eyes and the way she had dismissed Betty's worries. If only Granny and Father hadn't been under the spell, one of them might have known what to do.

"Because they would have known. With only the two of you free of their enchantments, they thought they'd get away with it. You're only children, after all. They counted on no one listening to you, and they counted on you not knowing what to do."

"Well, they haven't met the Widdershins sisters before," said Betty fiercely.

They had been curious enough to find the secret room, brave enough to break into the witches' house, and bold enough to steal the evidence. It was this last thought that prompted her to think of what she'd found that day in Foxglove Cottage. "Anyway, you haven't explained the straw figures. You even used Charlie's tooth!"

"For your protection. I was trying to shield you and Charlie from falling under any more of their spells and trying to prevent Fliss from coming to harm." A dark look crossed the woman's face. "Lucky I found the tooth before they did. I pretended I'd tipped it down the sink with the soup. They wanted it to go in their room of cobwebs."

Betty narrowed her eyes, still not trusting what she

was hearing. "But the straw figures and the spell bundle, they were magical. If you're really Ivy and not a witch, how can you do those things?"

"Because in the company of witches," the old woman explained, "you pick up certain knowledge. Like the little trick with the broom. Others I discovered when they didn't know I was watching. Nature can be powerful, too." She glanced across to the forest. "I used to sneak away to sketch in the woods when I could and learn about the plants there." She smiled sadly. "The straw figures vanished after you'd been in the house. I'm guessing you took them."

"Yes," Betty whispered, her cheeks flaming. She had never considered that the straw figures might have been good magic. "I thought . . . after you came into the cottage, that you meant us harm. Why *were* you in the cottage that day?"

"I knew you'd found it," Miss Webb said. "The secret room."

"How?" Betty's heart banged like a slammed door. "You were spying?"

"Not spying. I was at the cottage. *Their* cottage, in the kitchen, when all of a sudden I heard voices. But not in the room with me; they were distant, like in a memory or daydream. I closed my eyes, and that's when I saw you, in the room. Looking around, through my things. And then looking right . . . at me. At the painting."

The words whipped around in Betty's head. This woman knew about the secret room and the painting . . . and yet it was clear that nobody had been in there for a long time when the girls had discovered it. She shot anxious glances at Charlie and then at Fliss, who was still circling the pond, unaware of anything but her own bewitched path. Was there a chance, however small, that what Miss Webb was saying might really be true?

Betty swallowed. "If you *are* her . . . if you're really Ivy, then tell me what else we found in that room."

"A diary." She spoke quietly, her eyes far away. "Two parts. That was all I had left. There was another part, but Uncle Jem found it." She shrugged, the gesture oddly girlish. "He destroyed it, to protect me, perhaps. Or to protect himself. Not that it did much good."

Betty clenched her fists to stop her hands from shaking. "What else?"

"A note." Miss Webb's eyes sparkled in the moonlight, filling with tears. "Taped to the back of the painting, asking for whoever found it not to destroy it. Because . . . because I think some part of me is trapped in it." She gazed at Betty, her eyes urgent. "Is it somewhere safe? Somewhere they can't get to it?"

Betty nodded, not trusting herself to speak. The painting was with her, curled inside the map case she carried. She had no idea if it was safe. Right now it felt as though nowhere was.

What she did know was that she was starting to believe that the woman in front of her might just be telling the truth, after all.

"Ivy?" Betty murmured. "Ivy Bell?"

"Y-yes . . . ouch!" More pins and needles dropped from the old woman's lips.

"If it's really you, then why are you out here with our sister?" Betty asked. "Why did you bring her to the pond, to the tree?"

"I didn't." Ivy gestured at Fliss helplessly. "I came because I knew this might be my last chance to help her."

Last chance. The words made Betty shiver with dread. "What do you mean?"

Ivy nodded past her, in the direction of the Splintered Broomstick. Betty chanced a quick look back, not wanting to take her eyes off Ivy. It was enough to catch another glimpse of the unmistakable outline of the pub's bullish landlord through an upstairs window.

"Brutus Crabbe was just a boy when Rosa Ripples vanished," Ivy said quietly. "That was sixty-two years ago. But he still remembers seeing her from the window of his father's inn, walking around the pond at midnight. Since then, he's made it his business to be on the lookout for the village's next witch." She smiled faintly. "He saw me do the same thing at midnight two years ago, after others saw me circling the pond one summer day during our art class."

"And now he's seen Fliss," Betty said, her dread deepening.

Ivy nodded. "And like me, he saw her vanish before his eyes. And so the witch hunt begins."

The dolls. If anything, by making Fliss disappear, Betty had sealed her sister's fate.

She became aware that Fliss had stopped walking, having completed her circuit of the pond. She was standing motionless next to the Hungry Tree. Her face was blank, but her head was on one side. Not tilted in the flirtatious way Betty had seen her use many times before, but like a bird, listening. In the brief silence, Betty heard something, too. The same whispering she had heard in the moments she had shoved Ivy toward . . .

Toward the tree.

The gaping knot in the trunk was still there but hadn't gotten any larger.

"Is that . . . ?"

"The tree." Ivy nodded. "It's whispering."

Betty went closer, her ears straining to hear the faint words. Some she caught, and they were jumbled and urgent, like secrets being passed on.

"Help me . . . can't get out . . . they put me here, they did this . . . Eliza Bird, that's my name. Trapped . . . I'm not a witch, I'm not!"

"Jumping jackdaws," Betty breathed. "So it's true. The Hungry Tree grew from Eliza Bird's bones!" She stared at the different things embedded in its bark. Shoes, newspaper, rags. "But why—?"

"They're not there because the tree ate them," Ivy explained. "They're there because it's the witches' way of keeping the villagers away and stopping them from hearing Eliza's whispers. And people here are so superstitious and afraid that they believe it and do what they're told." She smiled sadly. "I should know. I avoided it like everyone else. I kept away because the sign told me to. I thought it was for my own protection, but really it was just one more trick of theirs."

"Betty!" Charlie's voice was a loud whisper. She pointed across the green. More windows in the Splintered Broomstick were lit, along with the buildings next door to it. The villagers were stirring, along with Betty's panic. And there was the faint yellow flicker of a lantern at the inn's doorway. Someone was outside the inn. Before Betty's eyes, the lantern was joined by another.

The villagers could take no more.
They gathered at Eliza's door . . .

"They're coming," Betty whispered, horrified. She and her sisters might be invisible, but Betty knew now it was no guarantee of safety—especially when Fliss was behaving so unpredictably. "We have to get Fliss out of here!"

"There is somewhere safe," said the old woman. "For now, at least." She nodded toward the dark mass of trees bordering the village green. "Tick Tock Forest. The villagers won't think to go in there, and even Pilliwinks and Lightwing won't follow. I can lead you through it, but you must promise to do exactly as I say."

"How will we get Fliss anywhere when she's like *this*?" Betty cried, forgetting to keep her voice down. "Look at her! And, besides that, how do I even know if I can trust you?"

"Unless you want to face *them*"—the old woman jerked her chin at the glowing lanterns—"you don't have a choice."

"Wait," said Betty. "I have an idea." For, as a new problem occurred to her, she discovered she had a solution to something else. The Widdershins sisters might be invisible, but the old woman wasn't. She could still be followed by the gathering mob. In order to make her disappear, too, it would mean revealing the Widdershinses' magical secret. It was a huge risk—but now Betty realized that she had a way to tell whether the person before her really *was* Ivy Bell. The flickering lanterns bobbing toward them made her decision for her.

She took the nesting dolls out of her pocket, then felt deeper until she found the silver coin that she'd dug out of the church wall.

"What's that?" asked the old woman, as the coin flashed in the moonlight.

"You should know," said Betty softly. "If you really are who you say you are, then this coin was yours. Placed in one of the corners of Blackbird Cottage before you vanished."

The expression on the old woman's face was unreadable.

"Hiding an item belonging to you in these dolls will make you vanish," said Betty. "So if you're not really Ivy, then you'll stay visible." *And I'll have revealed our only source of magic to a witch*, she thought. She put the coin into the third doll, with her sisters' hairs and Hoppit's whisker. There was just enough room. Betty crooked a finger. "Come closer to the water. I need to see your reflection."

Miss Webb stepped closer.

Betty reassembled the nesting dolls, twisting the outermost doll in place. She stared into the surface of the pond—and gasped.

Chapter Twenty-Two

Tick Tock Forest

"I TOLD YOU I WAS TELLING THE TRUTH," the old woman said, her voice soft and sad.

Their shadowy reflections had vanished from the pond. Betty looked away and into the woman's face. Into *Ivy's* face. Now that she knew, it was possible to see traces of the girl Ivy had been two years ago: the high cheekbones and forehead, the piercing eyes. How had she ended up like this?

"I'll tell you everything," Ivy said, appearing to sense the questions piling up in Betty's mind. "But not here. We have to leave now."

The glowing lanterns were getting closer. Betty counted six or seven and saw the light flickering over faces. Some were angry, others afraid. She recognized only Crabbe and the red-cheeked woman from the Sugar Loaf. The rest were too shadowy. They looked eerie, like Halloween jack-o'-lanterns. Even though she had hidden them with the magical dolls, Betty didn't feel safe. Being invisible in Foxglove Cottage hadn't protected them, and being invisible here was no guarantee of safety, either. All it could do was buy them some time.

"Fliss," Betty whispered, realizing her sister was standing motionless. She laid a hand on her sister's arm, but Fliss didn't respond. She simply stood, swaying lightly.

Betty shook her arm as the villagers drew nearer. "Come on, we need to move. Please."

Fliss stayed rigidly where she was, staring at the Hungry Tree.

"This is hopeless," Betty said desperately. "How do we get through to her?"

There came the sound of a scratch and a hiss as a match was struck in the darkness. Ivy held it before her, the soft glow making her appear softer, younger.

It was no ordinary match, Betty could see that. The yellow of the flame deepened, becoming a fiery red, and it burned far more fiercely than it should.

Ivy started to speak quickly and quietly.

> *"Little matchstick burning bright,*
> *Work your magic day and night.*
> *Gaze at this enchanted flame*
> *And follow when I speak your name."*

Ivy blew out the matchstick, sending a twist of smoke around Fliss.

"Felicity Widdershins," she said.

Immediately, Fliss stopped swaying. Her eyes became hooded and glassy, but they fixed on Ivy.

Betty shuddered, both relieved and horrified. "What *are* those matches? Another trick of Pilliwinks and Lightwing's?"

Ivy nodded. "I watch and I listen. And I steal what they won't miss." She threw the dead matchstick into the grass. "Come with me. Hurry."

They passed under the branches of the Hungry Tree. Its bare branches skimmed Betty's hair and faint whispers reached her but were drowned out by the approaching villagers. She could hear them now. Their footsteps quickening. Whispers of "witch" and "vanished" carrying through the still night. *Oh, yes,* thought Betty grimly. If a figure circling the pond at midnight was enough to raise suspicion, then one who vanished in a blink would have no chance. But what exactly happened to witches in present-day Pendlewick? Crowds of villagers couldn't just hunt a "witch" down . . . could they? She remembered Miss Pilliwinks's talk of dunking and drowning, and the way she had tittered about it. Surely things like that couldn't happen here, not now . . .

Ivy led the way across Pendlewick Green, heading to the far side, where the girls hadn't yet been. There was a straggle of cottages to the left. Ahead of them a vast area of trees stretched into the distance, thick and black under the moon: Tick Tock Forest.

"You're not . . . taking us in there?" Charlie asked, her eyes huge with fear. "Are you?"

"I have to." Ivy quickened her pace, but already Betty could hear she was becoming breathless, the same way Granny did when she climbed up the stairs. *Of course*, Betty realized. It made sense that Ivy's aged body would tire far more quickly than Betty and her sisters. "It's the safest place right now."

"But it's enchanted!" Betty gasped, remembering what Miss Pilliwinks had told her on their first day in Pendlewick. "I thought people were supposed to keep out of it."

"They do," said Ivy. "That's why it's our best chance of getting away. We won't be followed through it—not even by Pilliwinks and Lightwing. Even they don't trust its magic. The most important thing is to get you out of Pendlewick, and fast."

Betty glanced over her shoulder, first at the villagers, who had stopped a little short of the Hungry Tree, and then at Fliss. Between the witch-crazed locals and her bewitched sister, she could see there was little choice but to follow Ivy, even into the middle of an enchanted forest in the dead of night. She wasn't happy about it, though; if the two witches wouldn't risk it, then the woods felt even more threatening.

Soon they were on the fringes of the woods and the villagers had been left behind. Betty was glad of the distance between them and that she could no longer hear their accusing voices.

The neat grass of Pendlewick Green gave way to scattered pinecones, dropped needles, and a cloak of darkness. It was cooler in the forest, too. The coolest Betty had felt since stepping foot in Pendlewick and its blazing summer heat. She felt a smattering of goose bumps on her arms as they slipped between the trees and realized that, at some point, Charlie's hand had found its way into hers. Beside them, Fliss was gliding along, glassy-eyed and bewitched.

Things crunched underfoot, dry and brittle from lack

of rain. Something sharp snagged on Betty's stocking, scratching her.

"Ivy, this is impossible," she protested, longing to pull out the map of Pendlewick but knowing it was too dark for it to be any use. "We can barely see. How will we find our way through these woods? What's on the other side of them?"

"The crossroads." Ivy was hobbling a little way ahead. Betty kept her eyes locked on her, a shadowy shape moving between the trees. "Listen for the stream and follow the sound. A little farther in and there's a path."

They kept going, stumbling over roots and broken branches. A sound reached Betty—the rush of running water. She headed toward it, then collided with Ivy, who had knelt without warning by a blackened tree stump.

"What are you doing?" Betty hissed, suddenly fearing a trap and bundling Charlie behind her.

Another match was struck, but this time there was no red flame or incantation. Instead, Ivy stood up, holding a little oil lantern that she'd lit. Betty looked down and saw that the tree stump had a hollow space in its side, where the lantern had been hidden.

"I was just lighting this," said Ivy, lifting up the lantern and watching her. "You still don't trust me, do you?"

Betty lowered her gaze, saying nothing. Ivy may have

proven to be who she said she was, but it wasn't enough to completely convince Betty that the sisters were safe with her.

"You said you'd tell us everything."

"And I will," said Ivy, looking around for something. "But there are other things you need to know first."

They set off again. Betty kept her fingers wrapped around the nesting dolls in her pocket as they walked. If there was even a hint of danger, she could open up the dolls, toss Ivy's coin out, and . . .

"There's the path," said Ivy. She pointed to a dusty track close by. "We just have to follow it, but there are things . . ." She winced, reaching down to massage her ankle.

"What's the matter?" Betty asked, feeling slightly guilty now.

"It's nothing." Ivy straightened up and lifted the lantern, sending shadows skittering. On the path ahead, a fox's eyes glowed amber before the animal shot away into the undergrowth.

"Before we go any deeper, there are three things you need to know about this forest," Ivy said, her eyes meeting Betty's with a piercing intensity. "Three rules. It's called Tick Tock Forest for a reason — it plays strange tricks with the time."

Three rules. The words flashed into Betty's mind as she recalled Ivy's sketches. She had seen them jotted down on one, but she couldn't remember what the rules had been.

"First," Ivy went on, "don't fall asleep while we're in the forest."

Charlie and Betty glanced at each other. There was no way Betty could even think of sleep at that moment.

"What happens if we do?" asked Charlie.

"You'll lose time," said Ivy. "And that's the last thing you'll want once Pilliwinks and Lightwing discover you're gone. Second rule: don't, whatever you do, speak if you hear the sound of ticking. And don't touch any clocks you might find in here. Once the ticking stops, it's safe to speak again, but not before. You'll slow time down."

"And third?" Betty asked. She had been used to the strangeness of Crowstone, with its will-o'-the-wisps, marsh mists, and ghostly pirate legends, but Pendlewick's mysteries seemed even more otherworldly. A hungry tree, witches, and now this: a forest that played tricks with time. As much as the Pendlewick folk denied it, the very roots of the place were steeped in magic.

"Third—and this is the most important—*never* ask what the time is." Ivy looked at Charlie pointedly. "Or if we're nearly there yet. You could cause a time slip."

"But how—" Betty stopped herself just in time. *Idiot!*

she told herself. For she had been about to ask Ivy how long the journey through the woods would take.

Ivy gave her a knowing look. "There's no one answer to that. It takes as long as it takes and is different for everyone. The best we can do is not make the forest angry."

Betty looked around her, shivering. She could see now why none of the villagers went near the place and even the witches didn't trust its strange magic.

They continued along the path with Ivy in the lead. Fliss was next, staring straight at the light of the lantern, her eyes unfocused and dreamy. Betty and Charlie stayed behind her, keeping their sister firmly in sight.

"Three rules," Charlie muttered darkly. "Why three? It's always three."

Betty remembered something their grandmother often told them. "Bad luck always comes in threes. That's what Granny says."

They found the first watch a short way into the forest. It was small and square, with a cracked face and tarnished brass. It had been fastened around a low branch, at the end of which were five twigs that looked like fingers. These gave it the eerie appearance of a treelike arm wearing the watch. Charlie immediately stuck her fingers in her ears, but Betty shook her head, spooked as they slowed to look at it.

"It's not ticking," she said, wondering whom the watch had belonged to and whether they'd made it out of the forest. Whether they had followed the rules.

"People leave them behind," Ivy said, urging them on. "They try to leave clues for other travelers who've lost track of the time. It never works."

Betty wondered how long they'd been walking but dared not ask. There was something about seeing the path twisting farther into the trees that immediately stretched time, making everything seem longer. More tiring. And now that her mind kept coming back to time, she couldn't hold back her curiosity. What had happened to make Ivy lose so much of hers?

"Ivy?" she said uncertainly. "How are you so sure that Pilliwinks and Lightwing won't follow us through the forest? Are you going to tell us what happened to you? What they did?"

Ivy slowed a little, bending to rub her ankle once more. It reminded Betty so much of how Granny rubbed her aches and pains that Betty felt her eyes sting. She blinked back tears, thinking of her sharp-eyed, smart-mouthed Granny and wondering if they'd ever get that version of her back.

"Yes," Ivy said hoarsely. "It's time I told you what they did and why I can't let it happen to anyone else—but we must keep moving." She took a deep, shaky breath, and her eyes darkened. "First, tell me something. How old do you think Miss Pilliwinks and Mrs. Lightwing are?"

The question made Betty's skin crawl in a way that she couldn't explain. Like it felt . . . *wrong* to be questioning it. "It's hard to say." She remembered the first day in Pendlewick, when the girls had visited the village shop. "At first . . . old. Like my granny. Older than her, even. But then I realized I must have been mistaken when I saw Pilliwinks more closely. And then . . . when we were in the Splintered Broomstick, we saw something—a picture that made no sense." For now her mind was piecing together the clues and there was only one possible, horrible answer.

Ivy nodded. "The photograph," she said quietly. "Of the two of them at the Splintered Broomstick."

"It was . . . old," Betty whispered. "Really old. But they looked exactly the same as they do today."

"Really old," Ivy echoed. "Because it is. It was taken on the day the pub first opened."

Betty didn't need to ask how old the pub was. They'd seen the sign almost the moment they'd arrived in Pendlewick. In a couple of days' time, the Splintered Broomstick would have been open for one hundred years.

A hundred years in which the two witches had not aged at all.

"It's time to tell you what happened to me," said Ivy softly. "The night they stole my future."

Chapter Twenty-Three

The Diary of Ivy Bell

Sunday, June 22nd

I'VE BEEN STARING AT THE WORDS written down in front of me. Words that are in my handwriting. The ink is smudged in one corner. There is a trace of it dried on my thumb.

> *Next in line was Ivy Bell,*
> *Hers a sorry tale to tell.*
> *Love was what turned Ivy bad*
> *When she spied the blacksmith's lad.*
>
> *In Tick Tock Forest, she searched for hours,*
> *Picking plants that gave her powers.*

Then she chanted with a thrill,
"If I can't have him, no one will."

Out, witch, out!
Give up your wicked ways.
Out, witch, out!
For magic never pays.

What is happening to me? I've read the words over and over again, but I don't remember writing them. I don't remember hearing them or even thinking them. Yet here they are in a song I've never heard. A song just like Eliza Bird's and Rosa Ripples's. I found it among my drawings, and though each word is like a knife, I can't stop reading it.

So Poison Ivy cast her spell,
And sure enough it turned out well.
The boy was hers! Success was sweet!
Why win his love when she could cheat?

She wore a cloak of butterflies
Before her friends' astonished eyes.
She summoned rain and conjured fogs
And caused her cat to vomit frogs.

Out, witch, out!
Your mischief has to end.
Out, witch, out!
And time is not your friend.

My hand is shaking too much to write. I need to stop. Uncle Jem is downstairs, asleep in his chair in the kitchen. I can hear him snoring. Poor Tibbles is meowing, asking me for dinner and bumping her head against my knee, but I can't seem to get up or think properly. Writing this down is the only way I can try to make sense of everything. And I can't tear my eyes from that song and its horrible ending:

The villagers had seen enough
Of Poison Ivy's spooky stuff.
They set a trap and lay in wait
And used her sweetheart as the bait.

A fire was built from ancient wood.
They'd catch the witch and roast her good!
Yet Ivy saw the flames burn bright
And so she vanished that same night.

Out, witch, out!
We won't forget the past.

Out, witch, out!
Our village, safe at last.

There are two possibilities.

Could it be true, then? *Am* I a witch? Everything in my heart says no. Yes, I was fascinated with Tick Tock Forest, and perhaps I shouldn't have sneaked away there to sketch when it was forbidden, but I have *never* tried to work magic, never tried to bewitch or harm anyone . . . and yet the things that have happened can only be explained by magic. The butterflies, the stream, the frogs. And Todd. It doesn't matter if I write his name now, does it? Did I bewitch him without knowing it or meaning to? Are his feelings for me all because of a spell I cast but don't remember? Somehow the idea of this is one of the worst things of all. Because I thought our love was real.

The second possibility is that someone else is causing all this to happen. If that's true, then magic must also be involved. Does it mean that a real witch is at work, casting spells and making it look as though I'm guilty to avoid being blamed themselves? This is the explanation that makes most sense to me. And if this is what's happening to me, then I must fight fire with fire. Or magic with magic. But how?

Fire. The word fills me with horror. *They'd catch the*

witch and roast her good . . . Is this what they want to do? Burn me at the stake for witchcraft? That doesn't happen anymore . . . *shouldn't* happen anymore—but then just days ago, I never thought butterflies could take the shape of a word or that a stream could flow backward. My only hope is that the song doesn't say they succeed. It says I vanish the same night I see the flames. Could this be a clue? A warning? And if I wrote this myself, does it mean it's a premonition?

Since the incident at the pond, I have been searching through my sketches for one of a peacock butterfly that I spotted at the start of summer. I'd felt an urge to see the drawing again, to check if I'd noted anything of significance. I found it this afternoon, and while there was nothing unusual about it, on the same sheet I'd also painted some sage leaves. At the time, Uncle Jem told me a funny thing about sage. He said that some people believe it's linked to living forever. I liked the idea of this, so I made a note on the drawing.

There were other pictures, too, from over the years, where I'd jotted down Uncle's little sayings: all these odd beliefs people have about nature. There are lots, in fact. Roses symbolize love and friendship. Wizards' whiskers are said to invite wealth if hung in bunches over doorways. And my favorite: ivy, which is a symbol of protection and immortality. And so on. Today, I've looked through them all in the hope that something here might help me.

I'm also trying to remember all the strange little things that the villagers have said and done over the years. Things linked to witches and keeping them away. I once heard Brutus Crabbe telling Uncle that his father kept silver coins in the corners of the Splintered Broomstick. Real silver coins are supposed to blacken if a witch has been near. He gave up on the idea, though, because the coins kept getting stolen. Franny Boot strings up bunches of fennel over the door of the Sugar Loaf. *To keep evil out*, she says. And Magda's grandpa is always putting lines of salt by the windows and doors for the same reason. She says it drives her grandma crazy.

I will do all three things to try to protect Blackbird Cottage—and myself. I don't think it will be enough, but it might buy me some time.

It is late afternoon now. We didn't have any fennel in the garden, but I found some in the fields over by Peckahen Farm. I know exactly where to find it in Tick Tock Forest, but now I don't dare venture there unless it's under the cover of night. When I came back, something horrible was waiting for me.

The cottage windows were dripping with eggs. Rotten, by the smell of them. The heat had made the stench even worse and dried out the oozing mess. I scrubbed it off with hot, soapy water before Uncle Jem saw, but dried egg is almost impossible to remove, like glue on a blanket.

I'm not going to wait to see the flames. I'm leaving—tonight. I've packed a small bag: some clothes, food and water, and a little money. Maybe this is what the song meant by "vanishing." If I don't leave now, something is going to happen to me, and it'll be buried with the rest of Pendlewick's secrets.

But Blackbird Cottage has its own secrets. Ever since I was little, Uncle Jem has told me stories about the secret room—or the *witch hole*, as he calls it. It was made as a hiding place years ago, when people were afraid they might be the next poor soul to be accused. Maybe other houses have them, too. I don't know. That is where I'm going to leave my diary—my version of the story—for Uncle Jem or someone else to find. I just want others to believe me once things aren't so clouded by magic.

There's one other thing I'm leaving behind, but this will be for Todd, so he'll have something to remember me by. If he *wants* to remember me, that is. Perhaps once they've publicly accused me of being a witch, he'll prefer to forget. I'm leaving a painting I've been working on for a while. It's a self-portrait, the best piece of work I've ever done. I've painted my own little magical messages into it: roses for love; sage, to show I'll always be his; and, of course, ivy. Perhaps in years to come, when he is old with children of his own, he might still think of the girl he once knew and cared about.

It's time to go. I'm ready.

Chapter Twenty-Four

The Stone Circle

"WE NEVER FOUND THE THIRD PART of the diary," said Betty quietly as Ivy lapsed into silence. "I searched for it, but there was nothing else in the room. Only the songs and your drawings." She remembered how convinced she'd been that there must be more to Ivy's story and the strange connection she'd felt to this girl through her diary. To be here with her now, making their way through an enchanted forest, felt to Betty like a peculiar, feverish dream. "And the painting. You did it for Todd."

Ivy's eyes clouded. She gave a faint nod and gazed ahead along the path, but to Betty it seemed as though Ivy was staring into the past.

"I planned to leave the rest of the diary in the secret room, too," Ivy said eventually, her voice little more than a whisper. "But Uncle Jem got to it first."

"What is all this?"

Ivy blinked, confused. She was in her room standing by the bed. Through her window she could see it was dusk.

Panic rose in her throat. What am I still doing here? *she thought.* I meant to leave hours ago!

Uncle Jem stood at the side of the bed, his face twisted into a frown. In his hands he held crumpled pages. His eyes widened as he read them out.

"Next in line was Ivy Bell, hers a sorry tale to tell . . ."

"It's not what you think," Ivy croaked. She glanced around in alarm. She had drifted away again. Blacked out or whatever it was she kept doing. Thankfully, this time there were no new drawings or strange songs she didn't remember creating. Just the painting, the canvas rolled up, ready to give to Todd when she said goodbye.

Uncle Jem tutted. "You can't write things like this, Ivy." He wagged his finger at her like she was a naughty child, but there was a look in his eyes Ivy hadn't seen before. "People will think you're up to no good."

"People already think—wait, no! Uncle, stop!"

Her uncle had begun tearing the pages up into tiny pieces.

Not just the song, but the third part of Ivy's diary with it. Ivy watched, horrified.

"Why would you write these things?" There was a sing-song quality to Uncle Jem's voice that somehow scared Ivy more than if he'd been shouting. "You know how we Pendle-wick folk don't talk about magic, Ivy. After all, magic and trouble go hand in hand."

Ivy went very still. "Uncle Jem?" Her voice was tiny and hesitant. "You don't think I've done anything . . . bad, do you?"

The old man didn't answer. Instead, he carefully arranged the torn papers in the little fireplace, struck a match, and threw it into the grate.

"There," he said brightly. "Just a little kindling, that's all it was. Nothing to worry about."

Ivy watched as her words went up in flames, burning to ash. The look in her uncle's eyes was one she had never seen before. A glazed, closed-off look. It didn't suit her warm, jolly uncle at all.

"I'll fix this," she said softly. She didn't know how, but perhaps she could seek help from outside Pendlewick, for both herself and her uncle. Ivy got up and bent down slowly over the old man, who was still kneeling by the fire. She placed a light kiss on the top of his head, fighting back emotion. How she loved him, her dear old uncle who'd cared for her since she was a child . . . and yet now it was starting to feel as though that person wasn't there anymore.

Her uncle didn't react. Ivy backed away, collected her small packed bag and the painting, rolled into a tight coil, then headed downstairs. Silence stretched behind her. Uncle Jem hadn't moved.

She found Tibbles snoozing on the doormat. She reached down and scratched the old tabby behind the ears. "No more frogs," she whispered, her eyes blurring with tears. "Look after him, won't you?" Then she pulled on her shoes and stepped out of the house, closing the door quietly. Her ears caught a light creak from above. She looked up and caught sight of her uncle's face at an upstairs window. She held his gaze a moment. His face was distorted by a ripple in the glass.

At the gate, she hesitated, glancing down at the roll of canvas in her hand. Todd had been distant with her recently, since the witch rumors had taken hold. Perhaps he'd been about to break it off with her, anyway. It would be easier to leave without seeing him, that way she could at least pretend things were still all right. But she couldn't, she knew that. She loved him—and she had to see him one last time.

Before she could stop herself, she set off down Bread and Cheese Hill. It was still light on the green, a pleasant evening. Within minutes, the church was in sight. On the bridge, Ivy spotted Scally and Wags playing fish sticks and bickering over whose was the winner. They spotted her and ran over, both talking at once.

"Ivy! Come and play," Wags insisted, tugging at her hand. "Scally keeps cheating."

"Do not," said Scally, aiming a kick at Wags's shins.

"I can't play now." Ivy tried to keep her voice light, but it came out thin and strained. "Have you seen Todd? Is he still at the farm?"

Wags shrugged, dodging another kick. "He was earlier. Helping build a fire, a big one."

A fire? Ivy batted the word away. Surely there was no reason to worry. There were fires all the time at the farm: burning piles of animal manure or sometimes fields that caught light in the summer heat. It didn't mean anything . . .

She stopped, sniffing the air like a startled animal. Yes, there it was, stinging her nose. Unmistakable.

A curl of smoke rose up in the distance, in the direction of Peckahen Farm. Ivy watched as it blackened the sky. The smell was gone, but the smoke remained. Her heart began to beat a warning. She couldn't see any flames yet. The words of the song played in her head:

They set a trap and lay in wait
And used her sweetheart as the bait . . .

No. She wouldn't go to him. It would be madness, however much she longed to see him. She blinked back tears, holding on to her memories. They would have to be enough. She gazed toward the village green. Around her she heard noises of suppers being prepared through open windows. A few straggles of children played ball on the green. Scally and Wags raced off ahead, playfighting on the grass. Franny Boot was walking her dog. Everything was peaceful, as it should be. But the spire of smoke lingered in her mind.

Ivy stared across at the standing stones, the still pond, and the Hungry Tree. Beyond, Tick Tock Forest loomed and her heartbeat quickened. She had planned to take the road out of Pendlewick this evening, but after seeing the smoke, another idea came to her. She could go through the forest. Very few would dare follow her. Ivy had been going into the woods secretly for years now. It should be safe . . . provided the rules were followed.

A door snapped open nearby, making Ivy jump. Miss Pilliwinks stood blinking in the doorway of the village store.

"Hello, dearie." Miss Pilliwinks gave one of her friendly, picket-fence smiles. Her voice was warm and welcoming. It had been so long since Ivy had been spoken to kindly that it brought fresh tears to her eyes. She swallowed them away and stepped closer to the shop. It would have been closed for

over an hour, and the sign in the door said as much. Inside it was dim, but Ivy could see a heap of price labels on the counter and half-unpacked boxes.

Ivy rubbed her nose and stepped inside, dimly aware of the boys shouting on the green. The playfighting must have turned nasty, for one of them was crying.

"You look upset, dearie," said Miss Pilliwinks. "Something the matter?"

Ivy felt a rush of warmth, and at the same time was struck by an idea. Miss Pilliwinks had always been so kind and obliging with her ready smiles and pots of jam. Perhaps the sweet old lady would help her once more.

"Could I . . . could I leave this for Todd?" Ivy mumbled, clutching the painting. "Next time he comes in, would you give it to him for me, please?"

"Of course." Miss Pilliwinks beamed and eased the painting out of Ivy's hand. Without asking, she unrolled it to reveal the portrait. "Well now. Isn't this something? It almost looks . . . alive. What a lovely souvenir. That'll do nicely."

"I . . ." Ivy stared, unsure what to say. What could Miss Pilliwinks mean by that? "Please, just make sure Todd gets it." She turned, glancing through the shop window as she headed toward the door.

"Were you going somewhere, dearie?" Miss Pilliwinks persisted. "You really do look quite troubled." She patted

Ivy's arm and lowered her voice. "Perhaps we can help. We know the things people are saying aren't true."

"We?" Ivy asked, startled by the old lady's directness.

"Yes." Mrs. Lightwing stepped out from behind a shelf and smiled kindly. "We know you're not a witch. But it's not safe for you here any longer. Let us help you."

Ivy sniffed, nodding. How good it felt to have someone on her side at last, even if it was these peculiar old women.

"It's kind of you," she mumbled. "But I was leaving anyway. I'd hate for you to get into any trouble because of me."

Miss Pilliwinks gave a soft hoot of laughter. "Don't worry about us, dearie. We've been in Pendlewick longer than anyone else. Let us come with you, until we know you're safely on the path away."

Mrs. Lightwing came nearer. A wisp of gray hair had escaped from the bun on her head and hung like a cobweb near her neck. A sound reached Ivy's ears: a familiar shuffle-shuffle. Ivy stiffened, noticing a movement up above on the shelves above the wools and yarns. The tiny, ornamental spinning wheel was turning quickly, the little pedal moving up and down on its own. Shuffle-shuffle . . .

That noise. The noise. She must have heard it many times before, whenever she'd been in the shop. The sound of it made her feel panicky. What was going on?

"Quickly, child. There's no time to waste." Mrs. Lightwing swooped closer to Ivy and wrapped her arm around Ivy's shoulders. She felt surprisingly strong and Ivy was suddenly grateful for it. She allowed herself to be led out of the shop and across the village green toward the woods. It was curiously empty now, with not a soul in sight and not a sound in the still air. It was as though the entire village had suddenly been abandoned.

"Where are we going?" she mumbled, glancing back in the direction of the bridge. Had the two old ladies somehow guessed she meant to go through the forest?

"There might be a way you can stay," said Mrs. Lightwing. "There's something we can try to make everything right again."

Ivy stared at her, hope flickering. "Make everything right?"

The two older women exchanged a look whose meaning Ivy couldn't catch.

"It's been said," Miss Pilliwinks began hesitantly, "that whoever can correctly count those stones will release the villagers from the spell and turn them back to people again."

"I know," Ivy said. Impatience crept into her voice. She needed to escape, not be delayed by age-old superstitions, however well-meaning the two old women might be. "Everyone knows that. But no one has managed to get the same number twice."

"There is another less well-known part to the saying," Mrs. Lightwing added. "That it wouldn't just break the curse on the villagers, but on the whole of Pendlewick. It would release the village from the evil hold of Eliza Bird. And what's happening to you would never happen again to anyone else."

Ivy gazed at the stone circle. So there *was* magic being used against her. Was it true that there might be a way to undo it? For her to return to her old life with Uncle Jem and have a future with Todd?

"What if it doesn't work?" she whispered.

"Doesn't hurt to try, does it?" Mrs. Lightwing coaxed. Her arm was still around Ivy's shoulders, her bony fingers digging in a little too tightly now. Ivy glanced down at them. The old woman gave a tight smile and released her. "Of course, people say that the only way to see them properly is to stand in the middle of the circle."

"But . . . but that's forbidden," said Ivy. "We're not supposed to go near—"

"How can they be counted if you can't see them properly?" Miss Pilliwinks added. "Listen, we'll help you."

"Hold this," said Mrs. Lightwing. From under her shawl, she pulled out a coil of thin cord. "Having a connection to the outside of the circle will keep you safe. If things become dangerous, we'll pull you out."

"Dangerous," Ivy repeated. She eyed the stones, afraid.

311

She had grown up with this legend. Uncle Jem had warned her countless times never to step into the stone circle, but what choice did she have? She took the cord, finding it smooth and cool to the touch, and hesitantly stepped between two of the larger boulders into the circle. Nothing happened. Braver now, she moved to the center. The stones towered over her, tall and ancient, like giants holding a secret meeting.

"Count this way," called Miss Pilliwinks, hopping from foot to foot. Ivy had never seen her with so much energy. She moved to Ivy's left and began tapping each of the stones in turn. And then Ivy noticed something else: a roll of canvas almost hidden in the grass.

"My painting," she said, confused. "I thought I left that at the shop. Why did you bring it?"

"Oops!" said Miss Pilliwinks. "How silly of me. That's what happens when I'm chattering. Don't you worry, we'll take good care of that for you!"

Reassured, Ivy began to count, turning to follow Miss Pilliwinks's path. Mrs. Lightwing marched ahead of her, and Ivy could just see her in the corner of her eye. ". . . three, four, five . . ."

A movement caught Ivy's attention over by the Hungry Tree. She paused in her counting, forgetting her place. There it was again—a tearstained face peering out from behind the bark.

"Wags," she whispered. What was he doing here? He must have had a fight with Scally and stayed behind. His eyes were dark and watchful, darting between Ivy and the two old women.

"I . . . I lost my place," Ivy croaked. "I need to start again." She had turned a full circle now and became aware that the cord Mrs. Lightwing had handed her had tightened around her waist. She wondered if she should untangle herself, but the cord was fairly snug and there was a risk she would trip over it, with it trailing on the ground. Mrs. Lightwing and Miss Pilliwinks stood next to each other, outside the stone circle. Both were motionless and smiling.

"I said I have to start again," Ivy called.

"Oh, there's no need for that," Mrs. Lightwing said, so softly that Ivy wondered if she'd heard her properly.

Ivy frowned, then cried out as a sharp pain stabbed her thumb like a pin. Looking down, she saw that the cord she was holding was no longer smooth. Hundreds of tiny little hairs were pushing their way out of it, along with spiky, familiar green leaves. Nettle leaves.

"How . . . What?" she stuttered as the leaves continued to sprout all along the cord. Only it wasn't a cord anymore. It was one giant stinging nettle.

Ivy stared at it in horror, her fingers blistering. This was like the stream, the butterflies. Things behaving in ways they *shouldn't. She gazed at the two old women, trying to summon the words to convince them this wasn't her doing . . . but they didn't look afraid or even surprised. They looked . . . pleased.*

At once, Ivy knew, and she was terrified.

"You tricked me," *she whispered.*

Another sting bit into her thumb, forcing her to drop the nettle. As she did, it lashed itself around her ankle like a tentacle, forming a tight, painful knot. Ivy dropped to the ground and began pulling at it, trying to free herself.

"It's easier if you don't fight," *Miss Pilliwinks said pleasantly.* "It really won't take a minute."

"No," *Mrs. Lightwing replied with a cruel chuckle.* "It'll take a lifetime."

Miss Pilliwinks tittered. "Oh, you are naughty. Don't tease the poor girl."

"I can't help it," *said Mrs. Lightwing.* "It's exciting. We haven't had one for so long."

"What are you talking about?" *Ivy thrashed and kicked, but it seemed to only make the snare around her ankle tighter.* "Haven't had one what?"

A dull ache began in Ivy's leg, spreading up through her body. She suddenly felt overwhelmingly tired, and her vision blurred. She wondered if she was crying but couldn't feel any tears. She lifted her hand to wipe her eyes — and whimpered.

Her hand was wrinkling up before her very eyes. She felt her body shrinking and wizening in her clothes, saw a strand of dark hair rapidly turning white.

"That's it, nearly there," breathed Miss Pilliwinks, leaning in closer.

"No!" a voice yelled.

Wags came pounding over the grass toward the stone circle, his face pinched in shock. Ivy strained against the nettles, but they held her firmly in place.

"Stay back!" she shouted.

The two witches turned in surprise as the small boy leaped toward them and flung himself onto the nettle cord, wrenching it apart with his hands. At the same moment, Ivy felt a powerful jolt shudder through her body and Wags was thrown back by an invisible force. He hit the Hungry Tree and slid down it, dazed.

Gasping and crying, Ivy crawled out from between the stones toward the small figure at the foot of the tree. The cord, still tied to her ankle, trailed after her.

"What's she doing?" Miss Pilliwinks squawked. "Why isn't she dead?"

Dead? The word echoed in Ivy's head, taunting her. I might as well be. She dragged her weary body closer to Wags. "What have you done to him? What have you done to me?"

"I don't know," Lightwing hissed, studying her own hands, taking a tentative step. She was replying to her sister, not Ivy. "I don't feel any different. My aches and pains haven't gone . . . That stupid child!" She turned on Wags and Ivy, her eyes like fire and ice all at once. "You've ruined everything! That stupid boy has taken our years!"

"You mean . . . it hasn't worked?" Pilliwinks's voice quavered.

"Of course it hasn't!" Lightwing roared. She poked Pilliwinks in the chest with a bony finger. "Can't you feel it? You're still a wrinkled old hag, and so am I!"

"You tried to kill me?" Ivy gasped. "So you could live longer?"

"Not kill you exactly," said Pilliwinks. "There would still be something left alive." She gestured to the Hungry Tree. "Eliza lives on, see? Just in a different form. Same as Rosa, with the pond." She gestured to Ivy's portrait in the grass. "And you. Our little souvenir."

Souvenir. The word clicked into place as Ivy gazed at the portrait. Only it wasn't quite the same as before. It had been a good likeness — there was no question of that. But this . . . this was not the work of a sixteen-year-old girl. The resemblance was uncanny. It looked like something living, breathing, in a way that made Ivy even more afraid than she already was.

She looked around wildly. "Help," she called weakly. "Someone, please help us!"

"There isn't anyone," said Lightwing spitefully. "We made sure of that."

"They're at the farm, aren't they?" Ivy wept. "Waiting to burn me!"

"Oh, no, dearie." Miss Pilliwinks gave a broad grin, as if she were discussing a new jam recipe. "There's no fire, not really. We just made you think that with our little trick. Our little song."

A trick? And she had fallen for it. Ivy touched Wags's face. He was breathing quickly, his eyes full of fear.

"I'll-I'll tell," he stuttered. "I'll—oh!"

A shiny silver pin had dropped from his mouth. Ivy stared at it in horror as Wags clamped his lips tightly shut.

"No," Mrs. Lightwing said, smiling. "You won't say a word, boy."

She snapped her fingers. Wags rose eerily, his eyes narrowing to unfocused slits. Wordlessly, he approached the pond, and for an awful moment Ivy thought they planned to drown him. Instead, he began to walk around it in a trance.

"Perhaps we should kill him?" Pilliwinks suggested.

Mrs. Lightwing tilted her head, considering this as she might consider which flavor ice cream to choose. "We may not need to."

"What about her?"

The two witches turned their attention back to Ivy.

"I won't tell anyone," she gabbled, backing away. "I swear. I'll leave, and you'll never see me again—Ow!"

Miss Pilliwinks had stepped on the nettle cord trailing in the grass. It bit into Ivy's ankle once more, lacing her with fresh stings.

"Oh, no, dearie," she said, picking up the cord and wrapping it firmly around her wrist. "You're coming with us."

Chapter Twenty-Five

Hickory Dickory Dock

IVY STOPPED SPEAKING AND LEANED against a nearby tree. Recounting the tale appeared to have weakened her. Her eyes were haunted and she was short of breath.

"Perhaps we should rest," Betty suggested. Her mind was whirring with what she had just learned, the horror of it all. Poor, poor Ivy. "Just for a few minutes so you can get your strength back."

"My legs are tired, too," added Charlie.

Ivy chewed her lip, glancing worriedly at the path. "We should keep moving."

Betty touched her arm lightly. It was trembling. "Do you think Pilliwinks and Lightwing are onto us yet?"

Ivy took a shaky breath. "If they're not, then they soon will be."

Her words hung in the air like a bad smell.

"Will they fly after us on broomsticks?" Charlie whispered, pressing herself into Betty's side. Ordinarily, Betty might have laughed at the idea, but the memory of the broom sweeping her out of Foxglove Cottage was fresh in her mind. These witches had broomsticks, all right.

"They wouldn't do that," said Ivy. "It would risk them being seen, and they're too clever for that." She straightened up next to the tree in an attempt to set off again, but Betty could see the weariness in her eyes.

"Sit," she insisted. "Two minutes won't hurt."

Reluctantly, Ivy nodded. They settled down at the base of the tree, sweeping aside dead leaves.

"Fliss?" Betty called hesitantly. "Won't you sit down with us?" Here, more than ever, she wanted to keep her sisters as close as possible.

Fliss halted beside them, swaying slightly. Her eyes were half-closed, still dreamlike. She sat down obediently, not even checking for slugs or snails. Not like Fliss at all. Betty shuddered, then stared back the way they had come through the silent forest. Even though Ivy believed the witches wouldn't follow them, to Betty, every dark tree was a shadow as the horror of Ivy's story settled over her. Thoughts of the giant lashing nettle ran through her head. Her stomach knotted with fear at the thought of the same thing happening to Fliss. Already Betty wanted to move on, but Ivy still appeared frail.

"Maybe they'll forget about Fliss," Charlie said in a small voice. "If they can't find her."

Ivy shook her head bitterly. "Maybe. But I doubt it. They pick their victims with care. Now they've chosen Fliss, they won't give up on her easily."

"But we're safe from them in here, aren't we?" Betty asked.

"From them," Ivy replied. "But not from the forest itself."

"How come? Why does the forest have this strange magic?"

"The rules I told you about time?" said Ivy. "Pilliwinks and Lightwing are the reason Tick Tock Forest is this way. The roots from the Hungry Tree go deep, and the forest is so close. I've always wondered if the trees somehow speak to each other."

"Like dogs?" Charlie asked. She stifled a yawn, eyelids drooping. "When they sniff—"

Betty nudged her to be silent.

"The dark magic that created the Hungry Tree has consequences," Ivy continued. "That's why this forest is the way it is. Messed up, the time all higgledy-piggledy. Pilliwinks and Lightwing are afraid of time catching up with them. That's why they've cheated it for decades and why they wouldn't risk setting foot in this place. One mistake and it could undo all they've achieved."

Somewhere above, leaves *shushed* spookily, as though whispering their agreement.

"How did the painting end up in the secret room?" Betty asked. "Did you put it there?"

Ivy's eyes glistened in the lantern light. She nodded. "It hung in the cobwebbed room at Foxglove Cottage for several months. With all the witches' other enchantments." Her eyes darkened. "They kept me prisoner. They liked the painting being in the house, taunting me as a reminder of what they'd done. But sometimes I heard them whispering, about Wags and why I'd survived. They'd needed part of me alive, and that was the painting. And I think they kept *me* hoping that they might one day work out why their spell had gone so wrong, how to claim back all those years that Wags had accidently taken. But when your family came along, I knew Pilliwinks and Lightwing wouldn't need me for much longer. Not when they'd set their sights on Fliss. That's when I stole the portrait and hid it in the secret room. That way, if they did something to me, then . . ."

"Then the painting would still survive," Betty said softly.

"I'd already heard Pilliwinks and Lightwing talking about the new family and how the eldest girl would be perfect, how she would be their next one," Ivy continued. "When I saw Fliss, I knew it had to be her. I tried to warn her, to say something, but I couldn't. All you saw was a mad old lady muttering a curse."

"What about the mirror?" Charlie asked. She'd slumped heavily against Betty now, leaning into her shoulder. "Did you bash it because you couldn't bear seeing yourself all wrinkly?"

"Charlie," Betty scolded. It was a good question, but she wished her little sister hadn't put it quite so bluntly.

The lines around Ivy's eyes seemed to deepen. She shook her head. "It was an accident," she whispered. "We used to have a mirror hanging from that hook. Being back in my old house, I almost expected to see my old reflection when I glanced into it. Instead, I saw . . . this . . . and I accidently knocked the mirror off the wall."

"There's something else I don't understand," said Betty. "If they were keeping you prisoner, how did you manage to hide the painting in Blackbird Cottage without them knowing and how did you get away from them tonight?"

Ivy looked down at her wrinkled hands in the lantern light. They trembled.

"Oh, they kept a close watch on me," she said bitterly. "Especially at first. They bewitched the cottage to prevent me from leaving. I tried to escape a couple of times, but it was hopeless. They cast another spell, on me this time, to prevent me going too far. I knew then that I had to pretend to give up, to do as I was told." Her eyes flashed with resentment. "I began helping out in the kitchen to begin with. As the months went on, they allowed me a little more freedom. Just the odd walk down to the bakery or outside to hang laundry out, but always with a warning that if I tried to tell anyone what they'd done or who I really was, I'd regret it."

Betty recalled the pins and needles tumbling from Ivy's mouth and shivered.

"When the painting went missing, they knew it was me, although they couldn't prove it," Ivy added, her eyes haunted. "They locked me in the cobwebbed room for three days."

"All this time," Betty murmured, "you were right under everyone's noses. Ivy Bell had never left at all."

"No. Instead, I became Miss Webb. Or rather that's what they named me." Ivy grimaced. "Their idea of a little joke. "Webb was Uncle Jem's last name, you see. No one ever made the connection. Perhaps no one cared, or perhaps the enchantment had fogged everyone's minds too much for them to see it." She paused. "Have you noticed other people acting differently since those two set their sights on Fliss? That's their magic, shielding others from what's going on."

"Yes," Betty whispered. She'd noticed, all right.

Magic and trouble go hand in hand . . .

"And poor little Wags, too," Betty added, feeling a lump in her throat. "He got caught up in all this. That's what happened to him, why he hasn't grown since that day."

Ivy nodded. "If it hadn't been for Wags breaking the nettle cord and stopping the spell before it was complete, I think he would have gotten much, much younger. And I think that's the only reason I didn't die, like I was supposed to. All those years they took from me . . . they were never meant for someone as young as Wags. And he can't stay the way he is for much longer without people asking more questions. He'll be another one of Pendlewick's little oddities: the boy who never grew up."

The hairs on Betty's arms stuck up on end. After hearing more of Ivy's story, she was horribly afraid of what could happen to Fliss. There was something else, too. Now that she knew the significance of the painting—

how a part of Ivy lived on in it—she was suddenly aware of how precious it was. Had she made a terrible mistake by removing it from the secret room? Either way, Ivy had to know.

"Ivy," she whispered. "There's something I need to tell you . . ."

The words faltered as a peaceful snore reached her ears. Too late, Betty became aware of just how heavily Charlie was leaning on her. *Jumping jackdaws!* How could she have been so careless?

"Oh no!" Taking her little sister by the shoulders, Betty shook her, gently at first, and then harder. "Charlie, wake up!"

Ivy lifted the lantern, her eyes widening in horror. "I didn't realize she'd fallen asleep!"

"Neither did I," Betty replied helplessly, tapping Charlie's cheeks lightly. She remembered Ivy's warning about the three rules upon entering the forest: *Don't fall asleep; don't speak if you hear the sound of clocks ticking; never ask what the time is.* Now they'd broken one.

"It's all right," Betty muttered as Charlie's eyes fluttered open, then lazily closed again. "She must have only just dropped off. Perhaps—"

"She snored," Ivy said worriedly. "But *maybe*—" She

leaned over and flicked up the hem of Charlie's dress. "Oh no. This is bad!"

Betty gasped. A trail of bindweed had wrapped around Charlie's ankle like a leafy snare, and even as Betty watched, it continued to grow at an alarming rate, twisting up her leg. More strands snaked over the ground, moving at a speed that wasn't natural. They raced toward Charlie's other leg.

Betty swept them away, half-afraid they might wind around her. But the bindweed seemed only to want Charlie. As fast as Betty could throw it off, it came crawling back. She began tearing at the vines on Charlie's legs, urging her to wake up.

"Charlie, get up! Move—quickly!"

Charlie groaned and yawned, her hair tousled. Then her eyes snapped open and she began to struggle. "Betty, what's going on?" she wailed.

"You fell asleep!"

Ivy reached over and began tearing at the leaf strands, but even with her help and Betty's, Charlie was still not able to get free.

"It's no good," Ivy panted.

"There must be a way to make it stop," said Betty desperately. "Fliss, help us!"

But Fliss just stared dreamily at the canopy of branches above.

"There's one thing you can try," said Ivy. "But I don't know if this works or if it's just something Uncle Jem made up . . . I'm not even sure I'm remembering it right—"

"Anything!" Betty urged. "Tell me! Just hurry!"

"You have to recite something backward," said Ivy.

"Recite something *backward*?" Betty echoed, bewildered. "Like a . . . a page from a book?"

"No, it can't be written down," said Ivy in a rush. "It has to be from memory. A song, a prayer, a nursery rhyme . . ."

"But that's impossible!" Betty burst out. Panic rose up in her. She continued to tear at the bindweed, but it was growing twice as fast as she could pull it away. Already her hands were sore.

"It's eating me!" Charlie howled, tugging at the weed with her chubby hands. Hoppit had emerged from her collar and was squeaking in alarm. "Hoppit, save yourself! Betty, grab him . . ."

Betty grabbed the rat and threw him at Fliss. She didn't so much as twitch as Hoppit burrowed into her skirts and lay there, quivering, with only his whiffling nose visible. Betty turned back to Charlie, frantically trying to think. "Quick, Charlie, a song," she insisted. "Think of something!"

Her own mind had gone blank, emptied by fear. Prayers were out of the question. Betty had never paid much attention when the Widdershinses attended church, and most of the songs she knew were bawdy ones sung in the Poacher's Pocket, with some very rude words — but right now she was willing to give anything a go.

"Fliss!" she shouted. "What's that song Granny used to sing? The one about the sailor and the vicar's wife? *Fliss!* For crow's sake, help me!"

"Out, witch, out," Fliss said softly. "Be gone from Pendlewick . . ."

Betty fought the urge to shake her. It was no use. Fliss couldn't help them, and all she had succeeded in doing was filling Betty's head with *Out, witch, out,* which was hopeless. Betty couldn't have recited it forward, let alone in reverse. And with every second the vines were swallowing Charlie fast.

"Hickory dickory dock," Charlie gasped suddenly. "Betty, say hickory dickory!"

Betty knew immediately what Charlie meant. Betty had once made up a silly version of the old nursery rhyme, and it had quickly become Charlie's favorite. She'd demanded that Betty and Fliss repeat it over and over again, much to Granny's annoyance. So many times, in fact, that Betty had often remarked that she knew it backward. But that had been a joke, a throwaway comment. She hadn't really *meant* it.

But what choice did she have? She called the rhyme to mind, and hope sparked within her. She knew it by heart and, best of all, it was short:

> *Hickory dickory dock,*
> *A magpie ate the clock.*
> *He burped a chime*
> *To tell the time,*
> *Hickory dickory dock!*
> *Tick tock!*

"Tock tick," Betty said, squeezing her eyes shut and trying to picture the words. "Dock dickory hickory . . . time tell to—oh, meddling magpies, I've messed it up already!" She tried again, concentrating hard. This time she made it further, only to say *piemag* instead of *magpie*. Despite Ivy tugging at the vines, Charlie's lower half was now completely covered in green.

"Let me try!" Charlie howled, but Betty could see she was panicking too much. Sure enough, she couldn't get past the first mouthful of words.

"Hurry!" Ivy said. "It's getting thicker!"

Betty closed her eyes, shutting out the frightening

sight of what was happening to her sister. She tried to imagine the rhyme as though it were written down on a page and went through the words again, slowly and smoothly. ". . . Clock the ate magpie a, dock dickory hickory!" she finished, her eyes snapping open.

She'd done it! And just in time, for she saw with horror that the vines were now trailing around Charlie's shoulders and working their way up to her neck. For a heart-stopping second, they showed no signs of slowing, then all of a sudden, they stopped and began creeping in reverse. One by one they loosened, slithering away from Charlie and vanishing into the undergrowth.

Charlie sprang up and threw herself into Betty's lap, hugging her tightly. Her little body was trembling, and she smelled of earth and leaves.

"Jumping jackdaws," Betty whispered into her hair. "That was a close one."

"Too close," Ivy said in a quiet voice. "Let's get out of here."

They got up, brushing themselves down, and set off once more. Again, Ivy took the lead, but Betty could see she was still weary and it was fear that was driving her —only this time it was fear of the woods. Ivy might have managed to follow the rules when she'd entered the forest alone, but Charlie's slipup meant she had now seen the true dangers of it for herself. For a long time, none of them said a word, too shaken by what had happened. Betty gripped Charlie's hand, but she needn't have worried. All traces of sleepiness had vanished from her little sister's eyes, and they were now alert and watchful. Fliss followed behind, dreamily silent.

After about an hour, Ivy spoke. "The edge of the forest is ahead. We're nearly out."

"Thank goodness," Betty muttered, loosening her hold on Charlie's hand for the first time. "I was beginning to think this place never ended."

"We should have been out of here faster," said Ivy, looking wearier than ever. "But breaking the rules added extra time to our journey." Suddenly she went still, her eyes alert.

"What—?" Betty began, but Ivy whipped a finger to her lips.

There it was, a distinct *ticking* sound. Like hundreds of watches and clocks all hidden out of sight. The noise surrounded them, giving the impression that it was coming from everywhere at once.

Ivy motioned for everyone to stay silent and beckoned them on. Gradually, the sound faded into nothing, but Betty was unable to shake the sense of eeriness. How could Ivy have dared to spend time here alone, sketching? No wonder her behavior had caused whispers among the villagers. Betty would be eternally grateful once they were out of the woods and heading to the crossroads.

They were perhaps ten steps from the edge of the woods when Fliss tripped on a root and stumbled to the ground.

"Are you all right?" Betty rushed to her side, expecting another blank stare from her sister, but Fliss's soft brown eyes were clearing, like she'd woken up.

"I . . . Where are we?" Fliss touched her ankle, grimacing, then looked around in confusion, seeing Ivy for the first time. "What's *she* doing here, and why are we out so late at night? What time—"

"Fliss, no!" Betty began, but it was too late.

"—is it?" Fliss finished.

A loud chime shook the forest, like an enormous grandfather clock had struck. They had broken another rule.

"Run," said Ivy in a choked voice. "Quickly!"

Chapter Twenty-Six

The Crossroads

BETTY HAULED FLISS TO HER FEET, pulling her toward the forest's edge. Charlie was already ahead of them and, together with Ivy, was squeezing through the trees.

"Betty, Fliss, come *on*!" she yelled, but her voice sounded faint from within the greenery.

Betty ducked under a low-hanging branch, pushing Fliss in front of her. She felt it scratch against her head painfully and then the slow warmth of oozing blood. It was only when she saw the leaves ahead drawing together like a curtain that she realized she hadn't simply misjudged its height. The branch *was* moving and so were

334

the trees in front. In fact, the whole forest was shifting, shutting the outside out . . . and Betty and Fliss *in*.

"Go!" she yelled, shoving Fliss toward the space where Charlie and Ivy had slipped through. She heard Fliss wince as branches scraped at her skin. They tore at Betty, too, her hair and clothes catching on spiteful twigs intent on keeping them in. She felt fresher air on her face from beyond the leafy veil and knew escape was near . . . but underfoot the ground was now shifting as roots rearranged themselves and knotted together. Betty gave her sister a last hard push. There was a ripping sound and then Fliss was through. Betty heard her muffled gasping on the other side of the thicket.

Betty was alone in the forest, the exit sealed up and her surroundings darker than ever.

"Betty, over here!" Charlie's voice filtered through from somewhere to her left.

Betty stumbled toward it blindly, her arms outstretched and pushing branches out of the way. Something snared her foot and she kicked it off. She saw a patch of moonlight through a last tiny gap that was vanishing fast. She flung herself toward it, crawling on hands and knees. She glimpsed Charlie's bird's-nest hair and a jumble of legs, felt branches digging into her like fingers, pulling her back and tightening around her waist and legs. Panic engulfed her. She had seen what had almost become of Charlie—only this was worse. Because now, if Betty was swallowed up by Tick Tock Forest, there was no one else inside it to help her.

"Pull!" Charlie roared, seizing Betty's arm. More hands joined in, Ivy's and even Fliss's. Betty looked up into her sisters' faces. Charlie's teeth were gritted in determination, and there was fear and fierce love in Fliss's eyes that Betty hadn't seen since they'd arrived in Pendlewick, a look she'd feared she might never see again.

Her muscles screamed in agony as three pairs of hands yanked her arms. The forest pulled back, hard. Betty cried out, terrified of who would win this enchanted tug of war.

"Don't let go!" she begged. She dug her boots into the dirt, kicking herself forward. The vine around her waist tightened further, cutting into her and squeezing her breath. She bit her lip, kicked again, and, with an almighty tug from Charlie, Fliss, and Ivy, there was a succession of loud snaps as the vines broke apart and released her. She whooshed forward and landed in a heap on the grass, the forest behind her and the clear moonlit sky above.

"Betty!" Charlie gasped, kneeling by her side. "Are you all right?"

Betty sat up shakily, still feeling the sensation of the vines wrapped around her. Her arms ached and her head was sore. She lifted her fingers to her scalp and pressed a tender spot. They came away bloody.

"Let me see." Ivy tenderly examined Betty's head. "It's not deep, just a scratch."

Betty swallowed and clambered to her feet, brushing earth from her clothes. The smell of it filled her nose. She glanced back at the forest fearfully, seeing the branches shuddering and shaking as though enraged.

"We got out," she whispered. "Just in time."

Ivy shook her head. "We may have gotten out, but we won't have escaped it. Not properly."

Betty felt her stomach clench. "What do you mean? We're free."

"We broke the rules," Ivy replied quietly. "One way or another, it'll make us pay."

"You said it could cause a time slip," said Betty, remembering Ivy's warning. "What did you mean by that?"

"The forest might take years away," said Ivy. "Or add them."

"Why did you even take us through Tick Tock Forest?" Charlie protested. "It was a bad idea!"

"I told you," said Ivy. "To throw Pilliwinks and Lightwing off your trail, at least for a while. The forest's biggest advantage is that they wouldn't dare set foot in it. But the sooner we get you to the crossroads, the better."

"Granny has a thing about crossroads," said Betty. "She says that people were often hanged at them and buried nearby. It was thought that if their ghosts came back for revenge, the different roads would confuse them."

"If only the same thing worked on the living," said Ivy, her mouth in a grim line. "Or at least those who *should* be dead."

Betty shuddered. The idea of the two witches cheating death for so long was a terrifying one.

"Come on," said Ivy. "I'll get you to the crossroads. Once we're there, you'll have the best chance of getting away from Pendlewick."

Betty went to follow her, but Charlie pulled at her sleeve and pointed. Fliss was standing completely still, staring at Ivy.

"Not until you tell me what *she's* doing here." Her voice was confused and suspicious. "She's the old woman who pointed at me in the cottage! Why are we wandering around in the middle of the night with her?"

Betty glanced at Ivy, then back at her sister. It really seemed as though the enchanted fog over Fliss *had* momentarily lifted. Could the witches' spell have been broken now that they were farther from Pendlewick?

"We got it wrong, Fliss," she said softly. "She wasn't trying to hurt you; she was trying to *help* you. To warn you that you're in danger."

A dark look crossed Fliss's face. "In danger from what?"

"This," said Ivy, gesturing to herself. "I'm Ivy Bell. I'm . . ." Her voice cracked. "I'm eighteen years old. This is what they did to me."

Fliss slowly looked Ivy up and down, her arms folded. "What *who* did?"

"Witches, that's who," said Charlie.

"Oh, not this again." Fliss rolled her eyes. "You mean to say you believe this deluded old lady? You dragged me out in the middle of the night because you think *witches* are out to get me?"

"The only thing that dragged you out was magic," said Betty, her hopes fading in the face of her sister's cold manner. The witches' grip on her hadn't been broken, after all, and Fliss was still unable to see the danger she was in. "That's why you were circling the village pond at midnight."

Fliss frowned. "I don't remember that."

"Exactly," said Charlie. "Now come on!"

"Come on *where?*" Fliss asked, not moving an inch. "Where exactly is it you think we're going? Does Granny know about this?"

Betty glanced helplessly at Ivy. "Fliss, we don't have time for this. We have to get you away from them and out of Pendlewick, but we need to think of somewhere safe. Somewhere they can't find us."

"I know," said Charlie suddenly. "What about Father's cousin, Clarissa? She's always asking us to go and stay with her!"

Betty considered this, then shook her head. "It's a good idea, but Clarissa lives too far away. We need to get somewhere fast, where we can hide until we figure out how to break the witches' enchantment over Fliss."

"That's something you may never find the answer to," Ivy said softly. "I never did. I tried everything I could find to break their hold over me: plants, herbs, old superstitions. Some of it helped, but none of them could undo what happened to me."

"Are you saying," Betty asked, her voice starting to tremble, "that we can never go back to Pendlewick?"

"As long as Pilliwinks and Lightwing are there, you'll never be safe," said Ivy. "Not unless you can find a way to end their magic." A bitter look crossed her face. "And end *them*."

She gazed at Betty pleadingly. "When I realized you girls had your own kind of magic, I thought . . . I *hoped* you might know some way to defeat them. But now I'm starting to think that no one can. They're just too old and powerful. But you three have a chance to escape, even if that means leaving for good. I lost my chance! Don't waste yours."

A sense of doom crashed around Betty. *Never go back to Pendlewick?*

"What about Granny?" she whispered. "And Father? We can't just leave them there and spend the rest of our lives hiding!" But when Ivy stayed silent, she realized that was, in fact, exactly what Ivy was suggesting.

"Granny and Father will come looking for us, though, won't they?" Charlie asked, looking stunned. "They wouldn't just stay in Pendlewick . . . and forget us?"

Betty didn't answer. How could she when she didn't understand it herself? She and Charlie had both seen Granny's and Father's glazed, unblinking eyes. And she and Charlie had been unable to rouse them from sleep or even get them to listen when awake. The thought of Granny and Father too bewitched to search for them, or forgetting the girls altogether, seemed frighteningly possible. She felt lost, without a plan and without hope.

"Don't let this be for nothing," Ivy said quietly. "We got through the forest. Don't give them a chance to catch up with you." She took a determined step forward, then winced and bent down. For a moment, Betty thought Ivy was about to massage her ankle again, but this time Ivy lifted the hem of her skirt a little.

Betty gasped. Ensnaring Ivy's ankle was a thin, silvery cord. Even in the moonlight, Betty could see the angry rash of red dots that spread out from where the cord met the skin.

"Nettle stings," said Ivy quietly. "From the enchanted nettle cord. The farther I go from them, the tighter it becomes." A look of defeat crossed her face. "I think this may be as far as I can take you. And, besides, perhaps the less I know about where you're heading, the better. That way they can't force me to tell them."

The silvery cord gleamed almost triumphantly.

"You're . . . you're not coming with us?" Charlie asked.

"That's what you meant earlier," Betty said in horror. "When you said they'd cast a spell to prevent you from leaving!"

"This is the farthest I've been from them," said Ivy. "But the cord's getting tighter now. It's time for me to go back."

"But . . . but maybe there's a way we can undo it," Betty said desperately. None of this was fair! They couldn't just leave Granny and Father—and Ivy—to suffer in Pendlewick at the hands of the witches. And what if they chose another victim? "Maybe we can break all their spells—

there has to be *something* we can do. You can't go back to them! And they can't get away with this."

She gazed at the stars, hoping and wishing for a clue, but there was nothing. The helpless feeling deepened, beating down on her like a swarm of crows.

Crows . . .

Betty tensed as a thought took hold. "Crows," she whispered, her body beginning to tremble. This time it was not with fear but excitement.

"Betty?" Charlie asked uncertainly. "You have an idea, don't you?"

"Yes, I think I do." Betty cupped her little sister's face. "I've got the answer, Charlie, I'm sure of it! I know how we can undo their magic."

"You've thought of something?" Ivy asked, incredulous.

"Not something," Betty said, her voice rising. "Some-*where*."

She heard Charlie take a sharp breath, and their eyes met in understanding.

"Somewhere magic can't be done," Charlie said, starting to grin.

"You . . . you've heard of this place?" Ivy asked. "How can you be sure it's real?"

"It's real, all right," said Charlie, reaching out to claim

back Hoppit from an unenthusiastic and sullen Fliss. She placed the rat in her collar and stroked his nose. "We grew up right next to it."

"Crowstone Tower," Betty finished. As she said it, she felt more certain than ever that it was the answer—for all of them. "Ivy, you have to come with us. It'll break their spell over you, I'm convinced of it!"

Ivy stared longingly in the direction of the crossroads. "I don't know if I can make it that far. Even if I could, I don't have the portrait. It's still in the cottage. Part of me will be still be in Pendlewick, trapped."

"You won't," Betty said in a rush, sliding the map case off her back. "Because the painting isn't at Blackbird Cottage anymore. I put it in here to keep it safe when I saw your note. We'll take it with us."

Ivy's mouth trembled. "You really think this can work?"

"I *know* it can," said Betty. "We just have to get there."

Chapter Twenty-Seven

The Spinning Wheel

I T FELT TO BETTY as though they'd been walking all night, but she knew it could only have been an hour or so until the crossroads appeared in the distance under the moonlight. Since leaving Tick Tock Forest, she'd felt completely on edge, a mixture of fear and exhilaration. She had hope now, they all did, and Betty could see a determined look in Charlie's eyes that matched her own surge of strength. Even Ivy seemed to be moving with less discomfort, although Betty wondered how far she really could make it with the sinister nettle cord looped around her ankle. It trailed behind her in the grass like a thin, silver snake, vanishing into darkness.

The only one of them lagging behind was Fliss. Betty continued to shoot her anxious glances, noticing that her expression was growing ever more sour the farther they went. Once or twice, she saw her sister pause and look back in the direction of Pendlewick, muttering to herself with that familiar glazed expression Betty had come to dread.

The crossroads was silent and deserted when they reached it. The only thing there was a signpost riddled with woodworm, leaning to one side like a drunken scarecrow. It showed that they were now almost two miles away from Pendlewick, with a mile between them and the harbor. On the sign, someone had scrawled a childish drawing of a witch's hat next to the word *Pendlewick*.

"The harbor," said Betty, pointing. "That's where we need to get to. We'll take Father's boat. I can get us back to Crowstone in a few hours once we're on it."

"You can sail a boat?" Ivy asked doubtfully.

"We can sail anything," boasted Charlie. "Boats, bathtubs . . ." Then her forehead crinkled. "But, Betty, how will we start the boat? Did you bring a key?"

"No," Betty answered. "But I know where Father keeps the spare."

They marched past the wooden sign, leaving it behind as they took the road to the harbor. To their left were fields and winding lanes. To their right, tiny lights blinked in the distance from some faraway village or town. With a bit of luck, the witches would think the girls were traveling there, Betty thought. She lengthened her stride, eager to reach the harbor. But Fliss's cold voice caught up with her, stopping her in her tracks.

"You know I hate boats."

Betty whipped around. Fliss stood there moodily, hands on hips.

"I know," Betty said, trying hard not to snap. Couldn't Fliss see how urgent this was? "It's impossible to forget, seeing as you throw up every time we're on one."

"You go ahead." Fliss gave Ivy a withering stare. "Take whoever she is with you. I've had enough of Betty Widdershins's adventures. Count me out of this one."

"You *have* to come," Betty insisted. "So we can break the witches' hold over you. Don't you see? The more of their magic we can undo, the better chance we have. Maybe . . . maybe it'll weaken them."

"Well, I don't want to," said Fliss rudely. "I don't believe in your childish stories of witches and spells. I'm tired, fed up, and I've got achy knees. The last thing I want is to board some smelly, fishy, old boat!"

"We've got bigger problems than a fishy boat," Betty growled, taking a step towards her sister. "So stop your moaning and—" She broke off, noticing something strange. "Fliss? What's the matter with your hair? Did you get something caught in it, a cobweb?"

"Cobweb?" Fliss lifted a hand to her dark locks, panic entering her eyes.

Betty gasped. There was nothing *in* her sister's hair . . . but a streak of it near the front had turned pure white.

"No!" Betty shouted, her voice echoing over the empty land. She turned to Ivy, her eyes wild. "How can they be doing this? I thought they needed her there, within the standing stones like you—?"

"This isn't the witches," Ivy said, biting her lip. She approached Fliss, her eyes narrowing, working something out. "You're right, Betty. They can't perform their spell without her there. This is something else—Tick Tock Forest. I told you we wouldn't get away with breaking the rules, even though we got out."

Betty gazed at her sister in horror. *A time slip*, that's what Ivy had said. So this wasn't the witches. Fliss had caused this herself by asking what the time was while they were still in the forest. Betty swallowed down a lump of dread in her throat. "White hair, achy knees . . ." she whispered. Would it get any worse?

"This can still be broken," she said. "If we get you to

Crowstone Tower, it'll undo the magic." Suddenly she felt as though she'd had about enough magic as she could take. Perhaps the villagers of Pendlewick were right, after all—magic really *did* lead to trouble.

Fliss stared up, trying to peer at the strand of hair Betty had pointed to, but it was too short. "White hair?" she squeaked. "But I'm only seventeen!"

"Now you're starting to understand how it feels," Ivy said softly. "Think that's bad? Try being me, trapped in this old body for the past two years."

The horror on Fliss's face deepened, but Ivy wasn't finished. She took Fliss's hand in a grip that looked surprisingly strong. "This is only a taste of what could happen if they catch up with you—and I was the lucky one. The one who didn't die, even though they stole my life from me. So do as Betty says and get on that boat if you know what's good for you!" She released Fliss's hand and stalked along the road without another word.

Betty and Charlie followed, and without looking back, Betty knew Fliss was right behind them now. She allowed herself a grim smile, glad for once that her sister's vanity had won through. If the threat of being enchanted hadn't frightened her enough, the thought of prematurely aging certainly had.

The smile froze on her lips as a sound reached her ears. A distinctive *shuffle-shuffle-shuffle* that made her think of Ivy's diary. It was the very sound Ivy had heard and grown so afraid of.

"Ivy," she whispered. "Do you hear that?"

Ivy nodded, her voice thin with fear. "They're working the spinning wheel, trying to find out where we are. We have to hurry."

There was no time for talk now. They saved their breath and energy for the journey, moving along the dusky path as quickly as they were able. The moon hung like a pale lantern in the inky sky, lighting their way, but once or twice Betty had the strangest sensation that, when she glanced up at it, it was spinning in the sky.

"I don't like it, Betty," Charlie murmured, casting fearful glances over her shoulder. "That creepy *following* noise. It's like they're right behind us. Hoppit doesn't like it, either." She reached up to her collar and scratched the rat's head with her finger.

"I know," Betty whispered back. "But remember, they can't see us. And right now, they don't know where we are or where we're going. As soon as we get to Crowstone, we can start to fix everything. We're going to end this."

Charlie nodded stiffly but seemed comforted. Betty looked away, worry gnawing at her. She wished she felt as certain as she sounded, but Crowstone Tower was their only hope. There was no question that once inside it would break the enchantments over Fliss and Ivy— Betty had seen its unearthly power for herself. It was the thought of *getting* there that scared her. How long did they have before Pilliwinks and Lightwing, with their green smoke, cobwebs, and shrieking cuckoo clocks, caught up with them? She glanced at Fliss. Her sister was still staring at her hair, her lovely face creased in disbelief. There was still something in her eyes that wasn't quite Fliss, and Betty didn't like it. The sooner they got onto the boat and away, the better.

They reached the harbor as the first pale light of dawn was visible on the horizon, and already there were signs of movement. Fishing boats were preparing to go out for their daily catch, and hungry cats were scavenging around the boats, hoping for a dropped morsel that had been missed. The soft lapping of water helped drown out the *shuffle-shuffle-shuffle* that had followed them the entire way.

"There's our boat," Charlie whispered, pointing to *The Traveling Bag*. The cheerful sea-green boat bobbed before them, next to the harbor wall. The sight of it, something so familiar, sent Betty a small glimmer of hope. How different she felt from when they'd arrived in that same harbor only a week before. She'd been bursting with expectation then, but now she had only the tiniest of threads to cling to.

Gratefully, they trudged toward it. Ivy was limping badly now, her face pinched and pale. Betty wondered how tight the nettle cord was but was afraid to ask. She collected the spare key from a tiny secret hatch under one of the wooden benches and unlocked the wheelhouse. Even Fliss looked grateful to sit down as they clambered aboard the little boat and crammed into the cabin, though she did let out a little moan as the boat dipped on a wave.

"We should make ourselves visible," Betty said, setting down the map case. Taking care not to disturb Ivy's precious painting, she took out the map and laid it out behind the wheel. "Fishermen are superstitious. If they see the boat leaving with no one in it, there'll be stories of hauntings that could reach Pendlewick within the hour. We don't want to give ourselves away."

No one disagreed, so reluctantly, Betty took out the nesting dolls and twisted them out of alignment. Then, after stoking the boiler, she took the wheel and steered the little boat skillfully through the fishing vessels and out past the harbor wall to the open sea. The wheel at her fingertips steadied her. This was something she knew, something she could do. Even though the sea could be unpredictable, Betty felt surer of her chances on the water than with the witches.

Consulting the map, she traced a path with her finger down over the mainland to where the Sorrow Isles were. There it was, their destination: the prison island of Repent with the foreboding Crowstone Tower looming over it. Little had they known when they'd set out for their bright new start that they would be making a return journey to the very place they'd just left—let alone so soon.

The Traveling Bag gathered speed. Betty kept her eyes on the brightening horizon. Sunrise wasn't far off now. Within minutes, a pasty-faced Fliss pushed her way out of the wheelhouse and began heaving over the side of the boat.

It was shortly after this that Betty began to realize things were not quite right.

The first sign was the stream of dandelion seeds that somehow appeared in the wheelhouse and floated eerily in a perfect circle before Betty's eyes. Round and round they went, unnaturally, as though caught in a breeze that no one else could feel.

"Do you see that?" Betty whispered.

Charlie frowned, not quite understanding. Ivy, however, looked terrified. The seeds dropped to the wheelhouse floor, scattering. The wheel began to resist under Betty's hands. Was it her imagination, or was it moving of its own accord? She got her answer when, without warning, the wheel was wrenched from her grasp by an invisible force. It spun crazily, faster than should have been possible. So fast that it blurred. The little boat was sent into a spin, and dimly Betty became aware of Fliss hollering from outside on the deck for her to stop. But of course this had nothing to do with Betty. She couldn't tear her eyes from the wheel, and as it began to slow, her gaze settled. However, she no longer saw the steering wheel of a boat. Instead, the wheelhouse darkened around her and Betty saw cobwebs dangling from everything, surrounding an old spinning wheel.

Shuffle-shuffle-shuffle . . .

"No!" Betty screamed, clapping her hands over her ears. "Leave us alone!"

She lunged for the wheel, bruising her knuckles in her attempt to stop it spinning. There was a flash of silver, something pointed, and Betty cried out as a sharp pain pricked her thumb. Instantly, the wheel stopped turning and the cobwebs vanished, leaving Betty clutching the wheel with a shaking, bleeding hand. She stared at her thumb and saw a deep scratch that could only have been made by the flash of silver she'd seen. In that instant, she'd known what it was: the spindle of a spinning wheel. She dabbed away the blood on her dress, sucking her thumb.

The door to the wheelhouse burst open.

"What was *that*?" Fliss demanded, eyes wild. "Jumping jackdaws, Betty! Have you forgotten how to steer this thing?"

Betty shook her head. "It . . . it wasn't me," she said at last. "It . . ."

Her eyes went to the map. Something had moved there, a slight fluttering that caught Betty's attention. A brown butterfly had landed on the map where Pendlewick was. Before Betty's fearful eyes, the creature crawled purposefully over the map, following the path Betty had traced with her finger. When it got to Repent, it stopped and settled, flexing its wings to reveal the brightly colored eye pattern that lay in the corner of each one.

Beside her, Ivy had risen to see what Betty was looking at. Now, as they both stared at the peacock butterfly, Ivy let out a sound that was something like a sob. The eyes on the butterfly winked, and then the creature faded and seeped into the map, a little black-and-white butter-fly inked next to Crowstone Tower.

"They know, they *know*!" Ivy repeated, rocking her-self back and forth on the bench. "They know where we're heading. They're going to find us."

Chapter Twenty-Eight

Return to Crowstone

IT WAS A LONG WHILE before Betty's hands stopped shaking, although she hid this by gripping the wheel so tightly that her knuckles ached. The scratch on her thumb eventually stopped bleeding, but her eyes kept darting from the butterfly on the map to the view before her. She expected lightning, freak waves crashing over them, shipwrecks rising from the seabed, and any number of obstacles Pilliwinks and Lightwing might conjure up to jeopardize their journey. But there was nothing. The sea was flat and calm, sparkling in the early-morning light as the sun rose.

"Why aren't they stopping us?" she said, more to herself than anyone else. Her voice was a dry croak.

"They don't need to."

Betty looked around. Ivy was huddled on the bench next to Charlie, who had fallen asleep and was leaning, open-mouthed, against Ivy's shoulder. Fliss sat on the opposite bench, hugging a bucket on her knees. Now that the sun had risen, Betty could see the streak of white in her sister's short, dark hair more clearly. It seemed to have become thicker and was stark against the darkness of the rest.

"They're toying with us," Ivy continued, her eyes glassy.

"Then why let us get away?" Betty asked fearfully. Her eyes scanned the water again, looking for any evidence of fish swimming in circles or spindles rising out of the water to wreck the little boat.

"They won't," said Ivy. "You can be sure of it. They're taunting us — this is what they do. To them it's all a chase. A game of cat and mouse."

The words settled around Betty like the cold seawater that was rapidly losing its sparkle. The sky grew ever darker with thick clouds. Even blindfolded, Betty would have known where they were from the damp, drizzly air that crept in through the windowpanes. The sight that she had loathed all her life, longed to escape from and never see again, loomed before her: the Sorrow Isles.

Around them the clouds were drifting lower and denser, threatening to envelop everything in marsh mist.

Torment was first; the island where the banished folk were. The boat passed alongside stony beaches and caves in the cliffs. Close by was Lament, the burial island for all Crowstone's dead—including Betty's own mother. Her heart twisted at the hurt that would never heal, and she tore her eyes away to focus on the final island as it came into view.

Repent, the prison island. The huge building shadowed the island, its ugly gray walls covered in barnacles, narrow, barred windows housing dangerous prisoners. The sight of it had always filled Betty with foreboding. She knew all too well how deadly some of the inmates were, for her family had always lived in its shadow.

She steered the little boat around the rocky coast toward the ferry point, where visitors disembarked. There, reaching high up into the ever-thickening marsh mist, was the oldest part of the prison: Crowstone Tower. Nothing grew on its walls, for legend had it that the stones it was built from had been stolen from the graves on Lament. It was used only for holding suspected witches, for it stripped them of their powers. Now it stood empty.

Betty had never been so glad to see it. She remembered how she had felt the day they'd left for Pendlewick, how she'd wished never to set eyes on the tower again. Little had she known then that it might be the one place that could save her family.

She turned the wheel, bringing the boat into the dock. It was too early for visitors; the ferry didn't start running for another couple of hours. With it empty, the place seemed even bleaker and more desolate than usual. Yet it wasn't completely deserted. Their arrival had caught the attention of a lone sentry who had been shirking his duties at the gates and slipped outside for a crafty smoke. With a flash, Betty spied the gap in the huge wooden gate. That was their ticket in!

The sentry tossed his cigarette and began marching across the shingle toward them. Marsh mist drifted around his ankles like feathers, and Betty felt her stomach lurch. Only ferries were permitted to stop at the prison island. She needed to think of something, and fast.

Charlie stirred as Betty brought *The Traveling Bag* to a halt. Her eyes opened groggily, then she sat up straight and stared at the tower looming above.

"We're here," she whispered. "We're back."

"Urgh," Fliss mumbled, raising her head from the bucket. "Have we stopped yet?"

"Never mind." Betty picked up the map case that held

Ivy's painting and checked that the nesting dolls were safely tucked in her pocket. "Just get ready to disappear."

One by one they clambered off the boat and stepped onto the crunching shingle. The mist was coming in thick and fast now, and Betty was glad of it. She knew better than anyone how disorienting the Crowstone fogs could be.

The sentry squinted at them, waving a hand crossly.

"Can't you read?" he yelled. "No docking! That's for ferries only, that is. Get back on your boat and leave this minute!"

"Now," Betty whispered, twisting the outer nesting doll into place.

The result was instant. The sentry screamed, staggering back against the prison wall.

"Help! Phantom ship!" he cried, calling toward the prison gates. "Ghost vessel . . . *help, I say!*"

"There," Betty said breathlessly as the sentry was swallowed by the fog. "Get through the gate while it's still open. Hurry!"

They rushed to the huge wooden doors and squeezed through the narrow gap into a vaulted stone walkway. It was damp and stinking inside, and Betty heard Hoppit give a squeak as though he sensed the presence of other rats. Following the walkway, they passed a door with a rusted sign above it which read **VISITORS**. Farther on, the walkway opened out into a vast stone courtyard. It was here that Crowstone Tower stood within the walls, though it loomed higher than any other part of the prison. Betty had been in the tower room only once, and she now recalled the dizzying views from above—and the impossible drop.

There was a warder on guard outside the tower door, just as Betty had known there would be. She also knew that getting past him wouldn't be a problem, for most of the warders were superstitious. A little staged "haunting" was sure to work wonders. And this one looked young and inexperienced, which was unsurprising given that Crowstone Tower stood empty these days.

Betty raced toward him, grabbing Charlie to hurry her along. She glanced back. Ivy was limping, struggling to keep up, and Fliss, still hazy-eyed under the bewitchment, wasn't moving much faster. They passed doors and barred windows from which the familiar smells of the prison oozed: stewed cabbage, sweat, and sewage. Soon they were at the short set of steps leading to the tower.

The warder's head snapped up at the sound of their approach.

"Who . . . who's there?" he stammered, eyes darting.

"The spirit of the marshes," growled Betty, making her voice as throaty and menacing as possible. "Give me your keys!"

The warder tore the bunch of keys from his belt and threw them, stumbling away. "D-don't hurt me!" he whimpered, making the sign of the crow for protection.

Betty scooped the ring of keys up. They jangled eerily, like a ghostly chain being rattled. The warder turned and fled. Betty grappled with the keys, jamming one into the lock of the tower door. It didn't budge.

"Come on!" she cried in frustration. *They were so close now!* She pulled it out and selected another. There were just two keys left.

"Quick, Betty!" Charlie urged.

Knock, knock, knock.

The sound came frighteningly loud and close. For a moment, Betty thought it was from behind the tower door and, without meaning to, took a step back. The sound came again. It wasn't from the tower, she realized now, but from a small wooden door set back in one of the courtyard walls. A door that was now creaking slowly open.

Too late, Betty noticed something out of place: a woven doormat that lay before it. Why would there be such a thing in a place like this? she wondered fleetingly. The thought was snatched away as another sound came from the door: a cruel chuckle that sent splinters of terror into her heart.

Fingers of thick fog crept out as the door widened, but already Betty knew what—or who—was on the other side. Another sound arose from nowhere, a *shuffle-shuffle-shuffle*.

Miss Pilliwinks emerged from the thick wall of marsh mist and stepped across the mat, adjusting her thick glasses. Mrs. Lightwing followed, smiling widely as she wiped her feet on the woven mat, an exaggerated gesture done for show. The enchanted doormat disintegrated, becoming nothing more than a pile of limp nettles.

"It's *them*," Charlie whispered in horror, clutching Betty's sleeve.

"They can't see us," Betty whispered back, her hands shaking as she fumbled with the keys. They clinked in her hand, the sound unwelcome now.

"We don't need to *see* you to find you, dearie," said Miss Pilliwinks in a soft voice. Her owl-like eyes blinked. Betty wondered how she could ever have thought her a nice old lady. And just *how* had she heard Betty's whisper?

"Tut, tut, Ivy." Mrs. Lightwing's voice cut through the mist, sharper than her sister's. "You should know better than to run away by now. Did you really think you could escape with these *little girls*? Don't you know we're too powerful to let that happen?"

Like scuttling spiders, the two witches moved toward them.

A petrified moan escaped Ivy's lips as she pressed herself against the door of the tower. Betty selected another key and shoved it into the lock. There was only one other left, but she knew she was almost out of time. *Please, please* . . . she begged silently.

The lock shifted, clicking back. Betty gasped, lifting the rusted iron latch of the tower door and pushing it open.

"Go!" she yelled to Ivy, no longer caring about staying quiet. "Fliss, you too!" She shoved Ivy toward the door, triumphant. They were going to win . . .

Except Ivy never made it. Her hands caught on the doorframe as she was jerked back, her feet swept from underneath her. She cried out, hitting the stone steps with a dull thud, then rolled down them to land at Mrs. Lightwing's feet. Everything had gone eerily quiet, Betty noticed. As though the fog had blanketed the sounds of the warders . . . or perhaps their silence was the witches' doing.

"Whoops," said Mrs. Lightwing, grinning. Through

the deepening mist something shimmered in her hand: a length of pale cord wrapped around her fingers. The cord trailed away and led over the cobbles to Ivy, whose skirts had risen when she fell. Her ankle, bound with the other end of nettle cord, was now a horrid, bruised shade of purple. Every step away from Pendlewick must have been agony for her, Betty realized. A pain she had suffered almost without complaint. And for what? They had come all this way just to be captured like fish on a hook.

"No!" The word burst out of Betty before she even knew it was coming. She felt heat in her cheeks and fire in her belly. *How dare they?*

"You can't have her," she cried. "Or my sister. I won't let you!"

"Neither will I!" shouted Charlie bravely. She stepped away from Betty and stood by Fliss's side, shaking her fist at Lightwing, though of course neither witch could see her. Fliss, however, had gone rigid and was staring at the two witches with that haunting, glazed look in her eyes once more.

Pilliwinks made a scoffing sound. "Being invisible won't keep you safe, dearies. You might use it to sneak around in places you don't belong, but really all you have is a silly little parlor trick. You're up against *real* magic now."

"Yes," said Lightwing scornfully. "It's all very well talking the brave talk, but how brave are you *really*, Betty Widdershins? Because from where I'm standing, it looks as though you're too afraid to even face us properly."

Betty clenched her fists. She knew Lightwing was baiting her, challenging her to give up their invisibility. For a moment, her anger was so overwhelming she almost surrendered to it. After all, they'd captured Ivy. Being invisible hadn't helped her. But a shred of common sense remained. Invisibility might be the only trick the Widdershinses had, but it would be madness to give it up. And within the witches' web of dark enchantments, the Widdershinses' magic might be small, but it was theirs. And it was *good*.

Lightwing stepped toward Ivy, using the nettle cord to guide her, and knelt by her side.

"There you are," she said, as though she were addressing a child who'd got lost in a sweetshop. "Poor little Ivy. You really have caused us a lot of trouble." She jerked the cord spitefully, causing Ivy to cry out in pain. "You and your new friends. But it's time to put an end to this nonsense. I must say you've been rather clever, sneaking around and helping to scupper our plans." She glanced at Pilliwinks questioningly. "I think we might make a witch of her yet, don't you?"

Bravely, Ivy tried to roll away, but Lightwing's hand shot out with surprising accuracy and grabbed her hair.

"What do you mean, make a witch of me?" whispered Ivy.

"You could be one of us," Lightwing crooned. "We could show you the way. You could live forever." She cast a hand vaguely in the direction of Betty and her sisters. "These three girls . . . we'll share them. Three silly little runaways—no one would know." She licked her lips longingly. "So much *life*."

"Never!" Ivy yelled. "I'll *never* join you."

"Shame." Pilliwinks clicked her tongue. Clearly, she hadn't expected Ivy to agree for a second. "Oh well, we'll just have to get rid of you, then. How do you fancy an eternal swim in the marshes?" She grinned horribly.

"Betty," Ivy whispered, meeting her eyes. There was a pleading look on her face. At first Betty didn't understand it. "You know what to do . . . *the painting!*"

Lightwing's head snapped around, her eyes wide. "What painting?" she snarled.

"But . . . but . . ." Betty stammered. The plan had been to get Ivy into the tower. If she stepped inside with only the enchanted painting, what would happen? Would the spell on Ivy be broken, or would it finish her off for good? And there was another problem—once Betty entered the tower with the dolls, their magic would no longer work. Charlie and Fliss, as well as Ivy, would be visible, too, unless . . .

She motioned to Charlie, who sidled quietly closer. Betty took the nesting dolls out of her pocket and handed them to her little sister, pressing a finger to her lips. Charlie nodded fiercely in understanding. Keeping the dolls outside the tower would at least keep the rest of them invisible, even if Betty wouldn't be.

A tear spilled down Ivy's cheek.

"Please," she begged. "Just do it—now."

She doesn't care anymore, Betty realized. *Either way, she just wants this to be over. She can't stand to be their prisoner for another second.*

"Destroy it!" Ivy shouted.

Betty slid the map case off her shoulder and gripped it tightly. Then she stepped through the door into Crowstone Tower.

Dust

A S THE TOWER RENDERED BETTY VISIBLE, the two witches smiled triumphantly before their gaze settled on her.

"*What* painting?" Lightwing repeated icily.

"I think you know," Betty said softly. She took another step back into the dimly lit tower and felt the cold stone wall behind her. It smelled musty and damp. To her left, a set of steps twisted up and out of sight, leading all the way to the room at the very top. She watched the two old women carefully, waiting for them to make their move. She was ready to run if she had to, all the way to the top of the tower. But neither witch stirred, and in that instant, Betty realized something crucial: if either of them entered the tower, their own magic would be undone.

That's it! she thought. *If I can get them in here, then it really will be all over—not just for Ivy and Fliss, but it would mean they'd never be able to do this to anyone else.*

The thought sent fireworks off in her head. She'd been so focused on getting her sister and Ivy here that she hadn't considered what else the tower could do. She had to lure the witches in somehow, if they *could* be lured. With a sickening jolt, she thought of the map—and the peacock butterfly. How much of Betty's plan had Pilliwinks and Lightwing discovered? Did they know the threat Crowstone Tower posed to them?

"This painting," said Betty. "You called it your *little souvenir,* to keep part of Ivy and your horrible plan alive." She reached into the map case and removed the canvas. It unrolled in her hands to reveal Ivy's image, rosy-cheeked and forever sixteen years old. "The one you enchanted, just like you bewitched the Hungry Tree and the pond on Pendlewick Green when you took Eliza Bird and Rosa Ripples."

Pilliwinks gasped, stepping toward Betty. At the same time, something dripped onto the stone floor at Betty's feet. Her heart slammed, panicked at the thought of the risk she'd taken by stepping into the tower with the painting—could it mean the end of Ivy's life? For a moment, she wondered if the paint itself was flaking away and the portrait was undoing itself, but as she glanced down she saw that more tears were spilling from the painted girl's eyes. This time they were real, not just a part of the canvas. The edges of it felt warm, then warmer still in Betty's hand. She realized they were curling and blackening, like paper thrown into a hot grate moments before it burst into flames.

"You give that here!" Pilliwinks shrieked, staggering even closer.

Betty dropped the canvas to the stone floor of the tower, no longer able to hold it. A horrid singed smell rose up from it as it twisted and contorted, the face in the picture no longer recognizable.

"No!" Pilliwinks screeched again, her hands flying to her face in horror. "Look at what you've done!"

Betty watched in revulsion as Pilliwinks's picket-fence teeth blackened and rotted in her mouth. One fell away, clinking onto the cobbles. Her eyes darted to Lightwing. The old woman's gray hair was thinning like cobwebs and dropping out, her bony skull beginning to show through. Out of the corner of her eye, Betty saw a horrified Charlie backing far away, until she had pressed herself against the courtyard wall.

"It's working!" she yelled. "Fliss, quickly! Come into the tower!"

Fliss stared at her, like a fox caught in a trap. Then she shook herself and took a tentative step toward Betty. But Pilliwinks was faster, hobbling on wizened feet to the tower door with a look of desperation in her huge, owl-like eyes.

She's going to do it, Betty marveled. Destroying the painting hadn't been enough to stop the witches completely, but it was a start. She had made them desperate, so desperate that Pilliwinks had lost her senses and was about to make a terrible mistake. Her last mistake. She was a mere footstep from the tower door when Lightwing stood up, dragging Ivy to her feet.

"Do not step into that tower!" she screeched.

Pilliwinks froze, and so did Betty's blood. It had almost, *almost* worked.

Pilliwinks shook herself slightly, as if coming to her senses. She chuckled creakily. "You nearly had me there, dearie," she said in an equally creaky voice.

Words from the Pendlewick songs flashed into Betty's mind.

Oh, dearie me! How very grim . . .

"You made up all those things about Eliza Bird and Rosa Ripples and Ivy, didn't you? That they were vain and wicked, so no one would care when they disappeared. So no one would go looking for them. You lied about them and set them up to look like trouble so everyone would be glad they were gone!"

"And now you're trying to do it to our sister!" Charlie roared from across the courtyard, too angry to keep quiet.

Lightwing's eyes shifted craftily in her direction, but her focus returned to Betty.

"Eliza was nothing," she spat. "A nobody. An oddball. No one cared about her. What did it matter if she was gone?"

"She was a person," Betty retorted, horrified. "And whatever kind of person she was, it wasn't up to you to decide whether she deserved to live or not."

Pilliwinks shrugged. "No one missed her. It was simple, so simple. And the funniest thing of all is how easy it becomes to control a place when the people are scared. No one *wants* to see what's going on or ever suspects two sweet old ladies. How much easier it becomes to do things, especially when you're old. Unnoticed. *Invisible.*" Her mouth twisted bitterly. "Why shouldn't *we* have some of that youth and beauty?"

"And then you came along," Lightwing interrupted,

her eyes flashing. "Annoying family. Why couldn't you just be like everyone else and do as you were supposed to?"

"I told you someone with sisters was a bad idea," Pilliwinks pointed out. "After all, we know what sisters are like, don't we? They stick together." She lowered her voice to a mutter. "Even if they don't always agree."

Lightwing's nostrils flared angrily. "It was either the new family or a new village," she snapped. "And neither of us was up to that, thanks to everything with Ivy going wrong."

"You mean Wags, don't you?" said Betty. "Wags ruined your plans and took those years you wanted."

Lightwing narrowed her eyes. "You're far too smart for my liking. Perhaps we chose the wrong sister."

"That's what I said!" Pilliwinks cried. She reached up and wobbled another loose tooth. "I *told* you this one would be trouble, didn't I?"

"Then why *didn't* you choose me?" Betty asked.

"You're too young," Lightwing replied crossly. "People notice when a child goes missing, no matter how powerful our magic is. It raises too many questions. But when it's a teenager, especially a young girl in love, well, people will readily believe what you want them to. No one likes pretty teenagers like Rosa Ripples—"

"Or girls who wander off into forbidden forests," Pilliwinks added with a sly look at Ivy.

"Or your sister," Lightwing finished. "If you're really honest with yourself, you'd probably be pleased, deep down, not to have to see that sickeningly pretty face every day." She smiled wickedly at Betty. "The face people always look at first. You know you'll always be in her shadow, don't you? Wouldn't it be better if she was gone?"

Red-hot temper crackled in Betty's head like a storm, as every resentful, envious thought she'd ever had about her sister's beauty and charm pricked at her conscience. Yet Betty's anger wasn't directed at Fliss. It was at the witches, for she saw that this was another one of their tricks, another attempt to seize control.

"No!" Betty spat. "It wouldn't. The only people who should be gone are you two!"

Pilliwinks cackled, and again it was a horrid creaking sound like a rusted wheel. It iced over Betty's rage and made her feel small and afraid. How had she ever thought they could win against such evil?

"We've been around a long, long time, dearie," Pilliwinks wheezed. "And it's going to stay that way, I'm afraid."

What none of them saw coming was Charlie, charging across the courtyard with her arms outstretched. Lightwing looked this way and that as the sounds of the little girl's footsteps were smothered in the damp, swirling mist, realizing too late what was about to happen.

"Move!" Lightwing shouted. *"Away from that door!"*

It was too late. Charlie hit Pilliwinks at full speed, sending her flying through the door of Crowstone Tower. Betty barely had time to dart onto the staircase and out of the way before the old crone came lurching toward her, her awful teeth bared in a snarl. She hit the stone wall with a curiously hollow *poof!* and a bright flash of light that made Betty squeeze her eyes tightly shut. She heard Charlie thud against the wall straight after, then felt her sister's arms around her. When she opened her eyes, it was to a thick, gray dust in the air . . . that settled onto a pile of tattered rags and bones on the ground. All that was left of Miss Pilliwinks.

There was a heartbeat of pure silence and stillness as everyone stared in shock and disbelief at the dusty heap.

"Jumping jackdaws!" Charlie exclaimed.

"N-no," whispered Lightwing, swaying slightly. "No. My sister . . . you killed her!"

For the tiniest moment, Betty almost felt sorry for her. The horrible moaning that escaped her lips was like an animal in pain. Ivy, however, used the moment's distraction to her advantage. She lashed out with her elbow, striking Lightwing in the chest. The witch momentarily released her grip on Ivy's arm, but a moment was all Ivy needed. She ran for the tower door, throwing herself across the threshold.

As with Pilliwinks, the effect was instant. Only this time it was the opposite. The years fell away from Ivy like magic. Her skin became plump and youthful, her long, gray hair lush and dark. Her back straightened, her limbs lengthened.

"I'm . . . I'm *me* again," she whispered, staring at her hands. At her feet the nettle cord trailed to the doorway, frayed like an old rope. Ivy knelt and unpicked the knot from her leg, gathering up the wilting mass of nettles.

"Here," she said triumphantly, tossing them at Lightwing. "I'm not your prisoner anymore."

The witch didn't move as the nettles landed at her feet. She stared at them, not saying a word. Then her shoulders began to shake. At first Betty thought she was sobbing, but as her face turned to the tower door, it was clear she was shaking with rage, not tears.

"You," she hissed, pointing a bony figure at Betty. "You've ruined *everything!*" She snapped her fingers and a sound rose through the swirling marsh mist, the *shuffle-shuffle-shuffle* of a spinning wheel. The nettles lifted into the air by themselves, once again forming a neat rope. Lightwing snatched it and wrapped one end tightly around each hand. "You're going to pay!"

She staggered toward the tower, her eyes mad and full of death. Betty shivered with fear, but Ivy and Charlie pressed against her, clutching her tight. Giving her strength.

"Cowards," Lightwing ranted. "All of you! Hiding in there, too scared to face me. Too scared to *fight*! Why don't you come out here and find out how real magic is done?"

"It's *you* who's the coward," Betty answered, finding her voice at last. "And you who's afraid."

"I'm not scared of you!" Lightwing shrieked. "Little fool, you're *nothing*!"

"Not scared of me," Betty finished. "Scared of death. That's what all this is about, isn't it? You're afraid to die!"

Lightwing's face contorted like a mask stretched too tightly.

"Not anymore," she hissed, her eyes flickering to Pilliwinks's remains and then down at her own withered hand. "What else is left for me, thanks to you?" She grinned frighteningly. "But if I'm going to die, I'm taking you with me!"

With a terrifying scream, Lightwing flew at the tower, the nettle rope pulled as tight as a wire between her hands, arms outstretched, reaching for Betty's throat. For a heartbeat, Betty felt hands on her, clawing. But only for a second. No matter how much power Lightwing had once wielded, it was crushed by the weight of Crowstone Tower.

Her mouth opened in a silent cry of surprise before she, like her sister, fell away to dust and nothingness. Just a pile of tattered rags and bones in a heap on the cobbled floor. The Pendlewick witches' reign had finally ended.

"Fliss," Betty called in a choked voice. Her sister had watched, motionless, but now the cold, hazy look in her eyes had gone. She shook herself lightly, as if she were clearing her head of seawater. Then, as if in a dream, she moved toward her sisters and stepped into Crowstone Tower. At once, the streak of white in her hair darkened, but it was her eyes Betty marveled at. They sparkled with warmth and kindness, and everything that was just . . . *Fliss.*

"I'm sorry," Fliss whispered. "I'm so sorry."

Betty laughed, hugging her tightly. "There's nothing to be sorry for," she mumbled into her sister's short, dark hair. "I'm so glad you're back."

"Uh, Betty?" Charlie poked her, pointing past the door to the courtyard where a group of warders were gathering, their batons raised. "We've got a problem."

Betty tensed as the warders approached, but after what they'd just been through her worries were slight in comparison. "It's nothing we can't handle," she said, linking her arm through her sisters' and glancing warmly at Ivy.

"Come on, Felicity Widdershins," she whispered. "Time to work a bit of your own magic."

Fliss squared her shoulders, took a breath, and marched toward the warders. Her voice drifted back to the tower, full of charm and persuasion.

"I'm *terribly* sorry, but we seem to have gotten a bit lost. This blasted marsh mist came down out of nowhere and forced us to moor our boat. We were wondering if you could help . . . ?"

Betty grinned to herself. Her sister was back, all right.

Epilogue

THE SPLINTERED BROOMSTICK WAS BUSIER than Betty had ever seen it, and for once, even Brutus Crabbe had a smile on his face. The centenary celebration was in full swing, spilling out of the pub and onto the twisting streets of Pendlewick. Glasses clinked, beer slopped, and the floor became ever stickier.

On a rowdy corner table near the bar, the Widdershinses were crammed in cozily with familiar faces old and new. On one side of the table, Father and Charlie were squeezed between the Hubbards, Buster, and Henny, who'd brought an enormous paper bag of sweets with them, which Charlie was eagerly splitting between herself, Scally, and Wags. On the opposite side were Spit and Fingerty, who were filling Betty and Fliss in on all the latest Crowstone gossip. Granny was behind the bar, serving, just the way she liked it, but she could be heard hollering for people to wait their turn in every corner of the pub.

It had been three days since the Widdershins sisters had returned, and already Pendlewick felt like a different place. There were the obvious differences, such as the village store and post office being closed up with no explanation as to where its eccentric owners had mysteriously gone. The same went for Foxglove Cottage: several bottles of milk soured on the doorstep and spiders spun webs in the windows without interruption. It was, the villagers whispered, as though Mrs. Lightwing and Miss Pilliwinks had disappeared into thin air, and a mystery that would keep Pendlewick in gossip for weeks. More than this, however, were the other differences that perhaps only an outsider might notice. Such as how, when discussing the mysterious goings-on, there was a willingness to talk of magic, which hadn't been present before.

"Maybe they were taken by fairies," children whispered when passing the house. "Or eaten by the Hungry Tree!"

And though the hazy summer heat continued, Pendlewick felt lighter and more wakeful, as though its residents had never been under a spell at all. The happiest and perhaps oddest thing of all was that Wags was suddenly several inches taller and chattering nonstop. Ivy's return, too, had been even stranger in that it had been unremarkable—as though she'd never been away. Which she hadn't, in a sense, Betty mused to herself.

She looked over at Ivy now, catching the girl's eye. She was radiant, eyes shining with happiness and youth as Todd leaned over and whispered something in her ear. She gave a warm, grateful smile to Betty and then she and Todd slipped further into the throng of people as a table became free.

Betty felt Fliss shift next to her and glanced her sister's way.

"Cheer up," she whispered, giving her a gentle nudge with her elbow.

"I'm trying," Fliss mumbled, looking away as Todd and Ivy slipped out of sight. She attempted to smile, but her warm brown eyes were tinged with sadness. She sighed and took another sip of blackberry fizz, then fanned herself. "It's hot in here. Shall we get some air?"

Betty nodded, and the two of them got up from the table and threaded their way through the busy inn to the street outside. The air was fresher, but still heavy and balmy with summer. Pendlewick Green glowed pink and gold in the setting sun, and in the distance the surface of the pond glittered like fireflies.

"Oi," said Charlie, appearing behind them suddenly, her cheeks bulging with sweets. "Where are you two sneaking off to?"

"We're not sneaking anywhere," said Betty, holding out her hand expectantly.

Reluctantly, Charlie produced a rather squashed marsh-melt from the rapidly emptying bag of sweets. Betty popped it in her mouth and crunched contentedly. It was a little taste of Crowstone, a place that now felt fonder in her memories. A place that had saved them.

"It was good of Granny to invite everyone from back home, wasn't it?" said Charlie. "I wish they could all stay here forever."

Betty smiled. "So do I. But they'll come and visit again. True friends never leave us, no matter how far away they are."

The three of them stared across the green into the distance, where Tick Tock Forest was black against the dusky sky.

"I wonder if the forest will . . . *behave* now that the witches are gone," Fliss said quietly.

"Don't know," said Betty with a mischievous grin. "Perhaps we should take a walk and test it out?"

Fliss patted her glossy, dark hair in alarm. "No, thank you."

"Are you still sad, Fliss?" Charlie asked, rummaging through the sweet bag again and digging out a sticky beak toffee for her. "About Todd and Ivy?"

"No," said Fliss too quickly. She sniffed and then stuffed the sweet into her mouth. "Well, yes, a little. But it'll pass." She smiled faintly. "Eventually. Because I have you two to cheer me up, don't I? No matter what happens, I'll always have my sisters looking out for me."

"Even if we are annoying," Charlie replied.

"We're the lucky ones," Fliss said softly, gazing at the Hungry Tree. "Poor Eliza and Rosa . . . they weren't. They didn't have anyone to look out for them." The sadness in her eyes lessened and was replaced with something steelier. "I wish we could have helped them, like we did Ivy."

"Maybe there's a little something we can do," Betty suggested, pointing to a patch of wildflowers growing by a cracked wall nearby.

Wordlessly, the three of them gathered a selection of flowers and began walking across the grass, arranging what they had into two small posies. Arriving by the pond, Fliss dropped hers into the water, and they watched as it cut across the mirrorlike surface and lay floating at the center.

Charlie frowned. "The water's clear now. It was green before."

"Maybe something has lifted, after all," said Betty.

"Be at peace, Rosa," Fliss said softly.

They turned to the tree and moved beneath its vast canopy of branches. Betty reached out and touched its bark gently. It was warm and rough under her fingers. Things were still caught in its knobbly surface, but there was no movement. No gaping, mouthlike holes widening or whispering.

"She's gone," said Betty, and as she said it, she knew it was true. "Eliza's gone." The tree felt different now; the gloomy, miserable feeling had disappeared.

Charlie took the second bunch of flowers and placed them carefully at the foot of the trunk. It was then that Betty noticed something—something so tiny she almost missed it. "Look," she whispered.

For there, on a thin branch just above them, a single leaf had formed, new and green. The tree was growing again.

A familiar voice cut across the green from the pub, where a crowd was gathering outside.

"Ahoy!" yelled Spit, waving at them. "You're gonna miss the photograph!"

Arm in arm, the three sisters dashed back toward the

Splintered Broomstick. As they passed the stone circle, the dying sun cast deep shadows around it. They stretched into long, dark fingers across the grass and, at a glance, Betty could almost imagine they looked like spokes in a spinning wheel, broken into pieces . . .

But only for a second. She blinked and the illusion was gone. They were lichen-covered stones, ancient and crumbling. Nothing more.

And they were home.

Acknowledgments

As always, I'm indebted to my wise and wonderful editor, Lucy Rogers, to whom this book is dedicated. I'm convinced you're secretly a Widdershins girl. Thanks also to Jane Tait for another stellar copyedit, Leena Lane for the proofread, and Amy Cloud, my wonderful editor in the United States.

My fantastic agent, Julia Churchill—thank you. And Prema, Vickie, Alexandra, Mairi, and the gang at A.M. Heath for whisking my three sisters away to lands far and wide.

A big thank-you to Jack Bowers for naming the Splintered Broomstick pub. It's exactly what I was after!

Thanks to the real Mrs. Lightwing, whom I met at a

book signing in Waterstones Norwich (and who is lovely), for allowing me to steal her name. It was too good not to use!

Finally, I'm forever grateful to all the wonderful booksellers, librarians, teachers, bloggers, authors, reviewers, and readers who have been so supportive of my books.

Team Widdershins!